SOPHIE AND THE ODD ONES

SOPHIE FEEGLE BOOK 1

GWEN DEMARCO

Gwen DeMarco

Visit my website at www.GwenDeMarco.com

Printed in the United States of America

First Printing: July 2020

ISBN-97 986-6 435923-7

Copyright © 2020 by Gwen DeMarco

✿ Created with Vellum

CONTENTS

CHAPTER 1

⊂⨠

*B*lanketing the street, fog sat heavy in the air, so dense it absorbed the sounds of the city. Even though it was only late afternoon, the haze had steeped the day in gloomy shadows. Stepping out of the front door and locking it securely behind her, Sophie glanced back through the gloom at her apartment building. Once, a very long time ago, the large house had been a shining jewel, glittering in the city. However, like a forgotten aging starlet, the building had lived a hard life and it showed. Inside the building, all the house's original character had been gutted sometime in the '80s; bland function and quick fixes replaced its charm and craftsmanship. Someone had haphazardly divided the three-story mansion into small studio apartments in an attempt to fit as many renters inside its walls as possible.

At least they left the outside of the building alone, Sophie wistfully thought as she looked at the house's edifice. The steep Victorian gable with fanciful scrollwork was still intact, even if it was sullied with decades worth of grime and smog. Unlike the other painted ladies around the city, someone in their infinite wisdom had decided to paint the entire house one color: an unfortunate shade of tan, caught somewhere between cantaloupe and khaki. Sophie shook her head over this crime against her eyes and architecture.

"See you later, Brown Betty," she said to the building, patting one of the thick porch columns as she headed out into the street. Pulling on her worn black peacoat, Sophie stepped onto the cracked sidewalk.

After checking her watch, she sighed with relief to see that she still had plenty of time to walk to the nearest BART station and get to her job interview. She couldn't afford to blow this one. She didn't want to have to choose between eating and paying rent.

Sophie turned, ready to scurry to the Powell Street station when the sound of growling and hissing caught her attention.

What in the world is that racket? I don't have time for this shit, she thought, huffing out an annoyed breath.

Peeking her head around the corner into the narrow alley between Brown Betty and the adjacent building, Sophie saw nothing at first glance. As her eyes adjusted to the gloom, she realized a large dog had cornered some kind of small animal behind a few trash cans.

"Hey! Hey, cut that out! Get away from there!" Sophie yelled at the stray.

The dog whipped its head around, and spotting Sophie, snarled at her. She stumbled, taken aback by its aggression. Checking around her, she spotted a piece of metal that had broken off from the sad wrought-iron fence surrounding Brown Betty's small, neglected front garden.

Stepping back into the darkened alleyway, Sophie held the spear of rusted wrought iron in front of her like a sword. Sunlight barely penetrated the gloom of the alley, but she could see that the dog – some kind of oversized husky or malamute – was trying to work its way between the large trash cans. She worried that if she didn't hurry, she would be too late to save whatever animal the dog had in its sights.

"Hey! Fuck off! I mean it!" Sophie bellowed, putting as much authority into her voice as she could.

The dog swiveled toward Sophie. When it spotted her, it lowered its head and growled loudly, its hackles raised in aggression. The monstrosity looked like some mad scientist crossbred a husky with an Irish wolfhound. She wondered briefly if lightning was involved in the creation of this oversized canine.

"Fuck off! Please. I don't want to have to hit you with this thing, but I will," Sophie grated out, feeling stupid for talking to an animal like it could understand her. She continued to wave her makeshift spear threateningly at the dog. It looked at her and then returned its gaze to its trapped quarry. With a final narrow-eyed growl at her, it turned and trotted off down the alleyway.

As the dog disappeared around a corner, the piece of metal sagged in Sophie's fingers as a surge of relief swamped her.

"Oh thank god," Sophie muttered on an exhale.

Still clenching her rusted spear, she slowly approached the overflowing trash cans. The usual stacks of empty crates and piles of rubbish from the pub next door and small market around the corner occupied the narrow space of the alleyway. The pitch-black darkness and the walls slick with moisture and grease made the place feel forgotten and quietly menacing. Hearing small rustling noises emanating from the shadows, she cautiously peered into the small space between the cans. At first, she didn't see anything, but then a pair of eyes glowing in the shadows caught her attention.

"Hey there, are you okay? Did that asshole dog hurt you?" Sophie asked, keeping her voice soothing and soft.

An answering hiss made her think the dog had cornered a cat.

"It's okay. I'm not going to hurt you. I just want to check and make sure you aren't injured," Sophie inanely explained to the cat. She set her makeshift weapon nearby and crouched to see fully into the narrow space. A long white face with a pink nose and twitching whiskers glared back at her, hissing again in warning.

"Hey, you're not a cat! You're an opossum! What are you doing here?" she asked. "Are you hungry, sweetheart? I have an apple. Would you like a treat?"

Sophie slowly reached into the messenger bag hanging from her shoulder. Feeling around the bottom of the bag, she had a momentary pang when she pulled out the fruit.

"I probably shouldn't waste this on you; it's my last one, but I think you might be having a worse time than me," Sophie said, setting the apple on the ground near the still-hissing opossum. She slowly nudged it closer with a finger.

"What the fuck is going on out here?!" a familiar voice yelled from the alley opening.

Huffing out an annoyed breath, she stood up and faced the interloper.

"Nothing, Moe. A dog attacked an opossum," Sophie explained.

"Opossum! Gross! I hope the dog got it."

Moe's exaggerated shudder made Sophie narrow her eyes in irritation.

"Don't be a jerk, Moe. Opossums are wonderful creatures. You don't know what the fuck you're talking about. They're America's only marsupial," Sophie said, just to fuck with him.

Moe looked stupefied for a moment before growling at Sophie.

"Like I give a fuck about marsupials. The only thing I care about is rent. Are you gonna be late again? Because I'm getting sick of this shit. The other tenants don't give me the trouble you do," Moe said.

"Get off my ass, Moe. I'll have your rent. I'm heading to a job interview right now," Sophie said.

"In that outfit?" Moe asked incredulously, his lip curling in distaste.

"What do you mean? This outfit is perfectly acceptable for a receptionist at a tattoo parlor," Sophie said, looking down at her dark jeans and Ramones t-shirt.

"You look like a goth Tinkerbell who just finished gang-banging her way through a biker bar," Moe sneered.

"Really? Stop, you sweet-talker. You're making me blush," she said with a curtsy.

Just as Moe opened his mouth to retort, Sophie held up her hand to stall his words.

"Shit! I have to go!" Sophie cried when she saw the time on her watch.

As she rushed past a still sputtering Moe, Sophie glanced back at the trash cans, happily smiling when she realized the apple was gone.

~

A FEW HOURS LATER, SOPHIE MADE HER WAY INTO THE BAR NEXT TO Brown Betty. She dejectedly slid onto a stool at the glossy but nicked wooden bar.

She eyed the few men dotted around the interior of the bar, hoping to find someone willing to buy her a drink for a few minutes of conversation. With a slow exhale, she realized that the patrons were busy contemplating the contents of their glasses, eyes too glazed-over and watery to notice her.

"Damn it," Sophie mumbled under her breath.

"Hey Sophie, what can I get you?" the bartender asked, approaching from the other end of the counter where he had been talking to a stooped old man. Barrel-chested with a perma-nent no-nonsense scowl, the bartender should've intimidated Sophie, but they had hit it off the moment they met six months ago when she moved into Brown Betty.

"Hey Burg, so… I'm a little low on funds at the moment. And I've had a shit day. I don't suppose I could put a whiskey on a tab and pay you back later? Or maybe do a little work for a drink?" Sophie asked with a pleading expression.

"That bad, huh? Alright, just this once. You can help me wipe down the tables and sweep up later tonight. Deal? I should warn you, that'll only get you a glass of the cheapest whiskey I have in stock," Burg said, making his usual caveat. With a practiced flourish, Burg grabbed a half-empty bottle from the mirror-backed shelf.

Claws of indignity raked over Sophie as she sat, humbled and embarrassed at having to rely on Burg's good nature. But after the day's shitshow, she just needed a drink.

"Thanks, Burg. I owe you one. And yes, I will help you clean up later," Sophie said, taking a tiny sip of her drink. She raised her eyes to Burg when the whiskey didn't taste like the cheap stuff. Burg just shrugged his shoulders sheepishly.

"Alright, Soph, tell old Burg about how bad your day was," he said, leaning on the counter.

Just as she opened her mouth to start bitching, the bell over the front door rang and a man stepped into the bar. Sophie quickly took note of him as he sat a few seats down from her. He had thinning blonde hair, wide-set dark eyes, and seemed a little pudgy under his knee-length trench coat. The man emitted a feeling of kindness and timidity. He wasn't even a blip on Sophie's danger radar, so she dismissed his presence.

She turned her attention back to her surroundings, admiring the charm of the old pub while Burg poured the man a beer. Burg once told her the bar had been built decades before Prohibition. The walls were patterned with the original dark wainscoting and hunter green paint. Old sepia-toned photos, ancient posters advertising beers, a few neon signs and rows of shelves littered with all manner of tchotchkes – each one showing the patina of age – covered every square inch of the bar. There were a few dartboards she had never seen anyone use in the back section of the bar. On the opposite wall from the long wooden bar, a few Chesterfield sofas – which Sophie suspected might be original to the century-old bar – lined the wall. The only time Sophie had sat on one, it was lumpy, and a spring poked her in the butt. Lounging on crushed gravel would've been preferable to those couches. When she'd asked Burg about the sofas, he claimed they lent an air of 'sophistication' to the bar.

Sophie stared into the amber liquid of her glass while Burg finished serving the soft-spoken man. She admired how the multi-colored leaded-glass lamp hanging above her head reflected jewel tones off the ice in her drink. Swirling her glass on its cardboard coaster, she smiled as the colors blurred into a warm reddish-orange glow.

"Sorry about that," Burg said as he returned to his spot in front of Sophie. "Now, tell me all about your shitty day."

"I thought I had this receptionist job all lined up at a tattoo shop in the Haight-Ashbury. When I got there, five other people were also there to interview. I had to wait over an hour to get my turn, and I didn't even get the job. They gave it to this 1940s pin-up wannabe," Sophie said. "I really needed the job. My rent is due, and I'm fucked if I can't find anything soon."

"Haight-Ashbury," Burgs said with derision. "Why would you want to work there? Corporate America has crushed all the charm right out of the neighborhood."

"I don't have the luxury of choice. My rent's not going to pay itself. I can't afford to be snobby," she countered.

"Alright, I have nothing else to do right now. Let's look through the listings," Burg said, walking over and grabbing a laptop from behind the counter.

They spent the next hour going over job listings on various websites. Intermittently, Burg had to refill a patron's glass, including the quiet man seated three stools down in the trench coat, but mostly they spent the hour browsing.

"Why do these all sound like they are either scams or escort services?" Sophie complained.

"Don't be too glum, some of these also sound like pornos," Burg said like he was telling her a happy secret, making Sophie snort, before she thumped her head on the surface of the bar in defeat.

"I'm going to be homeless. Would you be so kind as to lend me a coffee mug, so I can properly beg for change?" Sophie mumbled into the wooden bar top.

"Have you considered becoming a stripper?" Burg asked in a serious tone.

She raised her head to look at Burg through one squinted eye. "Don't you have to be nice to people to be an exotic dancer? I don't think that's the right job for me."

"Well, actually, if you play your cards right, you could get paid extra for being mean. There's a certain type of guy who likes that kind of thing," Burg said with a wink.

Sophie gave Burg an intrigued, thoughtful look. A quiet 'ahem' interrupted whatever reply she was about to make. Both Burg and Sophie looked over at the man in the gray trench coat with raised eyebrows.

"I couldn't help but overhear that you need a job. I might have a job for you if you are interested," the man said.

"I'm not interested in being your sugar baby, but thank you," Sophie said, rolling her eyes at Burg.

"Uh, I don't know what a sugar baby is. However, I can assure you this is a regular job," the man stated.

She stared at the man for a few minutes, but only detected honesty in his dark brown eyes. He had the kind of round baby face which made determining his age impossible. He could've been anywhere from his thirties to his fifties. The man reached over and held out a pale hand.

"My name is Reginald Didel," he said.

"Sophie Feegle. This is Burg," Sophie said, indicating the bartender.

When she shook Reginald's hand, she noted it was soft and dry. The firmness of his grip was neither too strong nor too weak. *Nothing is more off-putting than a handshake that feels like someone just placed a dead fish in your hand,* Sophie thought, grimacing internally. *Almost as bad as someone who tries to crush your fingers in an attempt to exert their dominance.* The type of people who liked to give knuckle-crushers automatically activated Sophie's bitchy side.

"Okay," Sophie said slowly. "Tell me about this job."

"Well, it's at the city morgue," Reginald said with an apprehensive look. "Are you squeamish? Can you handle blood and body fluids?"

"Those kinds of things don't bother me," Sophie replied with a wave of her hand.

"I'm the Chief Medical Examiner in charge of the graveyard shift. I need an autopsy assistant. I specialize in unusual fatalities, so you would see a lot of unpleasant things," Reginald warned.

She snorted, thinking "unpleasant" was probably an understatement. "Doesn't an autopsy assistant need some kind of degree or training or something?" she asked skeptically.

"Normally, yes. However, I have not been able to keep this position filled. And I have a lot of say over who I hire. Mostly I just need you there to take notes, take photos of the bodies, weigh and measure things, take fingerprints and hand me instruments during autopsies," Reginald said. "You will receive training on the job."

"Why would you offer me this job? You don't even know me," Sophie said.

"Because, I need the help, and you seem like you need a break," Reginald said softly.

Sophie sighed because it wasn't like she could turn down the opportunity. Besides, all her intuition was telling her Reginald

and a silky blouse, daring her to say a word. Reginald had said that she didn't need to dress up for this job – that scrubs would be provided.

Sophie fought back the snarky words on the tip of her tongue.

Let's not fuck this one up right away. We need this job, she reminded herself.

"You're Sophie Feegle?" the woman confirmed. At Sophie's nod, she slid a black folder across the counter. "Fill out the paperwork and bring it back to me. If you have any questions, let me know. Once you're done, I will let Dr Didel know that you're waiting." The woman handed Sophie a pen.

Looking around the empty lobby, Sophie headed to the rows of chairs off to the side. Finding a seat against the wall where she could keep an eye on both the front door and the receptionist, she sat down and opened the folder.

She quickly filled out the application, grimacing slightly at her meager employment history. It had taken her a while to realize that customer service was not her forte. Dealing with idiots brought out the worst in Sophie. When the gods were handing out patience, Sophie must have been taking a piss. *They also skipped over me when they were handing out brain-to-mouth filters and appropriate humor,* she thought with a slight grin.

It took less than fifteen minutes to fill out all the paperwork and sign the document stating that she wouldn't disclose any details about the cases she would witness.

That's fair. Reginald said all his autopsies are for murders or unusual deaths. I wouldn't want to ruin a police investigation or anything, Sophie thought to herself. After signing the last document, she returned the folder to Miss Prim-and-Proper.

"Excellent. I will let Dr Didel know you are ready. He should be here in a few minutes if you would be so kind as to return to the waiting area," Miss Prim-and-Proper said, thumbing quickly through the papers in the folder.

Sophie strolled back to the waiting area and threw herself

back into the same chair. Glancing over at the small table covered in magazines, she rolled her eyes at the selection. She wasn't bored enough to read about how to make her own cleaning supplies or learn how to make five-ingredient meals in minutes. There was also a television in the upper corner of the room, but the screen was dark.

Picking at her cuticles, Sophie covertly watched the swinging double doors just past Miss Prim-and-Proper's desk. Finally, she spotted a shadow moving on the other side of the frosted-glass windows. Already rising to her feet, she smiled when she saw Reginald push through the doors. Reginald waved excitedly and scurried towards Sophie.

He must really need the help, Sophie thought.

Normally, she would assume this was all a ploy to get into her bed, but her dickhead radar hadn't pinged once around Reginald.

"Sophie! You made it. Are you ready to get started?"

"As I'm ever gonna be. Thank you again for this opportunity," Sophie said.

"Well, follow me. We will get you into some scrubs and get started. I have a lot of autopsies to get through before the shift ends tonight, so we're going to be throwing you straight into the deep end. A bit of trial by fire, I'm afraid, but I am confident you'll do great," Reginald apologized before turning and heading through the double doors.

Once Reginald had turned away, Sophie swallowed down her apprehension and followed him. The automatic lock buzzed just before Reginald opened the door and waved back to the reception desk with a loud "Thank you!" Looking back just before she entered into the restricted area of the morgue, she noticed the receptionist staring at her. The hall was quiet except for the squeak of Sophie's boots against the cream-colored linoleum floors.

"Huh," Sophie said in surprise as she entered the wide hallway.

"What is it?" Reginald asked over his shoulder as he led the way.

"This place doesn't look like I expected. I thought we would be in an ancient basement covered in pistachio-green tiles with bare fluorescent bulbs hanging above us. I think I've watched too many movies," Sophie said, looking around the bright white walls. It smelled faintly of bleach and disinfectants. The sharp chemical scent reminded Sophie of the way a hospital smelled, but without the odor of sickness. She was also relieved not to detect any smell of rot or decomposition.

"Well, if you had seen our old building, you might have been right. This facility was built just a few years ago. Everything is new and state-of-the-art. The toxicology department is even in-house now," Reginald said, pointing down an off-branching hall, pride evident in his voice.

Turning a corner, Reginald led her into an office with several desks arranged in a ring around the room. Perched at the desks were two men and one woman who all looked up as Reginald and Sophie entered.

"Hey, everyone!" Reginald said loudly. "This is the new autopsy assistant I told you about, Sophie. I hope all of you will make her feel welcome. Sophie, this is Amira. She will help get you set up. Normally, Amira is our Pathology Transcriptionist, but when I need help, she covers as my assistant. Today, she will trail us to show you the ropes."

The woman Reginald pointed out finger-waved at her from her office chair. Sophie admired the sophisticated-looking woman with a jet-black braid coiling around her head like a crown. Pursing her dark red lips, Amira stood up from her desk and sauntered up to Reginald. Her olive skin, touched with a hint of terra cotta, was flawless. Sophie admired her large dark eyes and prim features, feeling a bit like a weed next to a rose garden.

"Why do I have to show her how to do her job? Why couldn't

you find somebody who already knows what to do?" Amira complained with an air of regal disdain.

So much for the warm welcome, she thought sourly.

"We've been trying to fill this position for months. We need her. Unless you want to continue to be my assistant?" Reginald replied.

"No, thanks," Amira said with a delicate shudder.

"This is Azeban. Everyone calls him Ace. He works the night-shift in the Pathology and Toxicology lab," Reginald said, pointing to the man with brown hair sitting closest to the entrance. Reginald pronounced the name "ah-zuh-bahn". The man lifted his chin in a brief greeting before turning back to his computer screen dismissively. Sophie noted that Ace appeared to be around the same height as her, but she couldn't be sure since he was sitting. Ace looked like one of those compact men who, at first glance, doesn't appear tough, but when caught in a fight were scrappy and tenacious. His hair was cropped short on the sides but longer on top. The strands looked thick, almost wiry, and were sticking straight out as if electrified. His hair seemed to be comprised from every shade of brown in existence – from slate to dark chocolate – giving it a deep sable hue. The color and texture reminded her of a German Shepard from her old neigh-borhood. When you parted Axel's fur, the undercoat was a different lighter shade than the dark outer coat.

"And this is Fitz. He is our Transporter and Intake Specialist," Reginald said, indicating a blonde man sitting in a seat on the far side of the room.

Fitz rose from his chair and glided toward Sophie. Long-necked, with a prominent Adam's apple, Fitz gave her an impe-rious look down his long nose. Fitz was, by far, the tallest person in the room. He was very thin, almost gangly, with bony elbows peeking out from his shirt sleeves. Sophie figured he would be ungainly, but Fitz was surprisingly graceful as he approached. He had pale, milk-white skin, corn-silk blonde hair, and light, almost silvery eyes. He looked Nordic, but without the brawn she expected of someone with Viking heritage.

"It's nice to meet you, Sophie. That is my computer and desk over there," Fitz said, pointing to the station he had just vacated. "Don't sit at my desk or use my equipment. Oh, the sparkling water in the breakroom fridge is mine as well. Don't drink my water, and we won't have a problem, okay?"

"Sure thing. I will make sure to leave your stuff alone," Sophie promised, while silently trying to decide if it would be worth it to lick the tops of all his drinks. *Probably not,* she concluded. *At least Reggie is friendly*, she thought in exasperation.

"Amira, would you please show Sophie where to stash her things, get her some scrubs and show her to the autopsy room?" Reginald asked.

"Alright, follow me, new girl," Amira said, striding quickly out of the room.

"It's Sophie," Sophie said, glaring holes in the back of Amira's perfect head.

"Whatever." Amira sighed, looking back and rolling her dark eyes at Sophie.

Stopping by a small breakroom, Amira asked if Sophie brought a lunch.

"If you didn't, we can probably scrounge something up. There isn't anywhere to pick up food near here, and it wouldn't be open at our lunchtime anyway," Amira warned Sophie.

"Reginald warned me earlier today, so I packed a lunch."

Sophie pulled her lunch out of her messenger bag and tossed it into the fridge, laughing to herself when she saw a bunch of cans of sparkling water on an upper shelf, each one covered with an individual post-it note with Fitz's name claiming ownership.

Sophie followed Amira through the hall, taking several turns until they arrived at a small locker room. Amira moved like a ballerina – graceful and sure, with an economy of movement. She showed Sophie the stack of available scrubs and the lockers.

"You can get changed in here. I'll wait in the hall. I'd say get a lock so no one can steal your stuff, but I think you're safe," Amira said, slinking out of the room.

Sophie quickly shed her clothes and grabbed one set of dark-navy scrubs. Heading back into the hall, Sophie spotted Amira leaning against the wall waiting for her. Turning on her heel, Amira strode quickly away, crooking her finger to indicate that Sophie should follow her.

"It's good your hair is already secured back. Always make sure you keep it in a ponytail or bun, okay?" Amira confirmed. When Sophie nodded her head, Amira continued, "Here's the deal. I have an excellent sense of smell, and I am sensitive to bad odors, so I've been helping Reginald with the autopsies, but it's a struggle. That's why we need you here. How are you with unpleasant odors?"

"I live in the Tenderloin, so I'm fine with gross smells," Sophie replied, chuckling at her own joke.

"Well, we'll see," Amira said ominously.

As Amira opened a door and waved her through, Sophie detected the faint scent of disinfectant with an underlying hint of coppery sweetness and bleach wafting through the open door.

CHAPTER 3

"My life is so fucking weird," Sophie said four hours later, staring unseeingly at her peanut butter sandwich. A faint putrid film of rot still clung to the inside of Sophie's nostrils despite her having blown her nose several times before grabbing her lunch. Perhaps the smell would make most people lose their appetites, but Sophie had never thought of herself as particularly normal. And she was not one to let food go to waste. Mentally shrugging, she took a big bite of her sandwich.

"What do you mean?" Reginald asked from her left. Sophie, Reginald, and Amira were sitting at the round breakroom table eating their lunches.

"Well, I have now officially held three human brains in my gloved hands. I did not see this turn in my life coming," Sophie admitted, after swallowing her bite.

"Aren't brains interesting?" Reginald asked with a strange inner light brightening his eyes.

"Yes, they really are interesting. And weird. And way softer than I thought they would be," Sophie said with a slight shudder. "It was like holding an enormous block of tofu in my hands. Strange to think that the mass of tissue once housed what made a person who they were. This three-pound hunk of dead meat that I now have to weigh and catalog, generated every thought, every feeling, each insecurity and sense of self. It's just fucking weird."

"I'm just glad you could handle it. I'm happy to have someone else assist from now on," Amira said before taking a bite of her tuna melt.

Sophie raised one skeptical eyebrow at Amira. Amira gagged her way through every smell in the autopsy room, but then immediately came into the lunchroom and re-heated a tuna melt in the microwave, making the whole fucking room stink like canned fish. Sophie watched as Amira took a dainty bite of her sandwich, making a yummy "hmmm" noise as she chewed.

Sensitive nose, my ass, Sophie thought, rolling her eyes.

Sophie looked towards the room entrance when she heard some voices outside in the hall. The door swung open, and Ace and Fitz strolled into the room.

"She's still here!" Ace smirked. "Did she puke? Pass out?"

"Sophie was fine. Didn't struggle that much. She gagged a couple of times, especially during the second autopsy. That one had some advanced decomposition," Reginald said with a triumphant grin.

"Nothing? Really?" Fitz said in shock.

Reginald held out his hand and made a "gimme gimme" gesture.

"Ugh, fine," Fitz said, reaching into his pocket and pulling out a bill. Ace did the same, and they both handed Reginald the money.

"You guys bet that I would throw up?" Sophie asked with narrowed eyes.

"Not just throw up. I also bet you would cry. Fitz thought you would pass out and then run out of the building," Ace said, grinning sharply.

"So sorry to disappoint," Sophie said, scrunching her nose up at Ace.

"What did you bet?" Sophie asked, turning towards Reginald.

"I bet on you," Reginald said with a sweet smile.

"Damn right, you did," Sophie said, returning his smile with a grin of her own.

Fitz opened the fridge and pulled out an enormous plastic bowl, two cans of sparkling water, and a long baguette from the refrigerator.

Sophie watched as Fitz peeled the cling wrap off the top of what appeared to be a mixing bowl stuffed to the brim with only lettuce. Fitz had long fingers with pronounced knuckles, which somehow seemed almost elegant as he picked up a fork; the way he moved was almost graceful.

"Uh, do you want some dressing with that?" Sophie asked in fascinated horror as Fitz began to plow through his salad, dashing away Sophie's thoughts of his gracefulness.

"No! Why ruin lettuce by putting goop on it?" Fitz said around a mouthful of greenery. "What do you think of the job so far?"

"The first day has been good so far. Definitely weird. I will admit that I did not expect that conducting an autopsy would involve the use of power tools and gardening shears. That was certainly a surprise," Sophie responded, mentally shrugging off Fitz's eating habits.

"Oh, yes. The tools of the trade," Reginald said, rubbing his hands together like a villain in a movie, making Sophie snort.

"I'm still surprised the smell didn't make you sick," Amira said with a delicate shudder.

"Well, I worked in a water treatment facility for a month, so I got used to all kinds of awful smells," Sophie explained.

"You did? Why'd you quit?" Ace asked with a sharp look.

"I didn't quit. I was let go after I told my boss that it made sense he worked there since he was a huge piece of shit. It turns out they look down on that kind of thing," Sophie said with a shrug.

"What did you do there?" Fitz asked over the noise of Ace's guffaws.

"I turned floaters into sinkers," Sophie deadpanned.

Fitz, who was taking a drink of his sparkling water, started choking. Pressing a napkin to his face, it took Fitz a moment to recover his breath.

"Are you serious?" Ace asked, leaning closer to Sophie and pointedly ignoring his still-choking co-worker. Sophie was pleased to have shocked the air of irritation right out of Ace.

"No." Sophie laughed. "But you should see your face. I was in the custodial department – mostly I mopped the floors and took out the trash."

"I like her," Ace announced to the room with a smirk.

Reginald offered Sophie a bright green apple from his paper-bag lunch.

"I brought a few extras," Reginald explained.

"Thank you," Sophie said. Admiring the small shiny fruit, Sophie took a big crunchy bite. The apple made her smile, thinking of her opossum friend. After returning home from the bar earlier, she had checked for the creature, but it was nowhere to be found.

"Would anyone else like an apple?" Reginald offered, pulling another of the green fruit out of his lunch bag.

Ace snagged the fruit out of Reginald's hand, stood up and headed over to the small sink next to the refrigerator. Taking another bite of her fruit, Sophie watched as Ace vigorously scrubbed his apple.

"We should wrap this up. We need to get through at least four more bodies before the shift is over," Reginald said with a sigh, crunching up his empty lunch bag and chucking it into the trash.

"You got it, boss. Lead the way." Sophie got up from her chair.

"Hey, Ace, were you able to finish the toxicology report for the Jane Doe from earlier? The detectives from Richmond station will be breathing down our necks if we don't have something for them by tomorrow morning," Reginald warned Ace.

"Which detectives are on that case?" Ace asked, still scrubbing his apple.

I think the apple is clean by now. Maybe he's a germaphobe, Sophie thought with a mental shrug at Ace's borderline-rude behavior.

"Uh, I think Lancaster and Hernandez," Reginald said.

"Ugh, not those assholes," Ace scoffed. "Yeah, I'll make sure I have all the reports done in the next hour."

"Sophie, would you check the chart and bring the next scheduled body from the fridge into the autopsy room? I will meet you there," Reginald requested.

Sophie gave Reginald a jaunty salute. After checking the large dry-erase chart outside the autopsy room, Sophie headed to the giant walk-in refrigerator. Locating the next body, Sophie shuddered a little at the rows of stainless-steel tables. Each one had a body bag resting on it, waiting for its turn with Reginald and his scalpel. Quickly locating the correct gurney, Sophie hustled out of the fridge.

"You okay?" Reginald asked as Sophie pushed the gurney into the autopsy room.

"I just don't like being alone in the fridge. It skeeves me out a little to be alone with all those bodies. I keep expecting them to rise from the dead like zombies."

Sophie rolled the table into position. Turning, she grabbed the gloves, hair cover, safety goggles, and face mask she was required to wear for each autopsy. Returning to the gurney, she unzipped the bag so they can remove the body.

"Whoa. Look at that," Sophie said.

"What is it?" Reginald asked, looking up from his clipboard.

"The head is missing," Sophie responded, pointing at the corpse.

"Really? Interesting. I guess we won't be getting dental

records them. Oh look, no hands either!" Reginald exclaimed with a weird scientific glee.

"No hands *and* no head? I bet you the murderer is trying to make it hard to identify the body! What do you think?" Sophie asked.

"I don't know. That's the police's job. I don't tend to speculate. Hand me the scalpel, please," Reginald requested.

Sophie spent the next several minutes weighing, cataloging, photographing, and bagging up specimens destined for other departments.

"Hmmm. Interesting," Reginald said suddenly. "Come get a photo of this."

"Sure. What is it?" Sophie asked, picking up the camera and coming around the table to stand next to Reginald.

"Right here, on the upper bicep. It looks like someone cut a sizeable piece of skin off of him. Oh, look here. Another section looks like it was removed from his left forearm as well," Reginald said, pointing out the two areas.

"Probably had tattoos there. I bet this guy was in organized crime," Sophie mused out loud.

"Organized crime, huh? Like the mob?" Reginald asked as Sophie started taking photos.

"Yeah, like the mob. I think this guy was the head of a secret cabal, and they dealt in illegally imported goods. His rival was trying to take over his territory so he could have access to several warehouses strategically located on the bay!" Sophie said, making up a story on the spot about their headless corpse.

"I see. What were the tattoos on our alleged smuggler's arms? So, I can warn the SFPD to keep an eye out for pieces of flesh covered in specific designs," Reginald said, playing into Sophie's game.

"Hmmm. The one on his forearm was a stylized dragon surrounded by a sentence written in Vietnamese," Sophie said, pointing to one arm with the missing flesh. "The other... it wasn't actually a tattoo. It was a formation of five scars made from cigarette burns. It's part of the ritual for all the members when they join the gang."

"Does this gang have a name?"

"Of course it does. They call themselves the Bay Soi gang," Sophie replied, mashing together the names of her two favorite Vietnamese restaurants.

"Bay Soi is the name of the gang? I like it," Reginald said with a laugh. "And cigarette burns? Why burns?"

"It's an initiation thing. It shows commitment to the gang," Sophie said, making it up along the way as she wove her story.

"Well, maybe. Doubtful we will ever know," Reginald replied.

"What do you mean?" Sophie asked.

"Unless I am called to testify in court – which is rare – or the case is high profile, I rarely know the outcome of the investigation," Reginald said with a shrug.

"Really? I'd want to know!"

"Frankly, we see so many cases that I can't keep track of them anymore. It will probably be the same for you after a while," Reginald responded.

CHAPTER 4

⬡

*S*everal hours later, Sophie exited the Medical Examiner's office, almost skipping with happiness. She even held the door and smiled at several arriving employees as they entered the building, ready to start their day shift. Sophie imagined she must have looked like some kind of deranged hostess at a restaurant, giving each person a manic smile.

As usual, there was less fog on the bayside of San Francisco, so Sophie enjoyed the early morning sun warming her shoulders as she walked to the nearest bus stop. Her first night of work was such a success that she didn't even mind having to ride the bus from Bayview to the Tenderloin.

Sitting on the bus, watching a grungy homeless man coo at his pet rat, that was partially hidden in a grimy coat, Sophie couldn't stop smiling. Despite having to deal with cold dead bodies and power her way through some of the worst smells she had ever encountered, it was a good night. She liked her co-workers, even if they were a little strange and standoffish. Sophie especially enjoyed working with the soft-spoken Reginald. And she was surprisingly good at the job. Reginald even told her as they wrapped up the final autopsy that he thought she made a great addition to the team.

Things were finally, *finally* looking up for her.

Watching out the windows, Sophie took in the passing scenery. Squat ramshackle warehouses were sandwiched haphazardly between newer gleaming skyscrapers, all jumbled together with hole-in-the-wall burrito joints, convenience stores, check cashing places, clothing boutiques, and all manner of shops. If there was something you wanted to buy, there was a place somewhere in the city that offered it.

A large break between buildings gave Sophie a view of the glittering water of the bay. If she squinted her eyes against the reflective waters, she swore she could almost see the giant shipping cranes crowding the water's edge across the bay in Oakland. The giant steel structures always made her think of ancient dinosaurs' skeletons, hovering at the edge of a watering hole in perfect stillness, watching for nearby predators.

Masked by a new city block, the glorious body of water disappeared from view. Turning her attention away from the shipping cranes, she spotted an interesting-looking dim sum restaurant.

Licking her lips, Sophie made a promise to herself that she was going to buy some pork belly bao buns with her first paycheck. She could practically taste the fatty goodness complemented by the crisp pickled vegetables already.

A few blocks from her final stop, the man with the pet rat got off the bus. He walked past Sophie to exit the bus with the stench of rotting garbage billowing out behind him like a cape. Watching him kiss the rat on the nose and then tuck the animal into his jacket, a pang of envy hit Sophie.

I need to find a guy to look at me the way that man looks at his rat, Sophie thought wistfully. She could do without the long, stringy hair, and the sour scent of body odor mixed with a hint of urine, however. *If my dry spell keeps up much longer, I might be able to see past the rank body odor.*

Finally, Sophie's stop was coming up, so she yanked on the cord to request it. The graveyard shift started to catch up with her as she began the five-minute walk to Brown Betty. Stifling a yawn behind her hand, she spotted Burg up ahead, hosing off the sidewalk in front of his bar.

"Hey, you're up early. What're you doing?" Sophie called out to Burg.

Turning towards Sophie, Burg raised one hand in greeting while continuing to hose off the brick front of the bar, just under the large front window. The gold and green letters spelling out The Little Thumb on the window glittered in the morning sun. This morning, Burg reminded Sophie of the circus posters of old-timey strongmen from the turn of the century. His nose had a large lump in the middle, as if it had been broken more than once, sitting above a thick dark mustache. The morning sun was reflecting brightly off his melon-sized bald head.

"I'm always up this early. I don't need much sleep. You wouldn't know that since I've never seen you up before noon. And I'm washing piss off the wall. Some asshole just *had* to mark his territory last night. Disgusting beasts," Burg said, shaking his head.

"Gross. Well, I'm going to bed. Have a good day, Burg," Sophie said with a slight wave.

"Oh yeah! The new job. How was your first day?" Burg asked, gray eyes sparkling with good humor.

"It was great. I think it's going to work out. Soon I will be able to buy my whiskey rather than having to sweep your stockroom to afford it!" Sophie said with a wide grin and a laugh.

"Did you see anything gross?" Burg asked, bright glee shining from his eyes.

"I *exclusively* saw gross things! It was completely disgusting. You would have hated it. It was great." Sophie grinned unrepentantly.

"You are an odd duck, Sophie Feegle."

"Takes one to know one, Burg," Sophie replied, leaving Burg behind to deal with his urine removal.

Sophie slipped into the alley between the buildings and quietly looked around the trash cans, hoping to see her opossum friend. Disappointed that the animal was not there, Sophie left the half-eaten apple Reginald had given her earlier for the creature. The edges had turned brown, but Sophie figured opossums probably weren't particular about their produce.

When she entered the lobby of the apartment building, a small plaintive mrow caught her attention. Squatting down, Sophie spotted a petite tortoiseshell cat twined around the legs of the small table where Sophie usually sorted her mail. Holding out her hand, Sophie patiently waited for the cat to decide if it was worth his time to accept her paltry offering of chin scratches.

Approaching Sophie, the cat rubbed his cheek against her fingers in demand.

"Hey there, Ginsberg. Did you sneak out again?" Sophie asked, gently picking up the diminutive cat.

Hiking up the two floors, Sophie knocked on a shabby door across the hall from her apartment. After a long moment, the door opened a crack, and Sophie could see a milky blue, rheumy eye peek out at her.

"Good morning, Birdie. It looks like Ginsberg escaped again," Sophie said, holding up the culprit for Birdie to inspect.

"Oh, thank you, Sophie! He must have snuck out when I took out the trash earlier, the naughty little booger," Birdie said, opening her door and lifting Ginsberg out of Sophie's arms.

"You should have waited for me. I would have taken your trash out," Sophie scolded, channeling her inner schoolmarm.

"Please, girl. I can take out my own trash. I don't need a young piece of fluff like you babying me. I've been taking care of myself since before you were even a gleam in your father's eye," Birdie huffed. "Now, forget all that. Do you want to come in and have some tea?"

"That would be nice. Thank you, Birdie," Sophie said, stepping into the dimly lit apartment. The early morning sun filtered through the yellowed gauzy curtains in the living room, high-lighting the dust motes floating through the air. The apartment was clean, but it had the faint musty odor of old textbooks and stale lavender.

Sophie took a seat on the sagging sofa covered in large orange flowers. The old springs gave a low groan when her weight settled on them. Birdie puttered around her kitchen, setting a copper kettle on the avocado-green stove.

A moment later, the tea kettle gave its shrill call, and Birdie brought Sophie a delicate cup with steam curling from its contents. When Sophie noticed the chip on the lip of the silver and white porcelain, she pretended not to see it.

"Do you want a little brandy in yours?" Birdie offered, waggling a small bottle at Sophie.

"Maybe next time," Sophie said with no intention of ever taking a single drop of Birdie's special occasion bottle. She stared down at the tea bag floating in her cup, smiling to herself.

"What's got you smiling like that? Usually, only a man can put a look like that on my face," Birdie cackled.

"No man here. It's been so long since I've had a man, I'm forming cobwebs down there," Sophie teased, making Birdie chortle.

"Well, we should change that! Get you dolled up and get you out there," Birdie suggested.

"No, thanks. I need to just focus on keeping my new job and getting enough money for rent. No time for men right now," Sophie stated.

"I hear that. A man ain't nothin' but trouble anyway. Always distracting a woman from getting things done," Birdie said with a shake of her head, making the carefully curled strands wobble in place. "So, you got a new job then?"

"Yeah. You won't believe it, but I got a job down at the city morgue," Sophie said, taking a small sip of her tea. "I was beginning to think I would need to start stripping if I didn't find something soon."

"Nothing wrong with stripping. Did my fair share of dancing back in the day," Birdie hinted with a saucy wink.

"You did? I bet you had all the men panting after you," Sophie said, her lips curling up in a grin.

"Did I ever! I used to do burlesque back in the early '60s," Birdie cupped her bosom under her pink flowered housecoat and gave a little shimmy. "These old girls used to get me in a lot of trouble."

Sophie snorted into her tea, making Birdie grin widely. Seeing Birdie with that naughty smile, Sophie could almost picture the young woman she once was.

"These are what first lured in my dear old Darren. That man never was able to resist me," Birdie said, still cupping her breasts.

Sophie and Birdie fell into a companionable silence, enjoying the tea and the company.

"Do you want to stay and watch some of my stories with me?" Birdie asked as Sophie drained her cup.

"I can't, Birdie. I just got off work, and I need to get some sleep," Sophie said regretfully. "Do you need me to pick up some groceries later today?"

"No, dear. I have enough for the next few days. Go get your rest. We can visit another time," Birdie said, gently gripping Sophie's hand with aged fingers. Sophie stared down at the thin, pale vein-covered skin, placing her other hand on Birdie's and giving it a soft squeeze.

"Alright," Sophie said, standing up from the couch. "You have a nice day. I'll see you later."

Bending down to give Ginsberg one last scratch under his chin, Sophie let herself out and headed to her apartment to get some much-needed sleep.

Kicking off her boots by the front door, Sophie stripped as she walked across her small apartment, trailing clothes behind her. Falling onto her mattress in just her underwear, Sophie was asleep almost instantly.

CHAPTER 5

*S*winging her messenger bag over her shoulder, Sophie
skipped down Brown Betty's porch steps. As she
walked past the bar, she glanced inside, hoping to see Burg. He
was in his usual spot behind the bar, talking to a hunched
old man.

Waving her hand, she caught his attention. Burg looked up
and raised a hand in greeting. 'Work?' Burg mouthed at Sophie.
Sophie nodded and gave a thumbs up. She waved again and
mouthed 'See you later.'

Turning back to the street, Sophie jolted to a surprised stop
when she realized there was a group of teenagers standing in
front of her, blocking the sidewalk. She was surprised at their
silent arrival because she was usually good at sensing trouble
ahead of time.

"Spare change?" the young man in the middle asked her.

Sophie raised her eyebrows in disbelief. In front of her were
six people, not one of whom looked like they were old enough to
buy alcohol legally. Two were women, the rest were men. And
they were all glowingly beautiful, clad in pristine, expensive

clothes. They didn't need money; they needed a curfew and parental supervision.

"Sorry, I don't have any change." Sophie shrugged, looking over their artfully ripped t-shirts and jeans with evident skepticism.

The happy peal of the bell ringing from the bar door grabbed their attention.

"What are you doing?" Burg asked the group of kids.

"Just talking to the pretty lady. Mind your own business," the ringleader stated.

"She *is* my business. Now leave her alone and get out of here," Burg stated, stepping smoothly between the gang of catwalk castoffs and Sophie.

"We were just talking. Back off, Burg," said the pretty blonde boy-child flanking the ringleader.

"This is my block, and she's under my protection. Now run back to your territory. You're welcome here as long as you don't bother the people under my protection. Do you understand me?" Burg said with palpable menace. The anger pulsing off Burg in almost visible waves made him look even more massive than usual.

"You friends with this fucking ogre?" the ringleader sneered at Sophie, leaning around to see her face.

Rude! Someone should teach this brat a lesson, Sophie thought.

"Yes, Fabio, I am. At least he doesn't look like a reject from fashion week wearing leather pants that are two sizes too tight. Does it squeak when you walk? You'd better not fart, or you'll bust out all the seams," Sophie snarked.

"Fuck you, bitch! You better hope you don't lose Burg's protection," the ringleader said, trying hard to emulate Burg's menace but coming up short.

Burg took a step closer to the group. Fabio backed up a step with a huff, raising both hands in surrender.

"Fine! We're leaving. She wasn't worth it anyway!" he yelled as the group turned and slunk away.

"You should be more careful. They may not look it, but they are dangerous," Burg said, turning to Sophie with a frown.

"Yes, Dad. I will be more aware of my surroundings. Please don't ground me," Sophie said with an eye roll, channeling her inner fifteen-year-old.

"Smartass. Go on, go get to your disgusting job. I thought you were a slacker, but here you are all glowing with happiness about cutting up dead bodies," Burg said, stepping up and giving Sophie a small sideways hug.

"Gross! Your soft side is showing." Sophie laughed, elbowing her way out of the hug. "And even slackers like me can find their dream job! Later, Burg."

"See you later, Sophie."

With a wave, she headed off down the street.

~

"How's your second day going so far?" Ace asked, digging into a container of spaghetti at lunch, meticulously swirling up heaping spools of red-coated noodles and shoving them into his mouth.

"Should I get you a bib? Or maybe a drop cloth," Sophie teased Ace, who opened his mouth so Sophie could admire his half-chewed dinner. She quipped, "Looks like the intestines we had to dissect earlier. With this job, you're gonna have to try harder to gross me out than that."

With a sharp grin, Ace swirled up another heaping bite of pasta.

"The day is going great. I really like it. But I'm surprised at the amount of time we spend on paperwork. I guess I shouldn't be shocked, but it's a lot, even with Amira's help. Also, I'm amazed by how many victims of animal attacks we've gotten so far. This is only my second day, but I've seen three already," Sophie said, pulling her peanut butter sandwich out of her lunch bag.

"Oh, I can explain that," Reggie said, jumping into the conversation. "That's one of my specialties. I get all the animal attack autopsies, not just in SF county, but the surrounding counties as well."

"Oh. How do you become an expert in animal attack autopsies?" Sophie asked.

"Practice," Reggie said with a shrug. "How was your date with the data analyst guy, Amira?"

"Ugh," was all Amira said.

"Oh no," Reggie said with mournful eyes. "What happened?"

"He asked me where I'm from, so I said, 'San Francisco'. Then he said, 'No, I mean originally.' So, I said, 'I was born in Fresno.' And then he replied 'I mean like *originally* originally. Where are your people from?' I'm sick of it."

"Hey, at least you're getting dates," Ace argued.

"If one more guy calls me 'exotic' with that hopeful, perverted look in his eye, I'm going to start snapping necks," Amira said, dropping her fork in disgust.

"Is being called exotic so bad?" Ace asked with a confused frown.

"I'm no one's fetish, thank you very much. I'm sick of being objectified. They all think I'm going to fulfill their harem concubine fantasies. I'm sick of having to set them straight," Amira said with a sneer.

Somehow Sophie didn't think Amira let them down gently.

"You're lucky. I *wish* some woman would objectify me," Ace complained, making Sophie crow in laughter.

"Does it make you feel better to know that I find you objectionable? Is that close enough for you?" Sophie teased, trying to give Ace big innocent eyes, complete with coy, fluttering eyelashes.

"We've got a priority one autopsy incoming," Fitz announced, sticking his head through the breakroom door, interrupting whatever comeback Ace was working on.

"Ah, dang," Reggie said, standing up from the wobbly break-room table and dropping his meal back into his insulated lunch bag. "Come on, Sophie. We have to take care of this immediately. Priority ones take precedence."

Sophie stuffed her sandwich back in the brown paper bag and tossed it into the communal fridge. Following Reggie out into the hallway, Sophie heard him ask Fitz if a detective would be attending.

"Yes, it's Volpes," Fitz replied.

"Alright, it could be worse. Volpes is okay. He's more person-able than some of the others. It's good you get to meet him first, rather than one of the other more volatile detectives," Reggie confided to Sophie.

Sophie shrugged since she had no idea what he was talking about. She followed Reggie, getting suited up properly, before heading into the autopsy room.

"We've got a live one," a man next to a gurney said as they entered the room.

"I don't think that's technically true," Sophie murmured, eyeing the mangled-looking corpse on the table.

She turned her attention to the mystery man, presumably Volpes. He was about six inches taller than her five feet, four inches height, and looked to be in his early thirties. Even under the dark charcoal suit, she could tell he was trim but muscular. He looked like he had the lean, graceful strength of a dancer. However, the attitude emanating from him telegraphed cocky boxer just moments before a fight: all swagger and confidence. His light brown hair looked in need of a haircut in its disarray. As she watched, he ran his fingers distractedly through his disheveled strands pushing the waves back from his face. There was a few days' worth of beard growth gracing his lean jaw, making him look like he'd been too busy to take proper care of himself. If it hadn't been for the scowl, Sophie would have thought he was the boy next door all grown up.

"Who the fuck are you?" the man growled at Sophie, finally noticing her.

"Uh, what?" Sophie stuttered, jolted from her casual perusal by his angry tone.

"That's my new autopsy assistant, Sophie. Be nice. Leave her alone, *Malcolm*," Reggie said, peeling the open body bag back further to take a better look at the corpse.

"Mac," the detective corrected Reggie with a growl.

The man strode across the room to Sophie, stopping directly in front of her. His eyes traveled from her black hair, down her pixie face, stopping at her steel-toed boots. Sophie watched as his nose flared, and his lips curled slightly in distaste as if he'd just opened a package of moldy cheese.

"You don't belong here," Volpes said. "How could you hire her, Reginald? She's going to cause problems."

"Your name is Mac. Did I hear that right?" Sophie asked quietly. "So, Mac, do you have any say about my employment here?"

Mac didn't respond, just stared down at Sophie, silently trying to intimidate her. Sophie returned his tough-guy stare, but it bounced off him like pebbles thrown at a window.

"Is this your scary face, or are you trying to hold in a fart? I can't tell," Sophie said, smirking when Mac still didn't respond.

"You should quit while you're ahead. You're going to cause problems for this department, and you're going to see things you can't unsee," Mac said. Royalty talked to peasantry with less derision than Mac managed to infuse into every word.

"Ah, so that's a no; you don't have any say over my employment here. So, Mac... You can eat a bag of dicks," Sophie sneered, staring directly into his deep, ocean blue eyes.

"What?" Mac asked, jaw dropping in surprise.

"You heard me. Eat. A. Bag. Of dicks," Sophie repeated firmly, emphasizing each word.

Mac growled in his throat, taking a small step closer to Sophie. She squared up with Mac, ready to verbally tear him a new asshole. This was not her first time dealing with dickheads. The best policy was to cut their knees out from under them immediately and make sure they realized you wouldn't take their shit. Then, when they were still on the ground, trying to recover, you stomped on their ankles. Or somewhere worse.

If this is supposed to be the nice one, what are the other detectives like? Sophie wondered.

"Leave her alone, Detective Volpes. If you want to stay and witness this autopsy, you will be nice to my assistant. If you can't manage that, you can leave, and you will receive my report in the morning," Reggie warned.

"Fuck! Fine. Sorry, assistant girl," Mac said with pretend remorse. "I need some information on this death asap. Lancaster and Hernandez are trying to elbow in on this case, so give me something I can use. Fucking wolves," Mac spit, practically exhaling irritation with each breath.

He'd be good looking if he wasn't such a massive dickhead, Sophie thought sourly.

As Sophie helped Reggie with the autopsy, she noticed the detective flip open a notebook out of the corner of her eye.

"Based on lividity and degree of rigor mortis, estimated time of death is between five to six hours ago, so between six and seven last night," Reggie called out.

As Sophie recorded the estimated time of death on the chart, she watched the detective scribble in his little flipbook. Sophie was glad he was standing there silently, not interrupting their work. Reggie had a recurring set of steps, a systematic process he used to conduct each autopsy. She was glad Volpes wasn't disrupting the rhythm of their work.

"Cause of death appears to be blood loss from a wound to the neck," Reggie called out. "Sophie, please grab the ruler and photograph this laceration."

As Mac scribbled in his notebook, Sophie and Reginald measured the length and width of the gash.

"It looks like most of the wounds, including the removal of the appendages, appear to have occurred postmortem. It's possible they were removed using some type of sharp object, but it wasn't done cleanly. See these ragged marks?" Reggie said, pointing out the wounds and having Sophie take pictures of each one.

"It looks like something ripped him apart," Sophie murmured. "A monster sending a message."

"Do you have a story about this one?" Reggie asked, his eyes lighting up in anticipation.

"A story?" Mac interrupted, glancing up from his notebook.

"Sophie makes up the most delightful stories about the people we do autopsies on. It's kept me quite entertained these last two days," Reggie explained.

"Oh, the stories are delightful, are they?" Mac asked sarcastically, derision dripping from every word.

Sophie pretended to scratch her forehead with her middle finger, watching Mac's eye widen in surprise and then crinkle with a smirk.

"No stories today, Reg. I'm not here to entertain dickheads," Sophie quietly said to Reggie, unwilling to make up a story knowing that Mac would be listening.

She was still surprised that most autopsies took less than an hour to complete, from beginning to end. If anyone had asked her before she took this job, Sophie would have assumed an autopsy took multiple hours. Even though the autopsy took the same amount of time as usual, it felt like it dragged on interminably. Knowing the detective was watching their every move made Sophie's skin feel too tight and itchy.

Sophie breathed a silent sigh of relief when they finally

finished up with the body, and she rolled the victim into the walk-in fridge. Trudging reluctantly back to the autopsy room to finish the post-autopsy cleanup, Sophie was pleased to see that Detective Mac Volpes had left.

Several hours later, as the end of her shift drew near, Sophie gathered up the final specimens and samples to deliver to Ace. Thankful for the cart, she leaned some of her weight on the metal trolley as she pushed it down the hallway. Her eyes were feeling gritty and unfocused.

Sophie now realized that she had gotten through her first graveyard shift yesterday purely from the adrenaline of adventure and a desire to prove herself. Tonight, some of her job's newness was wearing off, and Sophie felt the pressure of exhaustion weighing on her. Her body hadn't adjusted to her new nighttime schedule yet, and she was feeling every minute of it.

Rolling the cart into Ace's lab, Sophie spotted him talking to Amira. She was leaning against Ace's desk, crowding him where he was seated. Ace was glowering at Amira, looking like he wanted to throttle her. Glancing at the narrow-eyed glare Amira was giving Ace, Sophie assumed they were bickering again. Amira stared defiantly at Ace, then reached out her hand and slowly pushed a pen off his desk with one finger, all the while maintaining intense, irate eye contact.

Standing, Amira flipped her hair in a dramatic swish and stalked past Sophie and out of the room.

"Don't fuck with me, *Azeban*," Amira threw over her shoulder.

"Don't call me that!" Ace bellowed after her.

"Why do you needle Amira? You know that cat has claws," Sophie said, shaking her head in exasperation, making Ace snort.

"Puh-lease, she's harmless."

"I've known women like her before. You push her too far, and she is likely to cut your throat and happily watch you bleed out," Sophie warned.

Ace gave a small, nervous glance toward Amira's quickly retreating back.

"You don't like to be called by your full name?" Sophie asked.

"Not really. It's hard to say, and assholes will purposefully call me Azkaban to piss me off," Ace said.

"What's Azkaban?" Sophie asked. "Never mind, I can tell by your horrified face that it's a movie or something I just 'have' to see. I'm not interested, so don't bother. I like the name Azeban. It sounds classy. What does it mean?"

"How in the world do you not know Azkaban? From Harry Potter? Have you been living under a rock?" Ace asked in bewildered shock. "Whatever. I have to pretend I didn't just hear that, or I will never be able to look you in the face again. My father named me after the Abenaki raccoon trickster god Azeban. He has a strange sense of humor. And my mother indulges him too often."

"Awww. It sounds like they love each other," Sophie said with a fake sugary tone, although she would never admit that their relationship did sound sweet, especially not to a grouch like Ace. "Here, I have the last of the samples for the night."

Handing over the specimens, Sophie headed out with a quick goodbye. Stopping by Reggie's office, she checked to make sure he didn't need anything else.

"No, we're all set here. I'm about to head out too. Have a good night... er... day, I mean. I will see you tomorrow," Reggie said with a wave.

"Hey, Reg," Sophie said, grabbing his attention with her serious tone. "I just wanted to say thank you for giving me this chance. You're not going to regret it. And I'm not going to cause problems. Detective Pissy-britches is wrong about that."

∾

THE RIDE HOME WAS A BLUR FOR SOPHIE, AND SHE HEAVED A SIGH of relief as she stepped off the bus.

Halfway up the final block to Brown Betty, shivers raced up Sophie's spine, and the hairs on the back of her neck all stood up at once. Pausing in front of the bar, Sophie pretended to peer inside the large bay window. Using the reflection of the glass, she tried to discreetly look around her and figure out what had her senses on alert. Out of the corner of her eye, Sophie spotted a dark figure dart into the alley on the far side of Burg's bar.

Sophie turned and raced into the alley on the opposite side of the building. The passage was barely more than a narrow corridor between the bar and Brown Betty. If someone was following her, they could circle around the back of The Little Thumb and intercept her before she reached the safety of home. Racing as quickly as her feet would take her, Sophie turned the corner and slid to a stop against the brick wall, hidden from view by a stack of teetering crates.

Back pressed against the rough wall of the bar, Sophie turned her head so she could see a sliver of the alley from behind a wooden crate. The alley was bright and backlit by the morning sun. She watched as a dark figure surged around the corner and quickly burst past her. Just as the man ran past, Sophie stepped out and, using his momentum to her advantage, shoved him hard between his shoulder blades.

The man stumbled to a stop, almost toppling over, then whirled around to face Sophie.

"Why are you following me?" Sophie demanded, assessing the man. He appeared to be in his early twenties, only a few years younger than her. Light eyes, light hair, farmer's tan on his muscled arms peeked from beneath the sleeves of his t-shirt. His face looked like it was still trying to hold on to his baby fat, making him look like a teenager despite the faded acne scars.

He stood, facing Sophie full-on, so either he hadn't been in many fights, or he was confident his larger size would be no contest against her. With his much taller height, probably over six feet, Sophie decided she would have to go low, or his over-confidence might end up being justified.

"Sebastian sent me to teach you a lesson," the man-child said ominously.

"Who the fuck is Sebastian?"

"You disrespected him last night," he said, dramatically cracking his neck.

"You mean Fabio? He sent you rather than coming himself. What a ball sack," Sophie retorted, carding her body sideways and dropping into a fighting stance.

Raising both arms to protect her face, Sophie bounced lightly on her feet. Sophie knew she had to end this as quickly as possible. Baby Face took two steps towards Sophie, shadow boxing to warm up his arms, expecting her to back up. Sophie managed to catch him off-guard when she darted forward instead and hammered a kick to his inner thigh. Sophie sank as much of her weight into the kick as possible. Baby Face dropped his guard, reaching both hands toward his thigh and started to curl his body down. Sophie took advantage of this by grabbing him by the back of his head and kneeing him straight in the face. She could feel the crunch of his nose breaking against her knee.

With a shove, Sophie pushed Baby Face so he fell against the brick wall. Smirking, Sophie picked up a familiar piece of rusted fencing and used it to raise Baby Face's chin, lifting his face so she could look him in the eyes.

"I have a message for Fabio I want you to deliver." She didn't bother recalling his real name. "You tell him that he has a problem with me, he needs to visit me himself. No more baby-faced flunkies. You're lucky I noticed you and not Burg. He would have really beaten your ass," Sophie stated. She threw the Burg thing in there just as reinforcement, but based on the way Baby Face's eyes went wide, Burg's name instilled fear in him.

"You're under Burg's protection?" Baby Face stuttered with watering eyes widening in an almost comical fashion.

"Yes. And Fabio knows this. Let me guess... Fabio told you that if you kicked my ass, he'd let you in his little gang, right? They are *never* going to let you in. They sent you out here to hurt me, fully knowing that the repercussions from Burg would fall squarely on you. You know in your heart, they would deny sending you, pretending you decided to attack me all on your own. They're never gonna make you a part of their gang. I've met them, remember? And frankly, you're not pretty enough. They're using you. And you're letting them," Sophie sneered in his face.

She was just making that part up but based on the look on his face, the barb must've rung true for Baby Face. He gave Sophie big, wounded, puppy-dog eyes, and she had to remind herself that not two minutes earlier, he had no problem with the idea of causing her pain.

With an annoyed snarl, Sophie left Baby Face in the alley to nurse his swollen nose and hurt feelings.

CHAPTER 6

*S*trolling into the lobby of the Medical Examiner's building, Sophie nodded a greeting at the prim receptionist Miss Zhao. All Miss Zhao needed was a pair of horn-rimmed eyeglasses perched on her delicate nose to perfect the stereotypical librarian look. Somewhere in her mid-thirties, the trim Asian woman never looked less than immaculate in her crisply pressed slacks and simple but elegant blouses.

Pulling off her knit cap and stuffing it into her bag, Sophie strolled past the receptionist's desk with a wave and pushed through the double doors as their locks buzzed open. Sophie brushed her fingers through her bangs, trying to fluff out her hair.

Amira was already in the changing room, stuffing her things into a locker when Sophie came in. As they exchanged a quick greeting, Amira dropped something. Since Amira's hands appeared to be full, Sophie stooped down and picked up a thin pink collar.

"Oh! Do you have a pet?" Sophie asked, then noticed that the tag hanging from the collar said 'Amira'. Feeling her eyes go as wide as saucers, Sophie looked at Amira and then back at the collar. It took a moment for Sophie to recover from her shock, but then a slightly horrified giggle escaped her.

Amira snatched the collar out of Sophie's hand with an exasperated, "Give me that!"

"Wow, Amira! Kinky. Didn't realize you had a master," Sophie said with waggling eyebrows.

"Oh please, I'm the queen of *that* castle," Amira said, pursing her burgundy-painted lips.

"I bet you are," Sophie chortled.

Amira flipped her silky hair in a dramatic fashion, making Sophie forcefully swallow a small ember of envy. She would never be so effortlessly sophisticated and glamorous. *That's okay, though,* Sophie thought to herself, *I'm sure there's a guy out there who wants a snarky, bitchy slacker with an affinity towards the morbid side of life.*

"Wait... I thought you said you were single?" Sophie asked in sudden confusion.

"I am. My situation is 'complicated.' You know how it is," Amira said, complete with air quotes.

Sophie raised her hands in surrender. "Ignorance is bliss. I don't need details!"

Shaking her head, Sophie quickly exchanged her clothes for scrubs, heading to the autopsy room to meet up with Reggie. She mentally prepared herself for whatever strange manner of death she was about to witness. Because Reginald's specialty was unusual cases, Sophie had seen every manner of death imaginable: from poisoning, to someone sawed in half, to a man drained of blood. In one week, Sophie had seen every manner of awful things one person could do to another.

The worst thing that ever happened to humans was humans. Sophie entered the autopsy room and saw Reggie already waiting for her with their first client of the day.

~

A COUPLE OF HOURS LATER, FITZ STUCK HIS HEAD INTO THE autopsy room. "Hey, just to warn you, we have a priority one. Code Red, Reginald," he announced with a serious expression on his imperious face.

"A Code Red? I see. Will any detectives be attending?" Reggie asked, looking concerned.

"Yeah. It's Hernandez and Lancaster. They'll be here in a few minutes," Fitz said with a small wince.

"Thank you for letting me know. If you could please tell the detectives that we should be done with this autopsy in about ten minutes, I would appreciate it," Reggie said.

Once Fitz turned to leave, Reggie gave Sophie a worried look.

"What's a Code Red?" Sophie asked with concern.

"Damn it. I had hoped to ease you into this," Reggie said, wringing his hands.

Sophie's eyes widened in surprise at Reggie's cussing. Reggie always seemed to handle every situation with an unflappable gentleness and kind regard. Even Ace and Amira's constant bickering didn't seem to create waves in Reggie's calm façade.

"Do you remember when I told you we handle all the strange and unusual cases in the city? Well, I don't want to alarm you, but there are some cases we receive that the general human population cannot ever know about."

"What do you mean, *human* population?" Sophie squawked.

"There are some bodies we get here that are not entirely human. You remember how you joked that vampires had drained the exsanguinated body the other day?" Reggie asked.

"Yeah," Sophie responded slowly, drawing the word out for several seconds.

"Well, you see, you were correct. That victim *was* killed by a vampire. They are real. A Code Red is a dead vampire. We are about to do an autopsy on one," Reggie explained, rushing his words like he had to physically push the words out of his mouth by the end.

"Bullshit," Sophie said through narrowed eyes. "You're just fucking with me. What does a Code Red really mean?"

"I swear I'm not kidding," Reggie pleaded. "I wouldn't play a cruel joke like that. I'm telling you the truth. Vampires are real."

Sophie opened and closed her mouth several times, but nothing came out. Dizziness and a ringing in her ears had Sophie bending over and grabbing her knees. It took several slow breaths before her head stopped spinning and the black dots blinking before her eyes started to fade.

"What the hell, Reg! Why didn't you tell me any of this sooner?" Sophie demanded.

"I know, I know! This is a lot. I should have told you sooner. I thought I had more time. Please don't panic. If we can just get through this next autopsy, I will answer all your questions, okay?" Reggie begged, clasping his hands under his chin in supplication.

"Vampires are real? You're not kidding?"

Reggie shook his head, still clasping his hands tightly under his chin.

"Holy shit. Okay then. Fuck," Sophie said, scrubbing a hand over her face. "Give me a second."

I can do this. I can pretend that finding out monsters are real is not scary and strange and unsettling. Just a typical day at the office, Sophie lectured herself.

"You *will* tell me everything when we are finished with this," Sophie demanded, pointing an accusing finger at Reggie, who nodded his head again.

A few minutes later, Fitz wheeled in a gurney covered with a black body bag, followed by two large men. Both were tall and broad, one in a gray suit and the other in navy. They both appeared to be about the same height as Fitz, but where Fitz was lean with elegant grace, these men were thick granite. The man in the navy suit was clean-shaven with salt-and-pepper hair. Under a thick brow, his piercing blue eyes skipped right over

Sophie and settled on Reggie with a scowl. In the slate gray suit, the other man looked like he was at least a decade younger than the other detective and had hair so dark it seemed blue-black. He was almost pretty – wide, masculine features, dark brown eyes, and long sweeping eyelashes – but something in his eyes made Sophie want to take a step back from him.

Normally Fitz helped get the body x-rayed and weighed when they first arrived, but Sophie watched as he made a hasty retreat.

"You're not staying to help with the intake?" Sophie asked quietly, approaching Fitz as he opened the door to leave.

"Uh, no. I have a thing I need to catch up on. Uh, paperwork, I mean I have paperwork I need to catch up on," Fitz said sheepishly, cutting his eyes toward the two detectives.

Fitz slipped out of the autopsy room on silent feet, leaving Sophie and Reggie alone with the detectives and a dead vampire.

Both detectives radiated menace and disdain in equal measure. Aggression transmitted through their clipped movements and tense posture. Sophie felt a little guilty for feeling glad that they both seemed to be ignoring her completely, focusing their combined attention solely on poor Reggie.

If she hadn't gotten to know Reggie so well this week, Sophie might not have noticed how uncomfortable and quiet Reggie was being. Not that she could blame him; these guys were way too intense.

Did they watch too many cop shows as kids? They need to chill the fuck out. Turn the menace down a notch, she thought snidely.

"Good evening, Detectives. Is there anything I need to know about this Code Red?" Reggie asked. Surprisingly, Reggie seemed to be holding up well under the dual stares from the evil wonder twins.

"We don't think so. It looks like a hunter interrupted a dine-n-dash," the navy-suited detective said.

"Will you be staying for the autopsy, Detective Lancaster?" Reggie asked in a cool professional tone.

Lancaster glanced over at the man in the gray suit who, by Sophie's master ability of elimination, she assumed to be Detective Hernandez. Hernandez gave a sharp dip of his chin in affirmation.

Sophie only just succeeded in holding back her sigh of disappointment. These two had managed to fill the entire autopsy room with an air of discomfort and barely restrained aggression. It was no wonder that Fitz beat a hasty retreat, rather than stay and help like usual.

Usually Sophie would've had something smartass to say, but she decided she would pretend to be mute. Silently, Sophie unzipped the body bag to prepare the vampire for autopsy. Peeling back the flap of the bag, Sophie paused when she glanced at the victim's face.

"What's wrong?" Reggie asked when he noticed Sophie freeze.

For a moment, she just stared at the young man's ethereal alabaster face. Then, her eyes skipped down to his artfully ripped jeans, confirming Sophie's suspicion. "I've seen this guy before."

Hernandez and Lancaster came alive like two hyenas spotting an injured gazelle wandering past.

"Explain," Hernandez demanded.

Sophie detailed her interactions with Fabio, aka Sebastian, and his merry bunch of assholes. The dead vampire was one of the pretty boys who had been standing with Sebastian when Burg rescued her from what she had previously assumed was a thwarted mugging.

"This Burg stepped between you and a vampire coven? What's Burg's last name?" Lancaster interrupted.

"Uh, I don't know. He owns The Little Thumb pub down on Hyde Street."

"This Burg said you were under his 'protection'. Are you sleeping with him?" Hernandez asked.

"I don't even know his last name, and you think I'm sleeping with him?! No, I'm not fucking Burg. We're just neighbors and friends," Sophie exclaimed indignantly.

"Do you think Burg knows they were vampires?" Lancaster asked, placing a quelling hand on Hernandez's arm.

Sophie opened her mouth to give a quick negative retort, then stopped for a second. "Uh, maybe?" she said slowly. "He did warn me that they were more dangerous than they looked."

While Lancaster quickly took notes, Sophie told them about the entire situation with Sebastian, including her exchange with Baby Face the next day.

"Do you think it was wise to fight a man bigger than you?" Hernandez asked with a disapproving frown.

"Gee, Dad. Should I have let him beat my ass without fighting back instead? I can hold my own. I've had a little bit of training. Plus, I only fought because I was able to get the element of surprise."

Lancaster snapped his small notebook closed and turned to Reggie. "We're heading out to follow up on this lead. Text me if the autopsy turns up anything unusual," Lancaster commanded.

Rude much? No please, no thank you? What a prick, Sophie thought.

"Don't leave town," Lancaster ordered, pointing a finger at Sophie.

With that last command, both detectives turned on their feet and strode out of the autopsy room.

"Don't leave town," Sophie mocked, rolling her eyes. "Do you think he gets a boner every time he gets to say that? Where does he think I'm gonna go?"

"You said you've had some fight training. Where did you learn to fight?"

"That might have been a little bit of an exaggeration. I was a receptionist at a boxing facility for a couple of months. The owner liked me and showed me the basics," Sophie said with a shrug.

"Why'd you get fired from that job?" Reggie asked with a knowing grin.

"It turns out that those big brutes had surprisingly fragile egos. Telling a guy that muscles don't make up for a lack of personality will send him running right to the owner to complain."

After initial photographs and x-rays, Sophie bagged up the vampire's ruined, expensive clothes. Peeling off his shirt revealed a large gaping wound in his stomach.

"Looks like we found the cause of death," Reggie nodded at the wound.

"Really? All the stories say you have to stake a vampire through the heart."

"Vampires can be killed just like anyone else; they're just harder to dispatch than a human. Staking them in the heart or decapitating them are just the most effective methods to kill them. Same as a human. Besides, I suspect this vampire *was* actually staked through the heart. You know how hard and thick the sternum is; it's easier to stab in through the abdomen and then angle the weapon up behind the breastbone," Reginald explained.

"Oh wow. So, the way to a man's heart really is through his stomach," Sophie snorted.

"Technically, yes. Also, vampires have all heard that joke before, and you might regret making it to their face," Reggie warned.

"What's a dine-n-dash?" Sophie asked as they moved the body onto the autopsy table.

"It's a crude term to describe how some vampires feed, especially lone vampires who are not a part of a Domus. They will drink a small amount of blood from a human and make that person forget the feeding. Part of a vampire's power is that they can erase small bits of memory. It's not dangerous for the human victim, but a lot of the other species have a problem with the practice," Reggie explained as he began the autopsy.

Sophie chewed on that information for a minute while looking at the pretty blonde vampire on the table. "Are all the vampires pretty like this guy?" she asked.

"No. But most are. Vampires prize beauty."

"You said a word I don't know. What is a Domus?" Sophie asked as they prepped the body and collected hair samples. A cursory examination did not turn up any fibers or any other foreign objects on the body.

"Most vampires are a part of a Domus, which is like a clan or small family. A vampire Domus usually keeps humans around to provide blood. The humans are there voluntarily in the hopes they will eventually be transformed into vampires. They are called Volos, but a lot of people call them Veins behind their backs. I think it is a cruel name, although I admit I cannot understand why anyone would want to be a Volo," Reggie said.

"Domus? Volos? Is this shit Greek or something?" Sophie asked as she took the vampire's fingerprints.

"Latin actually. Domus means house or family. And Volos means hopeful or want or something like that. Vampires are very pretentious so they love to use Latin when they name things," Reggie said with an eye roll.

"Lancaster said he thought a hunter killed the vampire during a dine-n-dash... What's a hunter? It sounds like a title."

"There is a sect of human fanatics whose only goal is to wipe out vampires. There aren't a lot of them left. Most of them were wiped out during the drug wars in the '80s," Reggie explained.

"This is all so fucking weird," Sophie said, while Reggie began the first Y-incision to start the autopsy.

∾

"Huh," Sophie said almost half an hour later.

"What is it? Do you see something unusual?" Reggie asked.

"No, nothing unusual. That's what's so crazy. If you hadn't

told me this was a vampire, I wouldn't have even known. I thought the internal organs would be different somehow. In all the books, they call vampires the undead. I thought... I don't know, that his internal organs would be shriveled or something." Sophie shrugged.

"Oh, don't ever call them the undead. They aren't dead; they're just transformed from humans into something different. Plus, they really don't like it when you call them that," Reggie warned.

"Transformed? What do you mean? How are they transformed?"

"There is a virus in their blood. Many people have tried to study it, but it evades our attempts to gain knowledge. It has magical properties that mess with medical instrument readings. It makes vampires faster, stronger, and age much, much slower. However, the vampire needs more blood than their body can produce on its own to survive. My theory is that their red blood cells cannot keep up with the demands of their enhanced body. The average lifecycle of a red blood cell in a human is 120 days. What little research we have suggests the lifespan of a vampire's RBC is half that. They are unable to produce enough blood on their own to keep up with their bodies' needs. Ace could probably explain this better than me," Reggie said, an excited light gleaming in his eyes.

Sophie smiled to herself over Reggie's excitement about the subject. *He should have been a teacher or a scientist*, she thought fondly.

"No, you're explaining it just fine. Will sunlight kill vampires, like in the movies?" Sophie asked, looking at the vampire's smooth, almost milk-white skin.

"Sunlight doesn't kill vampires. They do not dramatically explode into dust." Reggie chuckled. "Over time, their bodies stop producing melanin. The older the vampire, the less melanin they have. The paler a vampire's skin, the older they most likely are.

It's not a guaranteed way of knowing since people start out with varied skin tones. The older they are, the more they will avoid daylight since the UV spectrum in sunlight will cause discomfort. Based on the palor of this one's skin, I would guess he is over 60 years old," Reggie guessed.

"He doesn't look old enough to buy beer!" Sophie exclaimed. "Are they immortal? Do they live forever?"

"They are not immortal, but they do live an exceptionally long time. There have been a few vampires we know of who have lived to be over 300 years old. They do age, but very slowly. They stay youthful-looking for most of their life," Reggie said.

"Must be nice." Sophie grinned. "How can you even tell this is a vampire? Except for being so pretty and pale, everything about him seems human. Other than examining his blood, I guess."

"There's one foolproof way," Reggie said. He peeled back the vampire's lips to show Sophie the pointed canines.

"Fangs," Sophie gasped.

"Fangs," Reggie confirmed. "Vampires have pronounced canines. Upon their death, they don't revert to a fully human form like shifters do. That's the fastest way to identify a vampire."

"Okay, tha−" Sophie stopped and looked at Reggie. "Wait... did you say shifters? Like, uh, like werewolves and stuff?"

"Don't call them werewolves. They hate that. Call them wolf shifters," Reggie said.

"Wait a minute. Just... Are you kidding me?" Sophie looked at Reggie incredulously. "Vampires are real. 'Wolf shifters' are real. What else is out there?"

"Well, there are all kinds of shifters, not just wolves. There are also fairies, goblins, ogres, witches, sirens... Almost any magical creature mentioned in a myth probably exists," Reggie said.

"Holy shit. How do you know all this?" Sophie asked.

"Um, well... I'm not completely human myself," Reggie paused, cringing with worry. "I hope this doesn't change how you feel about me. I don't want to lose your friendship."

"Reggie, no," Sophie said plaintively. "You are my friend, and you are a good guy. I don't care that you aren't fully human. It doesn't change a thing between us, okay? You can't get rid of me that easily."

Reggie huffed a small breath of relief and blinked rapidly. Feeling awkward with Reggie's display of emotion, Sophie turned back to the vampire laid out on the stainless-steel autopsy table, staring unseeingly at his delicate, elfin features.

"Are you okay?" Reggie asked, placing a gentle hand on Sophie's shoulder.

Shaking her head, Sophie looked over at Reggie. "Yeah, I'm okay. I think all this crazy information has overloaded my brain. Just give me a minute, and I will be right as rain again."

"How about once we complete this autopsy, we take an early lunch, and we can talk more. I will answer any questions you have then."

"Deal," Sophie said with a quick grin.

"Would you tell me a story about the vampire? I think we could both use the distraction," Reggie requested.

As Reggie and Sophie got back to work, Sophie started to weave her tale. "This guy was Sebastian's right-hand man. Everyone called him Montgomery, but his real name was Jerry. In the 1950s, he renamed himself after the heartthrob Montgomery Clift. Jerry was originally named after his father, a man he despised, so he changed it. Just another guy with daddy issues."

Reggie snorted in amusement. "Was he killed during a dine-n-dash like Lancaster and Hernandez suggested?"

"B-o-o-o-r-ring," Sophie singsonged. "No, someone set this murder up to look like a hunter attack, but it wasn't. The murderer grabbed Jerry in Twin Peaks on his way to visit his secret human girlfriend: Bridgette. The killer used the same weapon the hunters use – a curved wooden stake."

"Curved? Why is it curved?" Reggie prompted.

"It's like you explained earlier. It's too difficult to pierce the heart through the breastbone. They use a curved wooden stake designed to enter through the abdomen and then naturally curve up to hit the vampire's heart in one solid thrust. They call the weapon a recurve stake."

"A recurve stake... I like that name. So why was he killed if not by a hunter?" Reggie asked.

"Someone powerful wants Jerry's Domus to sell them an important building. This is just a real estate deal gone bad!" Sophie teased.

A shadow passing by the frosted window of the autopsy door caught Sophie's attention. Hearing Ace's voice outside the door filled with gruff annoyance made Sophie smile widely. It sounded like Amira was messing with him again. Sophie loved watching those two take verbal sniper shots at each other at lunch each day.

It didn't matter if Sophie now had to deal with vampires and fairies and other magical creatures. She'd always felt weird and out of place around normal people, so it made sense Sophie would feel right at home here.

CHAPTER 7

⤬

Sitting at the breakroom table, Sophie watched as Reggie nervously picked at his lunch.

"You don't have to tell me what you are. It doesn't matter to me. Seriously," Sophie tried to assure Reggie. "As long as you don't hurt innocent people, I don't care."

"I'm an opossum," Reggie said in a rush, swallowing convulsively once the words were out.

"An opossum," Sophie repeated, surprise freezing her for a moment. One look at Reggie's nervous face kicked Sophie's thought processes back into place. "Like an opossum shifter, right? You can change from human into an opossum. Wait a minute... are you *the* opossum? From last week, the one the dog was after?"

"Yes, that was me. Although that was a wolf shifter, not a dog."

"That was a shifter too? It was attacking you!" Sophie exclaimed. "Are you in danger?"

"I'm not in any danger. He was just warning me away from his territory. It's already been resolved. I reached out to his Alpha. The Conclave grants me territorial immunity because of my work here."

"That was a warning! I thought he was gonna–"

The opening of the breakroom door interrupted Sophie.

"I'm just fucking sick of it. We shouldn't have to put up with him coming in here and spouting his bullshit," Ace was saying to Fitz as they entered the room, Amira trailing in behind them. Ace's eyes glinted with an intelligence wrapped in an ever-present air of annoyance – as if the whole universe got on his nerves.

"Hey guys, Sophie knows," Reggie announced to the group.

"Finally. I was sick of tiptoeing around her delicate human sensibilities," Amira said with an imperious roll of her eyes.

"Do I seem like I have *delicate* sensibilities?" Sophie asked, turning to Reggie with an exasperated huff and a raised eyebrow.

Amira sniffed daintily. "I guess not."

"Are any of you human?" Sophie asked Reggie quietly. Reggie gave a small shake of his head.

Sophie desperately wanted to ask everyone what kind of creature they were, but she held off, not knowing what the etiquette was regarding interspecies introductions.

"Whose bullshit should you not have to put up with?" Sophie asked Ace, deciding to wind him up rather than ask personal questions. Ace was at the sink, meticulously washing his lunch as usual.

"That asshole Malcolm Volpes. If he calls me TP one more time…"

"TP? Like toilet paper?" Sophie asked.

"No, he meant trash panda. It's a racial slur, I tell ya," Ace growled.

"Trash panda? Like, uh, a raccoon? Are you a raccoon shifter?" Sophie asked, feeling her eyebrows rise so high on her forehead she was surprised they weren't merged into her hairline.

Ace nodded his head, still growling under his breath.

"I'm a snow goose," Fitz placidly announced while stuffing a huge hunk of baguette into his mouth.

Sophie opened her mouth, but no words came out. Half-formed thoughts and questions swirled in a flurry inside her mind. Finally, her mind settled on a question: "Isn't bread bad for geese?"

Fitz snorted. "Bread is bad for everyone. But it's just so damn delicious." He stuffed another bite of baguette into his mouth with obvious relish.

"Wait... Can you fly?" Sophie asked, envy coating every word.

"Yes," Fitz said with a smug grin.

"That's so awesome. I'm super jealous," Sophie said with a smile.

Looking around the table, Sophie cataloged her friends, trying to mentally tie them to their animal halves. Reggie was an opossum, Ace was a raccoon, and Fitz was a goose.

Sophie looked at Amira taking small, delicate bites of yet another lunch consisting mainly of fish. She thought back to the pink collar, the aloof attitude, the time she deliberately knocked Ace's pen off his desk.

Sophie hesitated for a second, then pushed through. "Amira, are you a cat?"

"How'd you guess?" Amira asked with a pleased expression.

Sophie nodded her head at the fish on Amira's plate. "That. And the collar made me think feline."

Wisely, Sophie left out Amira's standoffish demeanor or her penchant for knocking things off counters when annoyed with someone.

"So you guys are all shifters... What else is out there?" Sophie asked.

"Pretty much any creature you've heard of from legend, it exists," Ace said.

"So like trolls are real?"

"Yep," Ace said.

"Centaurs? Leprechauns? Goblins? Chupacabras?" Sophie asked with a huff of laughter.

"Yes to all. Well, actually… I'm not sure about chupacabras. I've never met one, but that doesn't mean they don't exist," Reggie explained.

"Are there a lot of shifters and nonhumans in the world, and I've just never known about it?" Sophie asked.

"Not that many. There are a lot more humans than Mythicals in this realm. We tend to congregate in larger cities or near ley lines, so there are a lot more here in San Francisco than in other areas. The city's proximity to water and a strong ley line means this is the most densely Mythical-populated city west of New Orleans," Reggie explained.

"Mythicals? Realms? Ley lines?"

"Mythical is just another word for nonhuman. There are a bunch of other realms like the Fae realm, Shangri-La, Valhalla, and such. The other realms don't usually matter here. They mostly ignore this realm, and we ignore them. The Fae realm is the only one that interacts with the human realm with any regularity. Ley lines are channels of magical energy, crisscrossing all over the planet. Where the ley lines are the strongest is often where the path between realms is thinnest and closest, allowing people to cross over from other realms," Fitz explained.

"How can I tell if someone is a Mythical?" Sophie asked, pushing the idea of realms to the back of her mind. There were only so many weird revelations she could focus on at a time before she had a complete mental meltdown.

"Mostly, *you* can't. *We* can usually tell by scent, but even then, some are undetectable, like witches, brownies, and nymphs. Some you can identify if you know what to look for, like the teeth on vampires," Ace said with a negligent shrug.

"However, almost all Mythicals have biological and physiological differences that show up as anomalies upon closer scientific examination. That is why we are here: to make sure the general human population never learns about the Mythicals in their midst," Reggie said, picking up from Ace's explanation.

"Does that mean all the autopsies we've done this week were on Mythicals?" Sophie asked.

"Mostly. A few were human victims of an attack by a Mythical. One of the autopsies we conducted was because they weren't sure if it was caused by a Mythical or not, so they brought it to us just in case. I can see you're worried, but Mythicals are very strict about any human deaths. Any violence against humans is dealt with swiftly," Reggie assured her.

"Wait. That guy who had been torn apart by a bear in Yosemite, what was he?" Sophie asked suspiciously.

"He was a bear. Lost a dominance fight against another bear shifter," Reggie said.

"Dominance fight?" Sophie asked with raised eyebrows. "You know what, actually, I think I get the picture. What about that guy that was chopped in half?"

"He was Fae. He was probably cut in half using magic, but the autopsy couldn't determine that conclusively," Reggie replied.

"This whole thing is so crazy. Why did you hire me? Why am I – a human – allowed to know about all this?" Sophie asked.

"For a few reasons. You were kind to me when I was in my opossum form – many people are not. My instincts told me you could be trusted. Plus, I seriously needed an autopsy assistant. Amira was threatening to quit if we didn't find someone soon," Reggie said.

A random thought popped into Sophie's head.

"Is that why Detective Volpes said I didn't belong here? Because I'm human? That's why he thought I would cause problems," Sophie asked. The look on Reggie's face confirmed her suspicions.

"What is his problem anyway? Volpes was hassling me about Sophie earlier today. We don't answer to that prick about who and what we hire," Ace snarled.

"What do you mean he was hassling you?" Sophie asked.

"He just wanted to know more about you: if you showed up

for work on time, if you were causing any problems, if you've been acting weird. He's just an elitist prick," Ace sneered.

"Do I need to worry about him causing me problems?" Sophie asked.

"I will talk to Mac. Foxes are naturally distrustful. I'm not surprised he has honed in on you working here. You don't need to worry about him. I will make sure he leaves you alone. Mac knows he needs to stay in our good graces because of our work," Reggie tried to assure Sophie.

A fox? Sophie thought to herself, trying to reconcile the idea of the detective being a fox shifter.

Reggie glanced at his watch and sighed lightly.

"We need to get back to work. I'm sorry we don't have time to talk more," Reggie said.

"That's okay. I don't think my brain can process more information anyhow," Sophie said, pleased to get a chuckle out of Reggie.

~

SOPHIE WATCHED OTHER PEOPLE ON THE BUS FROM THE CORNERS of her eyes, wondering if anyone was a Mythical. The few people on the bus at this time in the morning all looked normal to Sophie. *Well, normal for San Francisco anyways*, Sophie thought as she watched a woman with glassy red eyes reach out and stroke the empty air in front of her.

It was a strange sensation to realize that creatures from myth and legend lived amongst the city like a secret society hidden in plain view. Shaking her head, Sophie went back to covertly observing her fellow commuters.

On the walk back to Brown Betty from the bus stop, Sophie spotted Burg lounging in the doorway to his bar.

"I've been waiting for you. We need to talk," Burg said, waving Sophie into the dim interior of the empty bar.

Burg pointed to a stool indicating that Sophie should take a seat. Stepping behind the bar, he plucked a bottle half-filled with amber liquid from a glass shelf. Snagging two tumblers from under the counter, Burg poured them each two fingers' worth of whiskey. Then he dropped a couple of ice cubes into the squat glasses. Just how Sophie liked it.

They clinked glasses and Sophie took a slow sip. She let the whiskey sit on her tongue for a moment, savoring the way it warmed the inside of her mouth. The taste made Sophie think of leather-bound books topped with a dollop of butterscotch and vanilla. She let it slide slowly down her throat. A whiskey like that needed to be relished.

"I had two detectives show up here last night asking about the vampire gang that was hassling you," Burg said. Sophie started choking and wheezing, the alcohol burning as it went down the wrong pipe. Burg handed Sophie a napkin with an apologetic grimace.

"Warn a girl next time you plan to drop a bomb on her!" she coughed. "I can't believe you know about vampires. Did you know they were bloodsuckers when you warned them away from me?" Sophie asked, finally getting her coughing under control.

"Yes, I knew. I didn't know you knew about vampires. Vampires don't wander into my territory very often. They usually stay in their fancy mansions in Nob Hill or can be found trolling for tourists at Fisherman's Wharf looking for a quick snack."

"Trolling for Tourists would be a great band name," Sophie said inanely, making Burg snort. "By the way, I didn't know about vampires until last night."

"You didn't tell me the vampires sent a Vein to harass you, Sophie," Burg said, channeling his Strict Dad voice.

"I handled it."

"You shouldn't mess with vampires."

"First of all, I didn't know it was vampires at the time. Second, *they* messed with me. I didn't mess with them." Sophie listed items off her fingers.

"Fair enough. But from now on, when someone bothers you – I don't care who – you need to tell me, no matter what. Most Mythicals look human, so you won't know who is dangerous," Burg warned. "Speaking of dangerous people, I had a second detective come talk to me last night, specifically about you. He wanted to know if you're a problem, where you've been for the last week, your habits and friends."

"That. Nosy. Dickhead! Was his name Malcolm Volpes?" Sophie asked. When Burg nodded his head, Sophie griped, "He just doesn't like me because I'm human. Don't worry about him. He's just complaining because he doesn't think a human should work at the morgue. He thinks my presence will cause problems. He can't do anything about my employment there except bitch and moan like a whiny toddler. If he keeps it up, I'm going to buy him a binky."

"I should have warned you that the man who offered you that job wasn't human. But I didn't realize he was recruiting you into the Mythical division. I thought you would be working in the regular human department, so it didn't occur to me to tell you," Burg said worriedly.

"Don't worry about it. Even if I had known ahead of time, I still would have taken the job."

Burg raised his glass, and they clinked the rims together.

Swirling her finger through the water left on the bar top by the condensation dripping off her glass, Sophie slowly sipped her drink while trying to gross Burg out by describing the sound a rib cutter made when it crunched through a rib cage. Watching the giant of a man shudder in disgust made Sophie cackle like a maniac.

When she finally recovered from the attack of the giggles, she stared down at her drink, trying to gather her courage.

"Hey Burg, are you human?" Sophie asked softly, purposefully not looking up from the polished, gleaming bar top just in case the question upset Burg. "Not that it bothers me one way or another. I'm just curious. You don't have to answer my question if it's rude. I don't know what the etiquette is yet," Sophie said in a rush.

"No, I'm not human, Sophie," Burg said with a kind smile. "I'm an ogre."

Shock snapped Sophie's eyes up from the contemplation of the wood grain under her fingers so quickly she almost dropped her drink.

"Wow. I thought… I don't know how to put this delicately. From the stories I've read, I thought that an ogre wouldn't look so human in appearance," Sophie said, swallowing the cringe that wanted to spread across her face. Sophie wisely didn't mention that in most fairy tales she could recall, ogres were also known for eating people, especially children.

Burg straightened out an arm, then began to crisply roll up his sleeve. He revealed a tattoo on his forearm of a boot encircled by words in a language Sophie did not recognize. The boot looked like a knee-high pirate captain's boot with a large folded-over cuff at the top. An ornate buckle held a thick leather strap across the top of the foot. The detail was so fine on the tattoo, Sophie swore she could see the grain of the leather on the boot. The foreign words were in a cursive language so elegant and fluid-looking it would probably give a calligrapher wet dreams.

"Boots feature in several tales about ogres – from Puss-in-Boots to Hop o' My Thumb. The image is often used to represent ogres now. I paid to have a Fae create and spell this sigil tattoo and imbue it with a glamor to give me a human form. This tattoo allows me to appear completely human," Burg explained.

The tattoo made Sophie think of the headless corpse from her first day at the morgue. At the time, Sophie had jokingly told Reggie that someone had sliced his tattoos off the body. Looking down at Burg's forearm, Sophie wondered if she hadn't guessed correctly. Burg's sigil was in the same spot as the missing flesh from the corpse.

"That is so cool." Sophie laughed. "Do you think I could get a magical Fae tattoo? So I could transform into something badass like a dragon or a unicorn?"

"Sorry, it doesn't work on humans. If you somehow talked a Fae into putting a magic-imbued tattoo on you, it would just be a tattoo. You need internal magic for sigil tattoos to work. Besides, most dragons are obnoxious assholes; you wouldn't want to be a dragon."

"What about unicorns? Are they real too?"

"No, sorry. But pegasi are. They come from the Mount Olympus realm. Extremely rare, though. I've never even seen one," Burg said with a wide grin.

"Pegasi? Mount Olympus? I can't tell if you are bullshitting me or not," Sophie said with a shake of her head.

Sophie and Burg finished their drinks in silence. Both lost in their thoughts. After the final sip of her whiskey, Sophie stood up and turned to Burg.

"I've got to go, Burg. Thank you for the drink. And thank you for looking out for me. I appreciate it," Sophie said.

"You may be an irritating bitch, but you're my irritating bitch. If anyone bugs you, I've got your back," Burg said with a wink.

"You may be a man-eating ogre, but you're my man-eating ogre," Sophie sassed back. "Hey, Burg, what does human flesh taste like?"

"I wouldn't know, but if I ever get a chance to try some, you'll be the first to know."

"Missed opportunity! You should have said chicken," Sophie said as she exited the bar with a wave, swept out on the tide of Burg's laughter.

Stepping into the apartment building's tiny lobby, Sophie wished she had been brave enough to have asked to see Burg's true form. Sighing softly, she decided it probably would have been a rude request; if he didn't offer to show her, then it didn't feel right to ask.

Ginsberg came darting down the steps and stopped in front of Sophie, curling his tail over his feet.

Squatting down to his level, Sophie stared intently into Ginsberg's bright citrine eyes. For a few moments, they both just silently observed the other. The fiery orange strip ringing his irises expanded as his pupils contracted into a sharp slit as he focused on Sophie's eyes.

"Ginsberg, are you a cat shifter?" Sophie whispered to him. "You can tell me. I know about these kinds of things now."

Sophie gazed raptly into his face, looking for even a small twitch to give Ginsberg's shifter status away, waiting for a response.

"Mrow," the tiny feline yowled at Sophie, clearly over the impromptu staring contest.

"Fine. Keep your secrets," Sophie huffed, tucking the cat under her chin. "Let's get you home to your mommy."

CHAPTER 8

◦⁂◦

$\mathcal{I}$t seemed to Sophie that the fog in San Francisco only came in two varieties.

Sometimes, it rolled over the city like a goliath unfurling a rug across the landscape. Once when she had been in Twin Peaks, Sophie had been high enough above the rest of the city to witness the fog as it rolled in from the Pacific. It looked like an impenetrable wall surging over the land, the city falling beneath its feet. This type of fog laid on top of the skyscrapers like a thick, gray wool blanket high above.

The second type of fog crept in on quiet fingers, slinking into all the crevasses of the city, draping the landscape until it covered everything in its dense, opaque shroud. It settled in your hair and on your clothes, making you want to wrap your coat tighter around you to keep its damp touch off your skin.

Stepping off Brown Betty's stoop, the fog kissed Sophie's face with cold, clammy lips. As Sophie walked swiftly down the sidewalk, the mist swirled behind in eddies and whorls, like she was a ship forging through dark waters.

I bet we'll see more murder victims than usual tonight, Sophie thought. This type of fog made people feel like it would hide their sins. Those people's sins ended up on a table in her workplace. Her job was now to help unveil them in an effort to catch the culprit and make sure they couldn't hurt anyone else ever again. Even though Sophie didn't know what happened with each autopsy once it was completed, there was a satisfaction in knowing she had helped. She didn't care if she was only a small, insignificant cog in the machine of justice.

Getting on the bus, Sophie pulled her messenger bag carefully onto her lap, not wanting to smush the ham sandwich inside. With her first paycheck, she was able to upgrade from peanut butter. The paycheck came not a moment too soon, since she'd been facing a rice week if she hadn't gotten some money.

Watching out the bus window, the city lurked dark and mysterious beyond the glass, tall buildings looming somberly overhead. The glowing balls of streetlights, smothered by the thick fog, regularly broke up the darkness with hazy, wispy light. Each golden orb quickly and silently gave only a momentary reprieve from the misty shadows. Darkened buildings arose from the gloom like tombstones lining a graveyard. Sophie smiled as the bus passed by a bar, bright light and cheerful voices spilled out into the night, a lively harbor in the darkness.

Sophie exited the bus with a sigh of relief, glad to almost be at work. After a spectacularly lazy weekend, for some reason, she'd been twitchy as hell; her nerves strung tight. Earlier in the day, as she paid Moe rent, picked up groceries for her and Birdie, and caught up on errands, Sophie couldn't shake the feeling that everyone was looking at her strangely. She kept looking over her shoulder, wondering if a vampire gang might be after her. The feeling of being watched had followed Sophie everywhere.

The itchy feeling between her shoulder blades finally dissipated as she walked up to the strange metal sculpture in front of the Medical Examiner's building. Glad to finally almost be in the safe cocoon of work, Sophie stopped to look at the piece of artwork. She'd never given the sculpture a second look until now.

The plaque at its base said the metal sculpture represented boat sails filled with wind. To Sophie, it looked like sections of silver fencing caught frozen mid-twirl in an invisible tornado.

Stepping inside the lobby, Sophie smiled as she saw that Miss Zhao was in head-to-toe pastel pink. Even the pearls covering her pretty side comb were a soft iridescent pink. Sophie raised her hand in greeting as Miss Zhao buzzed her in with a small enigmatic smile.

"I think Miss Zhao finds my punk-slacker look amusing," Sophie said to Ace, peeking her head into his and Fitz's shared office. Ace looked up from glaring at a report on his desk like the words on the document personally offended him.

"I find your look to be hilarious, so I'm not surprised," Ace said, the slight twist to his lips betraying his humor.

"Stop, you silver-tongued devil, you. You're making me blush," Sophie sassed at him.

Ace gave Sophie's black jeans with the ripped-out knees a pointed look, raising one eyebrow expectantly.

"What's Miss Zhao's first name, anyway?" Sophie asked, ignoring the barb.

Ace shrugged. "I don't think she has one. She's just Miss Zhao."

As Sophie turned to leave, Fitz brushed past her into the office space.

"Hey, Fitz. I picked something up for you today," Sophie said.

"You got something for me?" Fitz asked, surprised.

"It's not a big deal. I just happened to be near Boudin," Sophie explained, reaching into her messenger bag and pulling out a paper bag. Fitz practically snatched the parcel out of Sophie's hand, pressing his whole face into the bag's opening.

"Hmmm, sourdough." Fitz sighed, huffing his doughy gift like a junkie. "Sophie, would you like to be my wife? I would make you a fine husband."

"He's gay," Ace announced. "So, don't accept that proposal."

"You're not supposed to out people. You never know how they're going to react," Fitz lectured.

"If she doesn't care that you're a goose, she's certainly not going to give a shit that you like men."

"Alright now," Sophie interrupted before they both got started on one another. "No, I will not marry you, Fitz. The mutual love of bread is not enough to base a life together. And, Ace, stop being such an asshole."

"Are you talking about Ace? I heard something about an asshole," Amira said as she entered the room. Sophie turned and exited the room before things could get heated. As she walked away, she could hear Amira and Ace start their usual bickering.

After getting changed, Sophie grabbed her files for the night. She checked them against the chart on the wall, confirming the case number for the first scheduled autopsy, before heading into the fridge. Sophie quickly found the corresponding gurney and wheeled it into the autopsy room.

"Sophie! What have you got for me there?" Reggie exclaimed, looking up from a manila folder in his hands.

"Our first customer of the evening."

Getting the gurney parked next to the autopsy table, Sophie unzipped the body bag so they could move the person into place. The overpowering scent of the ocean – a combination of sunbaked seaweed, salty brine, and fresh fish with a hint of ammonia and cucumber – filled the autopsy room. Sophie shook her head, trying to rid her nostrils of the smell as she gave the woman in the body bag an intrigued look.

"Weird," Sophie said as they transferred the body of the woman to the autopsy table. "Why does she smell like that?"

"Because of what she is," Reggie said with an air of mystery.

"Let me guess… She must be a sea creature… Siren? Kelpie? Walrus shifter? No wait, I got it. Mermaid!" Sophie exclaimed. "She smells like a fish market… At least she smells like fresh fish and not like rotting seafood."

"You're correct. She was a mermaid," Reggie confirmed.

"That's so cool," Sophie breathed softly. "So weird, but still... so cool."

They worked in silence for a while, the quiet only punctuated with occasional requests for tools from Reggie and calling out information for her to jot down.

"Wait a minute... If she's a mermaid, where's her tail?" Sophie asked, looking at the woman's very human-looking legs.

"Excellent question," Reggie said, slipping easily into his mentor mode. "Mermaids are a type of shifter and most shifters will revert to their human form when they die."

"Is that why we get all these torn up human bodies? Because they were fighting in their shifter form, like a wolf or whatever. Then when they are killed, they turn back into humans but they keep their injuries?"

"That's correct," Reggie said with a pleased expression. Sophie suppressed the desire to preen like a teacher's pet.

"So, how did she die?" Reggie asked after a while, requesting another story about the victim.

"Hmmm... Let me think," Sophie said as she handed Reggie a scalpel, looking over the woman's form.

"Look at all these wounds on her side. I think they're bite marks," Sophie said, pointing to a series of ragged gashes and abrasions on the woman's torso.

"Bite marks?" Reggie said, taking a closer look at the wounds. "You might be right. Hard to tell yet due to the extent of the tears. What bit her?"

"An elephant seal," Sophie announced triumphantly.

"What?" Reggie's head popped up from examining the wounds, making Sophie chuckle.

"Yeah, she accidentally wandered into the territory of a male elephant seal during mating season. As a mermaid, she thought she could escape by running into the ocean, but it followed her and attacked," Sophie explained.

"Well, now I know never to cross paths with an amorous elephant seal. I shall visit the beach with more care henceforth," Reggie teased.

Sophie opened her mouth to retort but got interrupted by the squeak of door hinges, announcing someone entering the autopsy room behind them. "Oh great," Sophie breathed when she saw Mac Volpes enter the room.

"Detective Volpes, what can I do for you?" Reggie asked.

"I need to speak with you, Dr Didel," the detective said, giving Sophie a sour look.

"We need to finish this autopsy before I can speak with you. We're almost done. If you want, you can wait in my office or take a seat over there," Reggie said, indicating a chair on the far side of the room.

With an annoyed sigh, the detective took the seat. Sophie frowned in disappointment when he didn't head to Reggie's office, but decided to ignore him. She wouldn't give him the satisfaction of knowing that his presence bothered her. Reggie and Sophie continued the autopsy in silence.

"Huh, look at this," Reggie said a few minutes later. "Come take a picture of this area."

Sophie grabbed the camera and went over to where Reggie was pointing.

"Look at this mark on her outer thigh. These lacerations actually look like they could be bite marks. How strange. Maybe you were right," Reggie joked, spreading his hand to span over the circular area of the wounds, showing that the supposed bite was larger than the size of his hand.

"That an elephant seal killed her? That would be amazing." Sophie giggled.

"You never know. I've heard elephant seals can be quite dangerous," Reggie retorted.

"Maybe the seal thought she was sushi. Is it weird that I'm now hungry for a spicy tuna roll?" A muffled snort from across the room caught Sophie's attention. Looking over, Sophie caught Volpes scrubbing a smile from his face. Sophie was surprised she was able to break through the detective's solemn I'm-a-serious-man-that-does-serious-work façade.

Maybe he's not a total loss, Sophie thought doubtfully.

"Sophie, once you return the mermaid to the cooler, could you see if Fitz needs any assistance with weighing and x-rays? As soon as I am done talking with Mac, I will find you, and we can get back to work," Reggie said as they wrapped up the final steps of the autopsy.

"Sure thing, boss man," Sophie said with a jaunty salute, exiting the autopsy room with the mermaid. After depositing the mermaid back in the fridge, Sophie headed to Ace and Fitz's office.

Fifteen minutes later, as Fitz continued his animated monologue about the importance of a good sourdough starter, Sophie saw the door to Reggie's office open. Mac stepped through first, catching Sophie glancing his way. Mac gave her a long, considering look, which made apprehension skitter up her spine.

"As the microbes eat the sugars in the flour, they exhale carbon dioxide. That's what produces the bubbles. I will have to bring my sourdough mother for you to see some time soon," Fitz expounded.

"Your sourdough mother?" Sophie repeated back in confusion, looking away from Mac back to Fitz.

"Sorry! That's what we in the baking community call our sourdough starter. I've had mine for three years!" Fitz exclaimed.

"Wow. That is amazing," Sophie said, trying to feign excitement for Fitz's sake. Glancing back toward Reggie's office, she saw Mac had left. Reggie waved her to join him. "Sorry, Fitz, Reggie needs me."

She practically skipped away from Fitz and joined Reggie in front of his office door.

"Thank you for rescuing me. If I had known buying him a loaf of bread would make us bosom buddies, I wouldn't have done it. If I ever have to hear about the importance of a dense crust again, it will be too soon," Sophie whispered to Reggie as they headed back towards the main autopsy room. "What did Mac want?" She wheeled in the next gurney.

"He just had some follow up questions about an autopsy," Reggie said.

"Did you guys talk about me?"

"Why would you think that?"

"Just the way he looked at me when you guys exited your office."

"I think he's just trying to figure out how you fit in here."

"I'm sorry if my presence here is causing you problems." Sophie cringed internally.

"You are in no way causing problems. Having you here has been a tremendous help. I'm glad we get to work together. If Mac continues to be confrontational with you, let me know, and I will take care of it."

Sophie couldn't imagine sweet Reggie pushing back against Mac. She didn't want to put him in an uncomfortable position with that jerk, so she promised herself not to be a source of problems for him. "I can handle Mac. He's all bark, no bite. Besides, if he tries to bite me, I'll bite him back. And I'll do it somewhere it counts," Sophie chortled.

CHAPTER 9

She poured two drinks, making sure to stir a lethal dose of fentanyl into one of the vodka tonics. Squeezing an extra lemon into the glass to help cover any taste, she turned back to the man lounging on the plush couch.

Handing the large man his doctored drink, she sat down next to him.

"Share a drink with me. I've never done this before, and I'm nervous," she said with a small, timid smile.

She smothered a grin as he quickly tossed back his drink. She observed the man as he watched her with beady eyes, filled with repressed excitement. His neatly trimmed hair would look at home on an insurance salesman, and his slightly wrinkled suit was too tight across his gut. He reminded her of an aging high school athlete gone to seed, once-thick muscles devolved over time into hard fat.

"So, this is your first time answering an escort ad?" the man, who said his name was Dirk, asked. "What was your name again?"

"You can call me Snow White," she said, allowing her lips to curve into a secretive grin. She stood up and started to saunter towards her victim.

Sophie startled awake. "Fuck." She scrubbed her palms into

her eyes, looking at her clock and groaning at the time. She could sleep for two more hours before she needed to get up for work, but there was absolutely no way she could get back to sleep after the nightmare. She didn't want to think about the dream. Just remembering how much her dream-self had enjoyed toying with her victim made her feel vaguely ill.

"These fucking dreams... Why do you have to suck, brain?" Sophie asked out loud.

With a huff, Sophie peeled back her thick comforter, one of the few luxuries in her apartment. Darkness steeped her bedroom in shadows, the gloom created by a combination of the drawn curtains and the nascent dusk. In the dark, Sophie picked her way carefully around her room to her dresser, knowing where everything was placed in the small space by rote memory. Grabbing some clothes, she took a quick shower.

Afterward, Sophie glanced unseeingly into her refrigerator, but the unsettling dream had left her without an appetite. Glancing around her cramped, drab apartment, Sophie realized she couldn't spend another minute here alone with her thoughts.

Striding out of her apartment, she headed across the hall.

"Birdie, you home?" Sophie called out, knocking on her neighbor's faded red door.

"Girl, where else would I be?" Birdie said, opening the door.

Sophie snagged Ginsberg before he could fully escape into the hallway. Tucking the feline into her arms, Sophie scratched him under his chin. The buzzing of Ginsberg's purr did more to settle her nerves than anything else could.

"Birdie, do you want to go to the bar with me? I will buy you a drink. We can pretend its ladies' night and cause a ruckus," Sophie offered.

"There's a new episode of *The Bachelor* on tonight. I can't miss it."

"Of course. I wouldn't dream of getting between you and that bachelor you have your eyes on!"

"The things I would do to that man!" Birdie cackled.

"Down, girl. He'd probably never recover if you got a hold of him. You'd ruin him for other women," Sophie teased, handing Ginsberg back to Birdie.

"You're damn right I would."

"Maybe next time, then. Have a good night, Birdie," Sophie said, stepping back from Birdie's doorway.

"You too, sweetie. Go hit the bar and find yourself a man," Birdie yelled down the hallway as Sophie turned to leave.

THE JINGLE OF THE BELL ANNOUNCED SOPHIE'S ENTRANCE INTO the bar. Everyone glanced up at the noise, but quickly turned back to their drinks when they saw Sophie at the door. This was the type of bar where people minded their own business and weren't looking for any trouble. And Burg made sure it stayed that way.

Glancing around The Little Thumb, Sophie spotted a few lone patrons sprinkled throughout the pub and a group of burly men sitting around one of the tables in the back. There were a few familiar faces, but other than Burg, she knew no one by name. There was always someone in The Little Thumb drinking away their sorrows with cheap whiskey or a thick stout. Finding a stool at the bar with the obligatory two empty seats between her and the next person put her closer to the table of men than she would prefer. She was not particularly comfortable with a bunch of unknown men sitting at her back. However, knowing Burg was nearby meant she didn't need to worry. Plus, she didn't get the sense that they were paying her any attention.

"Hey, Soph. What can I get you? You want your usual?" Burg asked, approaching Sophie with a white bar towel thrown over his shoulder.

"Not today, Burg. I have to go to work in a few hours, and I don't want to drink beforehand. I need something without alcohol. Maybe just a soda?" Sophie said.

"How about a Lullaby Lady?" Burg suggested.

"Lullaby Lady?" Sophie repeated. "What is that?"

"It's like a Mythical version of your Shirley Temple. You wanna try it? I think you'll like it," Burg said.

"Sure," Sophie said with a shrug, plunking down some money to pay for the drink and to catch up her tab.

After a few minutes of fiddling with a drink, his back turned to Sophie so she couldn't see, Burg flipped a coaster onto the bar top and deposited a tall highball glass in front of her with a flourish, reminding her once again of an old-timey circus performer.

The glass contents were a cloudy white, similar in appearance to watered-down milk, topped with a bright crimson layer. As Sophie watched, the red floater slowly seeped its way into the white liquid below, looking almost like blood soaking into cloth.

"Beautiful, but deadly. Just like the Lullaby Lady," Burg said.

Sophie picked up the glass, turning it towards the light to admire the beauty of the macabre drink. Holding it to her lips, Sophie took a small sip. The first thing she tasted was some kind of floral fruit, like lychee or passionfruit. It was almost perfumey at first, but then the taste settled on her palate and morphed into something deeper, like a dark tea sweetened with honey.

"It's good. What's in it?" Sophie asked, smacking her lips lightly, before taking another larger sip.

"If I told you, I'd have to kill you," Burg said dramatically, baring his teeth at her.

"It's sad that you think you're funny," Sophie said, rolling her eyes. "Lullaby Lady… That's a weird name."

"It's named after a real person. She's a Fae considered so evil and power-hungry that only the Fae queen can leash her wrath. She's the name Fae mothers use to keep their children from misbehaving."

"So the Lullaby Lady is like the boogeyman – made up to scare your kids into behaving."

"I hate to break the news to you, but both the boogeyman and the Lullaby Lady are not made up. They're real. Every culture has some myth around a creature like the boogeyman. It's usually based on ghoul sightings or sometimes vampires depending on the country," Burg explained.

"Ghouls are real? Do they eat humans? You know what? I don't want to know. Tell me more about the Lullaby Lady. She sounds more interesting."

"She's supposed to be beautiful but deadly. I don't know anyone who has ever seen her for real, though. She lives in the Fae realm. There are rumors she is the Fae queen's favorite assassin. I've heard rumors that she kills anyone who has seen her face, so only the queen even knows what she looks like."

"She sounds kind of awesome. Are Fae the same thing as fairies? I've meant to ask someone. Everyone keeps talking about Fae this and Fae that and I keep picturing someone who looks like Tinkerbell," Sophie asked with wide eyes.

"Fairies aren't real creatures, but they were based on the Fae. If you ever meet a Fae, don't bring up fairies; they get quite pissy about the whole thing. Fae are dangerous. Some people might actually consider me a Fae creature since ogres originated in the Fae realm. However, I prefer to just think of myself as an ogre, an entirely different species than the Fae. Not all ogres are nice people by human standards but some of the Fae make ogres look like sweethearts. The actual Sídhe Fae themselves are usually cold, beautiful, power-driven, superior beings who consider everything else below them. Do *not* mess with them," Burg warned, leaning close over the bar top to whisper to Sophie.

"Sídhe Fae?" Sophie repeated slowly. It sounded like Burg had said Shee Fae.

"Yes, the Sídhe Fae. Thankfully, most stay in the Fae realm, sticking to their courts and fairy mounds, so the odds of us coming face-to-face with one is somewhat rare. Mostly, we only get the banished ones here in this realm. And their descendants."

Burg opened his mouth, clearly ready to issue more warnings, but a man down at the far end of the bar raised and wiggled his empty glass.

"You stay away from the Fae, okay?" Burg told Sophie, crossing his thick arms over his chest.

"You got it, Burg. I will keep far away from the Fae," Sophie promised, raising both hands in surrender. "How would I even know I'm dealing with a Fae? Do they look different?"

"Well, if you were Fae, you might be able to sense their magic. But since you're human, you have no way to tell. A lot of them pack a powerful magical punch, so they can be very dangerous."

"Do they look different from a human?"

"They mostly look human. They are snobs, so they usually dress lavishly. They are generally rich, especially the old established families. The best way to spot one – if you can't sense their magic – is they often dress in an old-fashioned manner, and they tend to treat all humans like servants," Burg advised.

"Oookay. I think that is enough information for me," Sophie whispered under her breath before taking another sip of her Lullaby Lady.

"I'm just sick of it, is all I'm saying. It's fucking bullshit, and you know it," a rough-hewn voice said from behind Sophie.

Looking into the antique-mirrored wall over the bar, Sophie located the voice. The mottled reflection showed a shaggy-haired man with ruddy weathered skin sitting at the round table a few feet behind her.

"They're pushing us out of Forest Knolls. Soon we'll only have Golden Gate Park and the Presidio to run in. If they keep trying to muscle us out, we're going to end up having to trek to Marin County or Muir Woods. And you know how the fucking packs are up there," the man growled.

"What would you have us do? We don't have any leverage or

power. I don't want to end up like Zee," another man with golden-blonde hair sheared close to his scalp said.

All the men looked like they just came from a job involving manual labor based on their dusty, grimy utility pants and well-worn work boots.

"We should take it to the Conclave. They need to know what's happening," the first man said.

"You're getting too loud, Wayne," the shaggy-headed man said. Sophie quickly dropped her attention from the mirror to her drink before they caught her eavesdropping.

Sophie waved goodbye to Burg, mouth already watering at the thought of a big bowl of ramen from the noodle house a few blocks over. They had some soups that were inexpensive enough to not put too big a dent in her budget.

As she departed, Sophie sensed a presence a few feet behind her. However, her danger intuition wasn't pinging. Glancing carefully over her shoulder, she saw the blonde man exit the bar right behind her, stumbling slightly. Striding quickly away, Sophie glanced back at the man to catch him peeing on the front corner of the building where the brick met the pavement.

Snorting, Sophie called out, "Burg hates it when you guys piss on his bar."

The man looked up from the intense concentration on his urine stream to see Sophie wagging an accusing finger at him. The man gave Sophie a shrug, a big shit-eating grin, and a lascivious wink. Shaking her head, Sophie turned on her heel to leave the man to his drunken pee fest.

CHAPTER 10

$\mathcal{A}$s Sophie approached the ME's building, she spotted a trench coat-covered silhouette with a familiar shuffling walk.

"Reggie! Wait for me," Sophie said, jogging to catch up to her friend.

Entering the main hallway, Sophie saw Ace and Mac ahead, facing off against one another. They were both scowling at each other and arguing in low, angry voices. Sophie tried to discern what they were saying, but she was too far away to catch any words.

I thought the two kings of irritability would get along like two bugs in a rug, Sophie thought, watching the men square off like junkyard dogs ready to fight over the same scraps.

"I need to talk to both of you," Mac said, not even glancing away from Ace to confirm who it was. Turning on his feet, Mac headed off down the hall toward Reggie's office. He didn't even bother to look and see if they followed.

Sophie looked at Ace and mimed blowing her brains out with two fingers, making him snort. Ace quickly turned his snort into a cough when Mac looked back at him with a glower.

Reggie took a seat at his gray metal desk while Sophie grabbed one of the two chairs facing him. Mac paced back and forth along the side of the room, looking more and more agitated. The few times Sophie had previously been around Mac, he had sported a scruff of a beard and tousled hair, but now he looked completely rumpled, as though he had rolled around in his suit. There were dark circles under his red-rimmed eyes.

"What can we do for you, Mac?" Reggie asked after delicately clearing his throat.

Mac froze in the middle of his agitated pacing like someone pulled his power cord; then he swung around pointing a finger at Sophie. "Explain to me how you knew about the mermaid."

Sophie stared at Mac for a moment in confusion, then looked over at Reggie to see if he understood what was going on any more than she did. She saw her uncertainty mirrored on Reggie's face.

"Uh… what do you mean?" she asked.

"How did you know an elephant seal killed the mermaid? I thought you were just joking around. Imagine my surprise when all anyone in my department could talk about this morning was the stupid woman who stumbled into the mating territory of an elephant seal and got herself killed. When they brought the body in last night, it was not common knowledge. So, explain how you knew," Mac demanded.

"I was kidding around. I didn't *actually* think an elephant seal killed her. That's preposterous. I made up the most ridiculous thing I could think of because I wanted to make Reggie laugh. It is just a very, *very* strange coincidence that an elephant seal killed the mermaid. I couldn't have possibly known the truth!"

"Okay. Say I believe you," Mac said, while Sophie huffed in exasperation. "Let's say it was just a strange lucky guess. Explain to me how you knew about the vampire."

"What do you mean?" Sophie said, apprehension working its way slowly up her throat.

"The staked vampire. It turns out he really did have a secret human girlfriend named Bridgette. No one even knew she existed, not even Montgomery's Domus. The only reason I found her is because I decided to do some checking around Twin Peaks after finding out about the mermaid's death. I overheard you say Montgomery was snatched in Twin Peaks. His body was discovered in Golden Gate Park. Twin Peaks was on no one's radar. Guess what I found after I did some digging? A secret human girlfriend named Bridgette Hudson living in Twin Peaks. How did you know all of these details?"

Sophie sat frozen in her chair with her mouth hanging open, her mind spinning in a thousand different directions at once. "His... His name was really Montgomery?" Sophie asked in a small voice.

Mac jerked his head in an affirmative. Sophie looked over at Reggie helplessly.

"I was making it up, I swear. I invented stories to keep us entertained. You have to believe me. I didn't know anything about these murders. Please tell me you believe me, Reg." Sophie turned, clasping her hands together so tightly her skin looked stretched taut over her knuckles.

"Of course I believe—"

"I know you didn't commit those murders," Mac said, interrupting Reggie's reassurances. "When the vampire was grabbed in Twin Peaks and then dumped in Golden Gate Park, you were here working. I checked. There was no possible way your absence wouldn't have been noticed. To grab a vampire, stake him, and dump his body would have taken enough time that someone here would have noticed you were missing. I already talked to Reginald yesterday, and your whereabouts can be accounted for the entire night of the vampire's murder. You would not have been able to leave the building without Miss Zhao being aware of it. I followed you the day the mermaid died, so I know you weren't there. Plus, there was a witness to her killing. My question is: how you knew all the details about their deaths. Has someone been feeding you information?"

"I don't talk to anyone about the details of the cases we work on, I swear. Couldn't it just all be weird coincidences?" Sophie asked, knowing deep down it didn't seem likely. Mac following her around the other day explained the feeling of being watched.

"I have an idea," Reggie piped up. Both Mac and Sophie looked at him with expectant gazes, so Reggie continued, "Mac, if you have access to all the police reports, I will get Amira to pull the files on all the autopsy cases Sophie and I have worked on. We will try to remember the stories Sophie told about each death, and you can compare her stories to the reports. Don't tell us the details of the reports so we can determine if she has rightly guessed the circumstances of any other deaths."

"Reg, this is stupid. We don't need to do this. They were just dumb made-up stories," Sophie said, apprehension making her words small and quick.

"I disagree. We need to see if it was just a fluke. If the other stories don't match up to the police reports, then we will know with certainty. But if you do get the other murders right... there might be something bigger happening, and we need to figure out what it is," Reggie said. He squeezed Sophie's shoulder as he headed out to get Amira to pull all the files from the last week and a half.

As Sophie curled forward and pressed her forehead to her knees, Mac cleared his throat and announced he needed to get his laptop. His command to not leave the office made Sophie silently flip him off.

When Mac returned, Sophie turned to him. "So, what does this mean? Either I'm a murder suspect, or I have a supernatural power. Are those my only fucking options?"

"You wouldn't be the first human to have powers. It usually means there was a Mythical somewhere in your ancestry," Mac said. Looking at her slumped shoulders, he said, "Would it be so bad to have powers? You could do some good with them."

"I don't want a complicated life. I just want to assist with autopsies, hang out with my friends, and occasionally drink whiskey at my neighborhood ogre bar. Is that too much to ask?"

Mac gave Sophie a sympathetic look she didn't appreciate one bit. She didn't want this jerk's pity. Especially since, in her opinion, it was all his fault anyhow.

"I have a question," Sophie said after a small awkward silence. "If it turns out the rest of the stories don't match up, what does that mean for me? Will I be a murder suspect?"

"Not for the mermaid, obviously. But we will need to figure out how you knew all the details of Montgomery's death. I can't overlook the fact that you knew detailed specifics. But don't worry about it yet. We'll cross that bridge when we come to it."

Sophie huffed in annoyance. *Easy for him to be nonchalant when his life isn't the one being upended.*

Reggie came hustling back in, clutching a stack of folders. Pulling Sophie's chair around his desk, they sat side by side with Mac separated from them by the bulky desk.

Reggie stacked the files one by one, keeping them in the same sequence the autopsies initially occurred, starting with Sophie's first one.

"When did I first start telling the stories?" Sophie asked him, trying to recall. "Wait… I think I remember. Was it that headless guy? I remember joking that the murderers cut off his tattoos."

Flipping through the stack, Reggie located the correct file and called out the case number to Mac. While Mac made notes in his little flip book, Reggie and Sophie told him the details of the story Sophie made up about the headless corpse.

When they got to the autopsy where she first met Mac, Reggie started to move it to the growing stack of reviewed files.

"Wait. Did you have a story about this one?" Mac asked. "I

remember you said something about a 'monster sending a message'. What would your story have been about this murder? This was my case, and I would like to hear your thoughts on the victim's death."

"I don't know. Whatever the story I was going to tell, it's gone. I don't remember what I was going to say." Sophie apologetically shrugged.

"Hmmm. Maybe you need to be in the presence of the body to get their story," Reggie suggested.

"You're assuming this isn't just a waste of time and that I'm getting these stories right," Sophie said pointedly.

"Let's just move on to the next one," Mac growled. "I can't spend all night here while you two reminisce. I've barely slept in the last twenty-four hours."

"I'm so sorry we're inconveniencing you! How about you shove–"

"None of the autopsies scheduled for tonight are high priority. I believe getting this resolved takes precedence. We will be able to get our work done just fine," Reggie interrupted quickly. Mac waved his hand imperiously for them to continue. Sophie was opening her mouth to tell Mac precisely what she thought about his attitude when Reggie caught her eye and shook his head minutely. Sighing in defeat, Sophie turned back to the next file. She recognized that her urge to pick a fight with Mac came from the desire to not have to face the possibility that her stories were anything other than made up.

Since they typically only completed about five to six autopsies per shift, it was less than forty files to review. Reviewing the autopsies took thirty of the longest minutes of Sophie's life.

"Well, Mac, tell us. Were any of Sophie's stories correct?" Reggie asked after he closed the last file. Sophie was thankful he said something, since her vocal cords appeared to be frozen.

Mac set his laptop aside and picked up his notebook. Silently Mac flipped through his notes, reviewing his information. Sophie was barely able to restrain herself from leaping over the desk and throttling him in impatience.

"Out of the 31 stories, you got 27 correct. One murder is unsolved, so there weren't enough details to confirm one way or another. I will be following up with the lead detective on that one. You had some minor details correct with the other three, but the majority of your story does not correlate to the police report. So it appears your gift isn't fool-proof," Mac stated.

"Gift..." Sophie sputtered.

"If we assume these numbers reflect your usual accuracy, you are correct over 80% of the time," Mac continued.

"But... they were just stories. They're not real," Sophie whispered, staring at Mac in horror.

"Don't you see, Sophie? This is amazing. You can do so much to help!" Reggie exclaimed.

Looking at Sophie's face, Reggie's delighted expression morphed into dismay, as tears filled her eyes.

"Oh, Sophie. It's going to be okay," Reggie said, pulling her into a hug. Sophie, not normally the touchy-feely type, clung to Reggie's shoulders for a long moment, swallowing thickly to get her emotions under control. There was no way in hell Sophie was going to cry, especially in front of the gruff detective who was looking decidedly uncomfortable with her display.

"I'm okay. Seriously, I'm okay. Thanks, Reg," Sophie said, pulling back.

Settling back in her chair, Sophie rubbed her temples, trying to stave off a stress headache.

"Okay, what happens now?" she asked, staring at Mac.

"For now, I want you to both carry on like normal. I need to follow up on these three cases that don't match your stories. I also want to see what I can dig up on the unsolved murder. In the meantime, I want you to keep telling Reggie your stories about each autopsy, then send them to me. If you can find a way to record them, do that. I want to make sure no details are forgotten or missed. Once I have more information, I'll be back. Also, don't tell anyone about what you can do yet. We need to decide together what to do about your gift. Don't tell anyone, Sophie – not your co-workers, not your family, not your ogre friend. No one. Got it?"

"Sure thing, Dad. Are you gonna ground me if I don't obey? Maybe take away my car keys?" Sophie said, voice dripping with derision.

"You're not as funny as you think you are. Just to reiterate, until we get a handle on this, we need to keep it a secret. There are dangerous people in this city who would happily use you or eliminate you if they know what you can do," Mac growled. "Speaking of what you can do... Are there any other hidden talents you possess? Have you ever been able to see the future or influence other people's moods?"

"Well, I do seem to be able to magically annoy you."

"Yes, that does seem to be a talent unique to you. What about gut instincts? Do you sense danger or easily get a read on people's intentions or personalities?"

"I don't know. I mean, I could tell you were a dickhead right away," Sophie teased.

"Sophie–" Mac started to snarl at her.

"Okay, okay. Sorry, you're just so easy to rile. Yeah, sometimes I get strong gut instincts about people or situations. But I don't know if it's any different or stronger than a normal person's intuition," Sophie said, raising her hands in defeat.

"What about dreams? Any premonitions?" Reggie piped up.

"No premonitions of any kind. However, I have a recurring dream where I'm a serial killer who works at Disneyland as Snow White. Occasionally, I have a dream where I'm a cutthroat stockbroker, too," Sophie said, making Reggie laugh.

"I can picture you as Snow White, but I can't imagine you in a suit." Reggie chuckled.

"Bizarro-World Snow White, maybe. You'd be handing out

the poisoned apples rather than eating them," Mac said, making Sophie snort in amused agreement. "Okay, I am going to head out. As soon as I have more information, I will find you guys here."

Without another word, Mac turned and stalked out of the office. Sophie eyed the stapler on Reggie's desk, fantasizing about chucking it at the back of Mac's head. She sighed, knowing deep down it was not Mac's fault that overwhelming information was now hanging over her head. The only thing he did wrong was he figured out that the stories could be real.

"I know this is a lot," Reggie said softly. "But you can do this. You can help people. The same woman who tried to rescue a cornered opossum and give it an apple is the kind of person who would use her gift to help people. I believe in you, Sophie."

"I just want to be normal, Reg," Sophie whispered.

"You were never normal, Soph," Reggie whispered back like he was confiding a well-kept secret.

"Ouch. Too true, though," Sophie chortled. "Okay, enough of this pity party bullshit. Let's go cut open some corpses."

"That's my girl."

The rest of the night felt a bit surreal to Sophie. Reggie used his phone to record her stories as they worked. He promised to take care of sending the recordings to Mac. She was glad not to have to worry about it. For the first two autopsies, the stories came out stilted and awkward until Reggie and Sophie started to relax and get into the strange rhythmic groove of their work.

As they sat down to lunch, neither Reggie nor Sophie participated much in the conversation, each lost in their own thoughts. Thankfully, no one seemed to notice that they were unusually quiet. A heated argument between Ace and Amira diverted any attention away from them.

"I don't care that you feel the need to obsessively wash your food like the OCD-riddled rodent that you are. That's not the point. The point is that you're getting fucking water everywhere.

The least you could do is mop it up, so the breakroom isn't a hazard. Someone could slip," Amira sneered.

"I can't believe *you* would dare to call me inconsiderate when you leave this room stinking like a fish market. Every. Single. Day," Ace ground out, baring his teeth at Amira in the beginnings of a growl. "I am *not* a rodent. I'm not going to put up with that specie-ist bullshit from the apex kingdoms, so I'm certainly not going to put up with that shit from you. You know better. The lesser kingdoms need to fucking stick together and watch each others' backs. Or are you too good for the rest of us, feline?"

"Apex kingdom? Lesser kingdoms? What are those?" Sophie asked, hoping to head off a brawl. The way both Ace and Amira had started to rise from their seats hadn't boded well for a peaceful resolution. Intellectually, Sophie had known they wouldn't actually come to blows, but she could imagine they both had their hackles raised in aggression.

"In the shifter world, there is a bit of a hierarchy. The apex predators like wolves, bears, and the big cats are in one kingdom. The lesser kingdom consists of the other shifters who aren't top predators. Like us, for example, an opossum, a raccoon, a goose, and a cat," Reggie said, pointing to each person at the table in turn. "There are quite a few of us from the lesser kingdoms in this realm. Despite our greater numbers, we are often treated like we are odd and inferior by the other species."

"Is Mac an apex shifter, since he's a fox?" Sophie asked.

"He's on the cusp. Not considered an apex predator by the higher kingdom, despite being a predatory animal. But he also doesn't fit into the lesser kingdom with the rest of us," Reggie said.

"It's all bullshit, of course. There is no 'lesser kingdom', and if you use that term, it means you're an asshole. The hierarchy doesn't really exist – it's all in their heads. The bigger the predator, the bigger their ego. Wolves are the worst ones because they are the most famous," Fitz said. "It's all those damn romance novels, I say."

"And don't forget the Fae who treat *all* shifter kingdoms like they're inferior," Ace interjected.

"What? Why?" Sophie asked.

"The Fae used their magic to create shifters to be their servants and warriors. They used to own shifters," Amira explained.

"Like slaves?" Sophie asked with distaste.

"Yes, exactly like slaves. They made apex shifters to battle for them, hunt, guard. The lesser shifters were used for a variety of purposes," Amira responded.

"Like what?"

"Depends on the breed. Scouting, domestic work, assassins… sometimes just as a pet. It was so long ago, it's mostly just speculation now," Amira said with a shrug. "But a lot of Fae still act superior to shifters, and our history with them has a lot to do with it. That, and Fae are often just arrogant assholes."

"What about humans? Where do they fit in?" Sophie asked.

She glanced around the table as no one answered. Everyone looked uncomfortable and vaguely embarrassed.

"We don't even count, do we?" Sophie asked in growing understanding.

"Well…" Ace said, clearing his throat. "Strength and power are what count with Mythicals. The bigger or more dangerous the individual is, the more they are respected. For example, shifters are physically strong, have teeth and claws; we're faster, stronger, and we heal quickly – even the lesser kingdom shifters. However, we respect the Fae because some of them have unimaginable power."

"Alright. So, what would happen if a small group of vampires faced off against an ogre? If the ogre told them to leave his territory, they would, right? Because the ogre is stronger or more powerful than them?" Sophie asked, remembering the interaction between Burg and Fabio.

"It would take a very old, very powerful vampire to be willing to tangle with an ogre. Or at least a sizable group of vampires," Amira said with a small shrug.

"Does that mean humans are the weakest and least powerful? To a vampire, are humans just warm, wiggly snacks who sometimes try to run away?" Sophie clarified.

"An individual human? Yes. But all of humanity? There is so much strength in the sheer numbers of humans within this realm. To stay safe, Mythicals must remain a secret. There are some individuals in the Mythical community who believe we should rule over humans. I believe those people are courting extinction. I just want to work here and live my life," Reggie said.

"Well... this weak, defenseless, tender human is ready to get back to work. We're behind because of Mac anyway," Sophie said, standing up. "By the way, those guys who think they're better than you because they think their animal side is bigger or badder... Those guys can go sit and spin. What you guys are and what you can do... Frankly, it's fucking amazing."

Tossing her trash in the garbage, Sophie exited the lunchroom, pausing in front of the chart to see what autopsy was scheduled next.

"Soph, wait up," Reg said, catching up to her side when she stopped outside the autopsy room. When she turned to face him, Reggie gave her a tentative smile.

"Thank you," Reggie said. "That meant a lot to us. We get sick of the way the apex shifters sometimes treat us; we appreciate your words. And we don't think of humans as less. Especially not you. You're our friend."

"You guys are my friends, too," Sophie said. "Now enough of this mushy-feelings shit. Let's go cut up a corpse."

~

STEPPING OFF THE BUS, SOPHIE ADMIRED THE EARLY MORNING FOG as it rose slowly from the street. Soon, the heat of the sun would chase away the last wisps of curling fog still stubbornly clinging to the buildings and sidewalks. Glancing briefly to the right, where Brown Betty and her bed were waiting for her, Sophie whirled on her heel and headed left. With the revelations of the night before, there was no way she would be able to get to sleep anytime soon. Exhaustion and a tension headache hovered along her temples, but she couldn't bear the idea of heading into her empty apartment with only her swirling thoughts to keep her company.

Her wandering path took her to a small curio shop on Leavenworth. Books, hats, and racks of random goods spilled out of the darkened doorway onto the sidewalk like a burst suitcase. Stepping inside, the narrow space was overflowing with clothes, cabinets crammed full of used books, and hundreds of hats stacked to the ceiling. With only one aisle, the store was barely wide enough to fit Sophie and her messenger bag. It almost felt like she had stepped into the overflowing closet of a hoarder. In the front window were several rotating displays, piled high with sparkling costume jewelry.

A thin, older man with a wash of dark brown hair peeking out from a tan ball cap, popped his head up from behind a small glass case, startling Sophie.

"Hello, welcome! Are you looking for anything in particular?" the man said in a warm, mellow voice.

"I'm just looking around," Sophie replied, shaking her head in wonder at this strange store. It felt as if she'd stepped into a pocket reality, separate from the rest of the world.

Sophie turned, cautious not to knock over a hanging display bulging with purses of every size and color. She was about to escape back into the open spaces of the street when something caught her attention. A citrine eye almost appeared to be gazing at her from behind a pile of sunglasses on a shelf. Picking her fingers through the clutter, she pushed the jumbled detritus out of the way. Sophie carefully slid a teacup and saucer to the front of the dusty shelf. On the outside of the delicate porcelain cup was a hand-painted cat, closely resembling Ginsberg.

Picking the cup off the shelf, Sophie examined it for flaws. Although it was clearly a handcrafted item, the image of the cat was quaint and carefully detailed. There didn't appear to be a single chip or scratch on either the cup or saucer. When Sophie glanced into the bottom of the cup, she almost lost her grasp on the handle and dropped it.

Cracking up, Sophie admired the dainty, cursive words painted inside: "Hot Pussy".

Unable to contain her grin, Sophie brought the long-lost treasure to the man who was waiting by an old-fashioned cash register. Sophie happily paid the store owner the few measly dollars listed on the bottom of the saucer. He meticulously wrapped everything in newspaper after giving the set an admiring look. With a conspiratorial grin, he handed Sophie her package.

Sophie scurried back toward Brown Betty, already looking forward to seeing Birdie's reaction to the gift. She was also excited to have a normal human conversation without a hint of any magical stuff, with a sweet, dirty-minded old lady.

CHAPTER 11

B arely an hour into their shift the next day, Reggie's phone dinged loudly as they finished up an autopsy.

Stripping off his disposable gloves, Reggie picked up the phone and looked at the screen for a moment before quickly typing something. Sophie smiled at the way Reggie's tongue poked out of the corner of his mouth in concentration as he typed.

"Detective Volpes will be here in about an hour. He wants to meet with us," Reggie informed Sophie. "I think we can get another autopsy done before he arrives."

"You got it, boss. Let me go fetch the next customer," Sophie said flippantly, trying to disguise her sudden nerves.

The next hour both dragged on and rocketed past at the same time. It didn't help that Sophie caught herself glancing at the large clock on the wall every few minutes. After a quick but thorough scrub, finishing up the paperwork, and returning the body to the fridge, Sophie headed to Reggie's office with dragging feet.

Stepping into the small office, Sophie breathed a sigh of relief to see that Mac hadn't arrived yet, even though it was only a temporary reprieve at best. Sophie tried to sit down to relax, but almost as soon as her butt hit the seat of her chair, she bounced back up. She started pacing the length of the office, much like Mac had the day before. Her eyes were dark with worry and stress.

"Mac says he'll be here in just a few minutes. He's in the lobby waiting to get buzzed in by Miss Zhao," Reggie said, purposefully looking at his phone to give Sophie her space.

"I have a question, actually," Sophie said, glomming onto a distracting thought. "Why don't you guys have more security for this building? So many of these autopsies could put someone in jail, you would think they would be better protected. All we have are buzzers and Miss Zhao."

"Miss Zhao is more than enough security. Only someone exceedingly foolish would attempt to force their way past her," Reggie confided.

"Miss Zhao?" Sophie repeated, thinking about the woman out front wearing kitten heels and a wool pantsuit.

"Oh yes. She's a dilong," Reggie said, as if Sophie should know what that means.

"A what?"

"A dilong is a Chinese earth dragon. Only a fool, or someone with a death wish, would try to fight a dilong," Reggie said, making Sophie's head whip around to stare at him incredulously. Sophie felt her eyes widen owlishly, but she couldn't control the reaction.

"A dragon. Like an actual live dragon," Sophie repeated, desperately wanting to go gawk at Miss Zhao like a tiger in a zoo. Sophie was unable imagine Miss Prim-and-Proper as a scaled and powerful dragon... Although there was something wise and formidable lingering in Miss Zhao's eyes.

Before Sophie could ask all the questions crowding her brain, the office door swung open, and Mac slipped inside.

"Did you know the receptionist is a dragon?" Sophie asked him, trying to keep the awe out of her voice.

"Oh yes. Whoever hired her to guard the entrance is a genius. No one is going to be able to sneak past a dilong, and they'll be incredibly sorry if they try. Just remember that respect and manners are very important to Chinese dragons. You do not want to be on their bad side."

Sophie plopped into one of the office chairs while Mac took the other one, pulling out his flip notebook. As Sophie watched him quickly review his notes, she wracked her brain, trying to remember if she'd ever let her mouth run away from her in front of Miss Zhao. She couldn't remember any instance where she might have been rude, but she made a mental note to treat the dragon carefully.

Mac still looked tired, and his hair needed to be tamed, but his dark suit looked freshly pressed with sharp creases. While he scanned his eyes over the writing crowding the pages, Sophie covertly took a moment to admire what the blazer did for his shoulders. Often, a suit disguised a man's physique, but this jacket emphasized the breadth of his shoulders nicely.

I bet he gets his suits tailored to make them fit so well, Sophie thought, letting her eyes linger for just a moment more.

"Here's what I have found so far," Mac announced. "Your story on the unsolved murder might be correct. Too soon to tell yet, but I stopped by this morning to talk to the presiding detective. I pointed out to her that there might be a hole in the boyfriend's alibi. She was not pleased about me butting in, but I talked her into giving him another look. We will see how that pans out. As for the three autopsies that don't match your visions, I can't figure out a way to prove which version of their death stories are correct: yours, or the police report."

Mac flipped back a few pages in his notebook and pointed to a name on the page.

"The first victim I want to review is Joseph Henson, the jaguar shifter. The police report says he died by suicide. He hung himself, but left a note. His younger brother Floyd found him the next day when he didn't show up for a family luncheon. Your story was that the brother Floyd got Joseph to take oxy and drink alcohol, then staged the hanging with two accomplices. According to the toxicology report, Joseph did have oxycodone and alcohol in his system. Floyd has an alibi for that night, but it's not rock-solid. He was with two of his friends, a John Dowling and a Mateo Perez," Mac said.

"Could those two be the accomplices Sophie saw in her vision?" Reggie asked.

"I have no way to prove that possibility. The case is marked closed, and there aren't any other leads to follow. I investigated both Dowling and Perez. Although they both have previous arrest records, there is nothing in their history that would lead me to believe they could commit murder. For the moment, it's a dead end."

"That doesn't mean Sophie's not right about what happened," Reggie argued.

"I agree, but I need to have more concrete evidence before I can do anything about it. To reopen a case, I have to have more than just Sophie's word. That brings us to Cynthia Forsythe. The report states that she interrupted a burglary in progress and was shot for her troubles. Sophie's version of the events was the person who shot Mrs Forsythe had been hired to do so. They were waiting for her to come home. They ransacked the house and stole some valuables, making it look like a robbery gone wrong. I don't suppose your vision happened to include who hired the gunman?" Mac asked.

"Not that I remember. If you got me access to the body again, I could attempt to get another... reading," Sophie offered with an apologetic shrug.

"I'm going to come back to that offer in a minute. Before that, I want to review the third autopsy story that doesn't match the police report: the vampire, Montgomery. You were correct about his real name, his human girlfriend, and I suspect you were right that someone grabbed him in Twin Peaks. I talked to Bridgette. The night he was murdered, she was expecting him to visit, but he never showed. The police report states it was a dine-n-dash interrupted by a human hunter. If he was feeding on a human, no witnesses have come forward. Hunters often recruit these victims to join their ranks, so it might not mean anything either way. I'm planning to follow up with Montgomery's Domus tomorrow to see if they have any enemies who are willing to kill members over a real estate deal.

"But it feels like a long shot. Most Domuses are extremely secretive. Even if they know one of their members was murdered, they wouldn't give any information to the police. They like to deal with problems themselves. It makes them look weak to accept help. With all of these cases, I'm stuck, and there are no more leads to follow. Plus, this is technically Lancaster and Hernandez's case, and they're hassling me for trying to muscle in on their territory. They're acting worse than usual, and that's saying something when it comes to wolves getting territorial. I think it's lazy police work just to accept the easy solution as they have."

"Wolves, like real wolves, you mean," Sophie asked. When Mac nodded, Sophie took a deep breath, counted to three in her head before breathing out. There were so many things jostling for room in her brain that she just had to put a pin in that information and deal with it later. "Okay, moving on. If the wolves aren't going to let you in on Montgomery's case, where does that leave us? It sounds like I can't help any more than I already have."

"I was hoping to get you access to one of these bodies to see if we can get another reading, but Joseph Henson and Cynthia Forsythe's corpses have been released back to their families. Both have already been cremated. Montgomery was released back to his Domus, and I have no idea what they do with their deceased members, but I would be shocked if they let us anywhere near Montgomery's body," Mac said.

"Well, shit. I thought you'd have better news. Or maybe some ideas about how I could help," Sophie said with a frown.

"There is something. Do you remember the first time we met? It was an autopsy for Zhang Liu. He'd been torn apart by a shifter. Based on hair and tissue samples, forensics was able to narrow it down to a wolf shifter. I initially thought it was gang-related or possibly a drug deal gone bad, but I wasn't convinced. I've been unable to find any real suspects, and the leads have gone dry. I want you to examine the body again," Mac requested.

"Absolutely. Just bring me the body, and I'll see what I can do," Sophie agreed immediately.

Mac cleared his throat a couple of times, looking more and more uncomfortable as he glanced at his notes.

"What's the problem?" Sophie asked.

"Well, we're going to have to dig him up," Mac said with a grimace.

"What do you mean, dig him up?" Sophie asked, her voice rising in pitch until it squeaked on the last word.

"He was interred at the Woodlawn Memorial Park down in Colma three days ago," Mac revealed matter-of-factly.

"You want us to go grave robbing!" Sophie screeched. "How the fuck are the three of us going to sneak into a cemetery and dig up a coffin?"

"I'm not sure yet, but we need to do it soon. I'll figure something out. I'm concerned the potency of your visions may wear off the farther you get from the time of death. I don't want to take the risk," Mac said.

"This Saturday, both Sophie and I are off of work. So are Amira, Fitz, and Ace. I think we need to inform them of Sophie's gift. They're going to start noticing what she can do sooner or later. I have worked with all three of them for many years now; we can trust them," Reggie suggested, looking at Mac and Sophie expectantly.

"Are you sure we can trust them? If we're wrong about

Sophie's gift, it could get very embarrassing very quickly. Possibly even damaging to our careers. Even if we are right about Sophie's gift, if word gets out before we can prepare, it would cause its own set of problems. Either way, until we can confirm this with more irrefutable evidence, we should keep it entirely under wraps," Mac warned.

"You know this isn't a fluke, Mac. You know her visions are right," Reggie almost snarled, making Sophie's eyebrows rise in surprise.

"I agree. She's the real deal. But... I need to figure out if her visions are 100% accurate or if she makes mistakes. Anyway, I need another lead on the Liu case, and she's my best shot," Mac argued.

"Did you review the audiotape we sent you this morning?" Reggie asked, switching subjects.

"Yes. All those visions appear to be correct. However, they were also pretty straight forward cases. Let's see what happens Saturday, and then we can figure out what to do next," Mac said. "Are you sure you can trust Ace, Amira, and Fitz?"

"Absolutely," Reggie confirmed with a firm nod.

Flipping his notebook closed decisively, Mac stood up from his chair and headed to the office door. "Alright, no time like the present. Let's go talk to your crew," he said, walking out of the office, leaving Reggie and Sophie to scramble after him.

"Hey dickhead, slow down and wait for us," Sophie bellowed.

"That's Detective Dickhead to you." He headed towards the lunchroom where the hum of conversation was buzzing.

When Mac walked into the lunchroom with Sophie hot on his heels, the conversation cut off like someone hit the mute button. Sophie observed from over Mac's shoulder as everyone stared in shock at his intrusion with slack jaws. The break room was the team's sanctuary, a place to relax and unwind from the occasional darkness of their work. Having the detective's thunder-cloud presence appear in the doorway had shocked everyone into silence.

As Sophie crowded in behind Reggie in the doorway, Mac grabbed an empty chair from the round lunchroom table and sat with a flourish.

"What the fuck?" Ace growled. "You are not welcome here, you–"

"We need your help," Mac interrupted before Ace could get on a roll.

Reggie and Sophie scurried over and took seats on either side of Mac.

"He's right," Reggie said, cutting over anything else Mac might have said to rile up Ace. "We do need your help."

Reggie and Mac spent the next thirty minutes laying out the facts for the team.

"So, our girl here is a superhero, huh?" Ace said with a grin after Mac finished speaking.

"I'm not–"

"Stop razzing her, Ace. This has been a tough couple of days for Sophie," Mac chastised, his quick defense catching Sophie by surprise.

"Fuck you. I'm not 'razzing' Sophie. You don't get to come in here and tell me how to talk to my friends," Ace sneered, starting to rise and lean over the table towards Mac.

"Enough, you guys. I can't take any arguments right now. You're going to give me a headache. We need to formulate a plan, not listen to you guys tear each other apart," Fitz piped up. He glared at both men until Ace sat back down with an irritated huff.

"We are going to have to dig up Zhang Liu so Sophie can get a reading on him. He's buried in the Woodlawn Cemetery down in Colma. The three of us can't pull this off on our own. We need your help. Since all of you are off work this Saturday night, we should do it then," Mac said.

"I'm in," Amira announced with a wide grin. "I've always wanted to break the law!"

"First, I need to find out the exact location of Liu's grave. Also, I want to scope out the grounds and cemetery security. Sophie, I need you to come with me. Let's see if you can get a reading without us having to dig him up first. I don't want to waste any time, so I'd like to go first thing in the morning. I will drive," Mac stated, treating the proposal like it was already a done deal.

"Uh, sure. That would be fine, I guess," Sophie said, swallowing any apprehension.

"If you're getting readings, it must mean you have some Mythical in your DNA. You look like you could have some Fae in your family tree. You got the right kind of eyes and bone structure. Now that I'm looking closer, maybe a pixie or a nymph," Amira said, giving Sophie a long look.

"Yeah, but pixies and nymphs don't typically have psychic powers," Fitz argued. "I'd put my money on Fae. Are any of your grandparents strange or particularly good-looking? Even disguised with a glamor, the Fae can't help but make themselves pretty. All that over-the-top ego wouldn't allow them to be plain-looking."

"No strange or magical family members come to mind," Sophie said with a grimace.

"Did anything weird happen to you in middle or high school that you were unable to explain?" Fitz asked.

"Other than puberty? No, I was a normal teenager," Sophie responded.

"You were normal as a teenager?" Amira snorted.

"Were you a cheerleader?" Ace asked, suddenly interested in the conversation.

"What? No. Can you picture me as a cheerleader?" Sophie said, shaking her head.

"I bet you were one of those socially awkward emo kids with

her nose always lost in a book. That's why you never get our pop culture references. You were too busy writing angsty poetry, preaching against conformity and experiencing existential dread over mindless consumerism," Amira announced, making Mac chuckle in agreement.

"No, I bet she was all about anarchy, taking down 'Big Brother' and raising hell," Mac snorted.

"You guys suck. I was a perfectly normal teenager and I'm not telling you anything else. You'll just have to live with the mystery of unrewarded curiosity because you're jerks. Besides, just trying to think about high school gives me a headache," Sophie said. "Can we please refocus on our grave robbing plans?"

For the rest of the lunch hour, they strategized on the plan in case Sophie couldn't get a vision from Liu the next morning. There was also an in-depth discussion of what tools and items they would need to dig up and rebury a casket in a single night.

"Just to reiterate, do not tell anyone about our plans or what Sophie can do. This has to remain a complete secret. I am counting on everyone in this room to step up," Mac stated. Once everyone nodded their agreement, he headed out to work on his part of the plan.

CHAPTER 12

When Mac pulled up in front of the ME's building precisely at 7, Sophie was surprised by the unremarkable, gray sedan he was driving. She had expected something flashy and overpowered.

"Good morning, Detective Dickhead!" Sophie chirped, getting into the car.

"Back at you, hellraiser," Mac retorted.

Sophie snorted at the lame attempt at a comeback. Looking around, she idly noted the meticulously clean interior of the car.

"Have you had any breakfast yet?" Mac asked as Sophie buckled up.

"No, but I'm not hungry," Sophie responded absently, still examining the car. Glancing over at Mac, she realized Mac was in faded jeans and a black t-shirt. His jeans and shirt looked like the kind of clothes that had been worn so often they would hold the shape of their owner's body, showing and hiding Mac's well-muscled form in equal measure. Trailing her eyes up from his clothes to his head, Sophie's eyes locked on Mac's face. This morning was the first time she had ever seen him clean-shaven. The ever-present bristles of his scruff had previously hidden the sharpness of his jawline and softened the hollows under his cheekbones. Sophie could feel her eyes go wide before she firmly pulled her poker face back on.

"What?" Mac asked, his dark blue eyes staring at Sophie suspiciously.

"Uh, I've never seen you out of a suit before. I assumed it was all you wore. That you probably slept in a three-piece suit," Sophie teased, glad Mac hadn't realized her reaction was the visceral effect his face had on her libido. Shaking her head, she reminded herself that a pretty face and a distinct lack of recent sexual release didn't change the fact that Mac was an asshole. She might have considered giving him a one-time try if she didn't have to deal with him at work occasionally. No way was she risking her job for a one-night stand.

"You're not as funny as you think you are. I'm getting us some food. You need to eat; you barely touched your meal last night. Plus, I don't know exactly how long this is going to take. Do you have any preferences for food?" Mac asked.

"No, I'm not picky. Let's just get something quick on the way," Sophie suggested.

After a few minutes of stifled awkward silence, Sophie opened the glove box and started rifling through the neatly-stacked papers inside.

"What are you doing?" Mac asked in confusion, glancing between the road and Sophie's snooping.

"I'm just checking to see if this car is registered to someone else. Did you steal it?" Sophie asked. "Or perhaps it is your spouse's car?"

"This is my car," Mac grumbled. "And I'm not married. I'm going to regret this, but why are you checking to see if the car is mine?"

"I just pictured you in something sporty, you know, something with a big rumbling engine, packing a bunch of horsepower. Or maybe a big shiny black motorcycle. Something with enough power to make up for any *short*comings you may have," Sophie said with a smirk.

"I don't need to compensate for anything," Mac growled. "This car is economical, gets good gas mileage, and will hold its resale value well. It was a smart purchase."

"Sure thing, All-American. Sounds like a very wise financial choice." Sophie grinned widely, watching Mac get fussy over his vehicle and her joking assumptions.

After a quick stop at a fast-food restaurant, Sophie ate her breakfast while watching the passing scenery. With an evil grin, she crumpled up and dropped the sandwich wrapper on the floor of Mac's car. The skyscrapers quickly faded from view behind them, morphing into the outskirts of the city. Interstate 280 arched high above the fringes of San Francisco, where the cheaper real estate populated the landscape. Dilapidated shopping plazas and worn-down service centers bisected endless cornrows of small houses.

The San Bruno mountain range rose on the left, dotted along the crest with a series of red-and-white striped towers. This time of year, the small mountain range looked dry and russet brown.

"Did you know there are more dead people in the city of Colma than living?" Mac suddenly asked, interrupting the comfortable silence that had fallen between them.

"What?"

"There are less than two thousand people currently living in Colma, but there are over one and a half million bodies buried there."

"Seriously?"

"Yeah, if there's ever a zombie apocalypse, Colma will be ground zero," Mac said, making Sophie chuckle.

Even with the morning traffic, it was barely a 30-minute trip to Colma. Most of the rush hour flow was heading into the city, not out of San Francisco, making it an easy drive. Entering Colma, Sophie noticed a distinct trend regarding the scenery of the town. Tombstones, florist, tombstones, another florist, more tombstones.

"Why are there so many graveyards here?" Sophie asked.

"There is almost no undeveloped real estate left in San Francisco. Plus, what land is available is too valuable to be used to hold dead bodies. In the early 1900s, San Francisco banned any new burials within the city limits. Then in the twenties, there was a huge push to close most of the existing cemeteries and move the bodies. The real estate was too valuable, and many of the graveyards had fallen into disrepair. Colma was established solely to house San Francisco's dead. Most of the bodies buried in the city were exhumed and moved to Colma by the end of the 1930s. They moved well over one hundred thousand bodies. Can you imagine?"

"I can imagine the smell." Sophie shuddered.

"I bet," Mac snorted. "Though it didn't happen all at once. One big secret most people don't know is a bunch of bodies got left behind. So, every once in a while, a construction site will stumble upon a bunch of remains. In 1993, the Legion of Honor was undergoing some renovations, and they found over seven hundred bodies."

"Holy shit! That must have been one hell of a weird day at the job site," Sophie exclaimed. "So, Colma is an actual necropolis."

When Mac flicked his turn signal, Sophie looked to the right and gaped in surprise. Across an expansive green lawn was a cream-colored building that looked like someone took the top half of a gothic, medieval castle and dropped it in front of a long driveway lined with rows of palm trees.

In between two wide-arched stone drive-throughs, which served as some kind of unmanned gatehouse, was a stunted octagonal tower topped with a red-tiled, sharply pointed roof. Something about the rough-hewn white granite bricks, vaulted windows, and wide gabled arches made the building look like it should be several stories tall instead of a squat, sprawling minia-ture castle.

Driving slowly under one of the arches, Mac pulled a piece of paper out of his pocket and handed it to Sophie. "Liu is in the Moon Gate Garden. I have it marked on the map. Give me direc-tions so I can get us as close as possible," Mac requested.

Following the turns on the map with her finger, Sophie called out directions to Mac, trying to look at the surrounding land-scape while navigating. Gently rolling hills were covered in rows upon rows of tombstones, interrupted only by ancient-looking cypress trees. The San Bruno mountain range reared above the cemetery in the distance like an ever-watchful guard dog.

"This place is huge," Sophie exclaimed.

"Yeah, the information I looked up said it is over 60 acres."

Sophie got them as close to Liu's gravesite as she could, then they got out and started walking.

"I think the Moon Gate Garden is through there," Mac said, pointing towards a rough stone wall with a large round opening, leading to a lovely rose garden. As they strolled through the stone arch, Sophie reached up to touch the gray keystone as she passed under it. It was gritty and coarse under her fingertips.

In one of the last rows of graves, they located Zhang Liu's final resting place. The grass mounded over the gravesite was new. The seams where the sod was laid out were still clearly visible.

Pointing out the square sections of sod, Mac said, "If we're careful, we should be able to pull off the grass and lay it back in place, so no one will ever know the site has been disturbed."

Glancing around to make sure no one was observing her, Sophie knelt next to Liu's tombstone and put her hands on the recently disturbed grass. Closing her eyes, she tried to relax and let the story emerge into her consciousness. Until it was revealed that her visions were real, Sophie never paid attention to how the tales originated. Now that she knew the truth, she'd been trying to concentrate within herself when a story materialized. There was a wellspring in her mind where the stories emerged, fully formed, into her consciousness. Being careful not to push at the chasm, Sophie watched the dark empty abyss in her mind neutrally, waiting to see if anything bubbled forth. After a few minutes of quiet quasi-meditation, Sophie sighed in defeat.

Looking up at Mac, she shook her head, swamped for a moment with uncertainty. She didn't want to let anyone down. The possibility of not being able to help solve the crime against Zhang Liu made Sophie's heart ache. She vividly remembered his torn-up body and bruised, cut face. And somehow, she didn't want to disappoint Mac either.

"Don't worry about it. It was a long shot with him being six feet under anyways. I think you just need to be closer to the body – possibly even in direct contact. I'm still hopeful for Saturday. But even if it doesn't work out, we'll just keep trying," Mac said, in response to the disappointed look on Sophie's face.

"Stop being nice to me, Detective Dickhead. It just makes it weird," Sophie said, sitting on the soft grass, letting her eyes trace over Liu's red granite headstone. Seeing the engraved words "Loving Son and Brother" hit Sophie hard. When she did her autopsies, it was hard to see the corpses as anything but a job to accomplish. But seeing those words hammered home that a family lost someone they loved. If Sophie could give them justice, or even just some answers, she had to dig deep and do what she could to uncover the truth of his murder.

"You got it, hellraiser. No more words of encouragement from me. So, get your ass up and stop wasting my time. We've got more shit to do before we can get out of here," Mac said with a challenging rise of his eyebrows. Sophie watched as his lips twitched as he fought off a smile.

Sophie flipped him the bird with a grin, then stood up and dusted her hands off on her jeans. "Where to next, dickhead?"

"Detective Dickhead," Mac jokingly reminded Sophie. "Let's

walk around and see if we can figure out the best way to sneak onto the property. Also, keep your eyes out for cameras and security."

Strolling around the grounds, Mac nodded over to a chain-link fence separating the cemetery from the back of a shopping center. They found a spot that was mostly hidden from the rest of the cemetery by a thick copse of evergreens.

"We could park behind the store and hop over the fence here," Mac said, pointing to the parking area behind the home improvement store. "I think they planted all these trees to hide the plaza and keep the aesthetic of a peaceful resting place. That works in our favor. Let's go check out the cemetery's entrance and see if we can spot any security personnel. Then let's go scope out the back of that store. Tonight, I'm going to come back and see if Woodlawn uses any nighttime security guards. I need to see how well-lit this area is at night."

After about an hour of wandering around the gardens surrounding Liu's grave, they visited the mausoleum and chapel. Then they headed back out to look for higher ground further into the cemetery. Standing on the highest hill in Woodlawn, they tried to determine if Liu's gravesite was visible from their perch.

"This looks like the only area where someone might be able to spot us at Liu's grave. If the Moon Gate Garden isn't well-lit, we should be okay. We will just have to be careful about flashlights," Mac said, shading his eyes with a hand, staring intently at the area with Liu's grave.

After finishing their tour, Sophie and Mac headed to his car. The back of the large hardware store appeared to be free of security cameras.

"Look, we can park on the far side of this shipping container if it's still here on Saturday. That way, we'll be hidden from the street," Mac said, pointing out the gray steel container plonked across two employee parking spaces behind the store.

"This might not be as difficult as I was worried about. I mean, it's going to be a pain in the ass to do the actual digging, but there's just not much security here. I expected cameras or something," Sophie said.

"I don't think grave robbing is much of a problem nowadays. I bet the worst thing the cemetery has to worry about is teenagers partying on the graves and vandalism," Mac said thoughtfully, pulling out of the store's parking lot and back onto Colma's main drag.

"Did you ever party in a cemetery as a teenager? I can totally picture you partying with your football team," Sophie asked with a grin.

"I partied a couple of times. But never in a cemetery. Our parties were always at the base of the local water tower. Also, it was with my baseball team. Not football." Mac laughed. "I didn't party much in high school because my father was the chief of police in our town. He would have tanned my hide if he caught me 'sullying' the family reputation."

"Chief of police, huh? You're not from around here?" Sophie asked.

"I was born in a small town called Civitas, about two hours south of here. What about you? Did you party with your angsty emo friends in a cemetery?"

"Not in a cemetery. I was a typical teen. I did the same things as everyone else. I just wanted to fit in, I imagine. Nothing special there," Sophie responded.

Mac snorted quietly but didn't say anything else. Once they got back to the city, Sophie accepted Mac's offer to drive her home. Pulling up to the curb in front of Brown Betty, Sophie spotted Birdie standing out front, clutching a paper bag emblazoned with a grocery store logo. Birdie gave the car a suspicious stare until she recognized Sophie sitting in the front seat. Then she hustled over to the car faster than seemed possible.

"Sophie!" Birdie exclaimed, stopping Sophie before she could finish getting out of the car and executing her escape. "Who is this?"

"Birdie, this is my colleague Detective Malcolm Volpes. Mac, this is my neighbor and friend Miss Alberta Gafferty."

Birdie dramatically grabbed her chest. "How dare you! *Never* call me by that name. Everyone calls me Birdie. I thought I could trust you. Or should I tell the detective here that your full name is Josephina?"

"That is *not* my name. Mac, ignore Birdie. She is well into her dotage and gets easily confused," Sophie said, grinning widely when Birdie stuck her tongue out at her.

"It's nice to meet you, Miss Birdie," Mac said politely from his seat inside the vehicle.

"Oh my. A detective, you say? It's nice to meet you too, Detective Volpes," Birdie said with a flutter of her eyelashes, Sophie's apparent betrayal of her birth name already forgotten. "I noticed that you should have been home several hours ago. Sophie, did this nice young man give you a ride?"

Birdie couldn't have sunk more innuendo into the words if she tried.

"He did. It was a smooth ride. Not as much horsepower as I was expecting." Sophie grinned wickedly when she heard Mac sputtering through the open passenger door behind her.

"Hmmm. Too bad. I do hope you got to try out his handcuffs," Birdie purred, making Sophie crack up. Sophie laughed even harder when she glanced back and realized that Birdie had made the hardened detective blush.

"Come on, you naughty old lady. Let me help with your groceries," Sophie said, shutting the passenger door and carefully grabbing the paper bag from Birdie's clutches.

"It was nice to meet you, Detective Volpes," Birdie said with a flirty finger wave. Mac, who had stepped out of the vehicle and was leaning against the roof of the car, smiled at the old lady.

Threading her arm with Birdie's, Sophie turned them both to head up to Brown Betty.

"Please call me Mac, Miss Gafferty. I can hardly wait to see you Saturday night, Sophie. I'm counting the minutes. Don't forget the outfit I want you to wear, and I'll make sure to bring my handcuffs," Mac called out to Sophie and Birdie in the most wicked, panty-dampening voice possible. Sophie knew the outfit Mac was referring to was all-black clothes, but she couldn't possibly explain that to Birdie.

While Birdie hooted and hollered next to her, Sophie whipped her head to give Mac a "you're a dead man" glare. He gave her a sinful grin in return before getting back into his sensible car and pulling into traffic, away from Sophie's death stare.

CHAPTER 13

*S*ophie looked around the interior of the battleship-gray minivan with a bemused smile from the passenger seat. She glanced over at Mac behind the wheel, and then over her shoulder at Amira, Reggie, Ace, and Fitz spread out behind her. The inside of the minivan was the exact opposite of the pristine interior of the last vehicle Mac used to take her to Woodlawn cemetery. There were toys and books and a plethora of crumbs and stale french fries strewn about the car. In the console's cupholder was a sippy cup. It was half-filled with what appeared to be apple juice.

"It's my sister's car. I had to borrow it. I didn't want to take more than one vehicle tonight, and this is the only one I could get my hands on that is big enough to fit all of us," Mac grumbled.

"Judgement-free zone here. I don't even have a car, so I have no room to criticize anyone else's," Sophie said, raising her hands in surrender.

"Hey, listen to this." Amira giggled from the back seat. "I found a fortune leftover from someone's fortune cookie. It says, 'You will travel to many exotic places in your lifetime.' We've already started! Such a life of glamor we lead. People will be so jealous when they find out."

"Did you know the fortune cookie was invented here in San Francisco?" Mac quietly asked Sophie.

"Really? I thought it came from China," Sophie responded.

"No, there are some disputes about it, but the cookies are definitely not from China. What's interesting is both men who claimed to have invented the cookies were Japanese men. The cookie was based on a traditional Japanese sweet cracker served in temples. They sweetened the cookie to cater to American taste buds. Most people believe it was first served in the Golden Gate Park Japanese Tea Garden," Mac said.

"You're just full of interesting facts, aren't you?" Sophie said, a grin tugging at her lips.

"I like history," Mac said with a self-conscious shrug.

"Me too, actually. Do you have any other interesting facts about fortune cookies?"

"You're going to regret asking," Mac warned. "Did you know you can still see some of the original cookie-making machines from the '60s in use today at the Golden Gate Fortune Cookie Factory in the city? They do tours."

"Okay then, explain to me how a Japanese cookie became synonymous with Chinese food?" Sophie asked.

"The theory I've heard is that most of the Japanese population were forced into internment camps during World War II. Chinese-American manufacturers spotted a business opportunity and stepped in to start producing the cookie. They began serving them in Chinese restaurants where they became hugely popular."

"Damn, that's kinda dark," Sophie responded, a pensive look plastered on her face.

"So much of history is," Mac agreed.

Turning into the hardware store parking lot, Mac cut the lights and pulled around to the back of the blocky building. The shipping container blotted out the streetlight and cast the interior of the car in shadow.

Turning in his seat to face the rest of the vehicle, Mac said, "Okay, here's the plan. When we get out, Amira, can you transform and quickly check out the area for any security personnel or other potential problems? As far as I could tell, a security guard patrols the cemetery on a golf cart every two hours. If they stick to their usual schedule, they will drive past at midnight, two, four, and six. We need to be done long before six. I have shovels for everyone in the back, along with gloves and flashlights. Those of us who can transform can take turns keeping a lookout. The best spot for that is on the stone entrance to the Moon Gate Garden. If anyone sees anything, make an animal call. Just to reiterate, whatever happens, don't get caught even if you have to abandon the site and run away. The most important thing is that we *absolutely* cannot get caught. Any questions?" Mac asked. Sophie swallowed an inappropriate grin when she realized that Mac was a "just to reiterate" guy.

After piling out of the van, everyone headed to the back to gather the shovels.

"I'm going to go transform over there," Amira said, pointing to a thick clump of low-growing evergreens. "I will be back after I scope out the area."

"Do you remember how to get to the Moon Gate Garden?" Mac asked.

"I got this," was all Amira said before skipping off.

Mac slung a large duffel bag over his shoulder before distributing shovels to everyone. It didn't take long before Sophie heard rustling coming from behind a nearby tree, and she spotted a flash of tan skin. A minute later, Amira reappeared fully dressed from behind the trees and let them know it was safe to get started.

Tossing the duffel bag and tools over the fence, everyone climbed over the chain-link barricade. Without the need for discussion, everyone fell in line behind Mac. Sophie was glad the moon was three-quarters full so they weren't walking in complete darkness. Earlier, Reggie explained to Sophie that most shifters have excellent night vision, so they were hoping to skip using any flashlights.

At Liu's tombstone, Amira took the first shift as a lookout. A few minutes later, Sophie heard a feline screech, the agreed-upon signal to let everyone know Amira was in position. Looking over at the stone arch, Sophie was slightly disappointed that she couldn't spot Amira in her feline form. She imagined Amira was an adorable cat; not that she would tell her that.

After carefully peeling back the sod, Mac laid out several large tarps for everyone to pile the displaced dirt. With a sigh Sophie pulled on her thick gloves, picked up a shovel and got to work.

Two hours later, Sophie regretted ever agreeing to this hare-brained scheme.

"This sucks," she announced. She adjusted the grip on her shovel in the hopes she could prevent the blister forming on her left palm from getting any worse.

A piercing animal scream interrupted their work. Mac and Sophie dropped behind Liu's headstone while Fitz and Amira hid behind an adjacent gravestone. Sophie peeked around the side of the large granite slab, staring out the opening of the stone arch. A moment later, a golf cart slowly rolled past the garden entrance. Dropping back behind the shield of Liu's headstone, Sophie saw the beam of a flashlight pass quickly over their hiding spot. Glancing over at Mac, Sophie realized that his eyes were gleaming with excitement.

"Are you enjoying this?" Sophie hissed under her breath.

"Of course! This is fun. It's an adventure. We're like Indiana Jones," Mac said, giving Sophie a sharp grin. "What? You don't like being a law-breaking treasure hunter?"

"I've never seen any Indiana Jones movies," Sophie whispered, while Mac clutched his chest in abject horror. "Besides, I doubt we're going to find any treasure tonight."

∼

DESPITE DIGGING WITH AS MUCH SPEED AS POSSIBLE, IT STILL TOOK almost four hours to get to the coffin.

"Are you ready to do this? Would you like to take a moment to catch your breath first?" Mac quietly asked Sophie.

Sophie looked down at her aching hands, covered in leather gardening gloves. Flexing her fingers a few times first, she replied, "No, let's get this done so we can go home."

Trying to wipe the sweat from her forehead, Sophie only managed to smear dirt across her face. Looking around at her friends, she realized they all looked like swamp monsters.

"Sophie, do you want to switch out your gloves for nitrile ones?" Reggie offered, holding out a pair of thin blue gloves. Sophie accepted them with a quick word of thanks.

Mac hopped agilely into the deep hole and helped steady Sophie on her feet when Reggie and Ace lowered her onto the casket. Kneeling on the coffin, Sophie waited while Mac ran his fingers around the edge of the casket. The dirt walls crowded close on either side of them. As Sophie shifted on her knees, her arm brushed the pitted, jagged walls of soil. They loomed tall over her, making Sophie feel like she was at the bottom of a deep well. Fitz leaned over the opening, training a flashlight beam on the casket so they could see what they were doing.

"Ah, here it is," Mac said under his breath as he fiddled with a metal clasp. Flipping the fastener, Mac had Sophie move back, so they were both side-by-side, halfway back on the coffin.

"I'm just going to open the top half of the coffin. That way, we can keep kneeling, okay? Are you ready?"

Sophie took a deep breath and let it out slowly before jerking her head in a nod. Reaching along the side of the casket, Mac dug his fingers into the crack of the coffin door and pulled. Mac huffed in irritation when the door didn't budge. Readjusting his grip, he clenched his jaw, straining to open the door. The seal on the casket door gave so suddenly Mac almost lost his balance and fell on his ass.

A cloud of foul, rotten air exploded out of the inside of the coffin directly into Sophie's face. Both Sophie and Mac scrambled back from the opening, gagging and coughing. Sophie quickly pulled the collar of her shirt over her nose and mouth in the hopes of filtering out the stench. The beam of light disappeared as Fitz, Reggie, and Ace fell back from the opening of the hole with exclamations of disgust. Sophie was glad it was Amira's turn to keep watch again so they didn't have to deal with her delicate sense of smell.

Giving the coffin a few minutes to air out as much as possible, Sophie and Mac slowly crawled back to the opening and peered inside at Zhang Liu. Fitz's flashlight highlighted Liu's sagging, discolored features in stark detail. Sophie quickly switched her focus to a red silk pocket square tucked gracefully into his suit jacket.

"Ready?" Mac asked. When Sophie nodded her head, he pulled his phone out to record. Carefully keeping her eyes from straying back up to Liu's face, Sophie softly placed her gloved hand over one of the hands crossed on Liu's chest. Pushing back the shudder of revulsion as it tried to work its way up her spine, she closed her eyes.

Sophie couldn't seem to concentrate enough to find the place in her mind where the stories emerged. Frustration started to mount within her as the minutes ticked past. Pulling her hand from Liu's cold one, Sophie shook her hand out in irritation.

"Are you okay?" Mac asked softly.

"It's just hard to concentrate when I know everyone is watching. Plus, we went to all this trouble, and I don't want to let you guys down. You all have a lot more to lose than I do if we get caught," Sophie whispered. "Also, this is creeping me out."

"You cut up dead bodies for a living," Mac said, softening the statement with a grin. "Why would this be any different?"

"I don't know. I guess this is supposed to be this guy's final resting place. I feel kinda bad that we're disturbing it."

"I don't think Zhang cares, Sophie," Mac said, bumping her shoulder with his. "Plus, if it were you, wouldn't you want someone to do everything in their power to solve your murder, even if it meant disturbing your grave?"

"Yeah, I guess so."

"Okay, then. I know you can do this. But if you don't get a reading, it's okay. My case is no worse off than it was before. This was just us taking a shot in the dark," Mac said, gently patting Sophie's shoulder.

"You're right. Let me try this again. Thanks for the pep talk, Detective Dickhead."

"You're welcome, hellraiser. Now get me my story."

Placing her hand back on Liu's, Sophie closed her eyes again. Breathing in slowly, Sophie focused on loosening her tense muscles before turning her focus inward, trying to relax her mind.

"A monster sending a message," Sophie whispered out loud, hoping that saying the words would reignite the story in her mind. As she did, an image began to form.

"Zhang is running with his pack. They are racing through the hillsides, trying to see who can reach the base of Sutro Tower first. He is wild and free, embracing the animal within. He wants to howl in triumph when he reaches the tower first but smothers the impulse because there are too many human houses nearby. Two more wolves tumble out of the underbrush, wrestling and playing. The three wolves transform into their human selves. 'This won't be so bad. We can run here,' Zhang says.

"One of the men says: 'Lake Merced Park was better. It's bullshit that we got pushed out. They're already attempting to grab this land as well. If we don't make a stand soon, we won't have anywhere left to run.'

"Zhang reassures the two men: 'Marcus, we can't afford to start a war with the Sunset District Pack. We would lose in a confrontation against them. We don't have the numbers to beat them. I will take care of this. I have a plan.'" Sophie tried to absorb every detail she could.

"They transform back into the three dark-furred wolves and head back down the hillside, racing and jumping over obstacles. The other two wolves get sidetracked when they startle a rabbit and decide to give chase," Sophie said, falling deeper into the rhythm of her storytelling. "Zhang shakes his head at his two packmates. If they're tired on the job site tomorrow, that's on them. Zhang gets to the edge of the small forested area where he left his clothes. He transforms into his human form again and quickly gets dressed. He's jogging back to his apartment in West Portal when six wolves ambush him. They herd him behind a school of some kind. He fights with everything within himself, but he already knows there isn't any chance of winning this fight. Six against one is too difficult to overcome. Each time he gets a good strike on one of his attackers, there is another one pouncing on his exposed flank. The fight is brutal but short," Sophie finished the tale with a shudder.

Sophie opened her eyes and looked at Mac. "Did that help?" she whispered.

"Yeah, it did. Thank you, Sophie," Mac whispered back. "Before we go, did you get much of a look at any of the wolves who attacked Zhang? Any specific wounds he inflicted on his attackers?"

Sophie closed her eyes, trying to picture the attacking wolves. "Hmm. They all had fur that was dark brown, maybe even black. Except for the one I think was the leader: his muzzle had a lot of gray or white fur. Almost like with age, if you know what I mean.

They moved and shifted around a lot, so it's hard to focus on just one. They all looked very similar."

"What about injuries?" Mac asked.

"Zhang tried to bite the throat of one. The wolf turned his shoulder at the last second, so Zhang ended up biting his nape instead of ripping out his throat how he wanted. I think he managed to get ahold of one of their ears, but I don't know how much damage he inflicted. I'm sorry, Mac, it was all such a blur, and Zhang was completely overwhelmed by his assailants. He didn't get many hits in before they killed him."

"You don't need to apologize, Sophie. You've given me more information than I had before. This whole night has been worth it," Mac said. "Alright guys, we got what we came for. It's time to let Zhang get back to his eternal rest."

Returning dirt to a gravesite was a much easier, faster process than uncovering one. It didn't take much more than an hour to return Zhang's gravesite to its previous state. If anyone happened to inspect the area, all they would find would be depressions in the ground and some loose dirt between the blades of grass.

"No one will think people came in here and dug up a grave. At most, they'll think vandals or teenagers were partying in the cemetery. Let's get out of here," Mac reassured the group as they inspected the area.

They gathered up their equipment and slunk silently between the rows of headstones, back to the chain-link fence separating them from their escape.

On the drive back to the city, there was a jubilant air of celebration in the minivan. Everyone was laughing and joking, congratulating themselves on a job well done.

"So, Amira, I know you wanted to know what it felt like to be a law-breaker. Was it everything you hoped it would be?" Reggie teased Amira.

"More physical effort than I would like. I mean, look at my poor nails," Amira bemoaned, showing Reggie nails that looked perfectly fine to Sophie. "I'm meant for a life of leisure, not manual labor."

"What? You thought digging up a grave was going to be more glamorous?" Ace snarked at Amira from the back seat.

"Don't start with me, TP. At least I pulled my weight last night," Amira growled back at Ace.

"Don't fucking call me TP, feline," Ace leaned forward across Reggie's lap to get in Amira's face. Sophie looked back and smothered a grin when Reggie rolled his eyes at their friends' antics.

Turning back around, Sophie tuned out her bickering co-workers as she gazed out the front windshield. She couldn't figure out what it was, but something was tickling at her consciousness. A nagging thought that she was missing an important detail danced around the edges of her mind.

"So, Mac, tell us. Did Sophie get the story right, you think?" Reggie asked, quieting down the argument between Ace and Amira.

"I believe she did. They discovered Zhang's body in Hawk Hill Park just on the other side of the fence behind Herbert Hoover Middle School. There is a large paved area behind the school with a running track and basketball courts. We found evidence of a fight and blood all over the courtyard," Mac said. "I interviewed the alphas of the local packs. They all stated that Zhang Liu was a pack-less shifter. An unaffiliated lone wolf. Sophie's story paints a different picture of a small pack being pushed out of territories. I will be revisiting the alpha of the Sunset District pack very soon. Plus, I need to see if I can track down a shifter named Marcus."

Mac offered to drive each person to their homes, rather than drop them off at the ME's office since everyone was covered in dirt and grass stains. He headed to Noe Valley first to drop off Reggie. Noe Valley was one of Sophie's favorite neighborhoods in the city, so she looked around Reggie's street with a little bit of envy. She spotted a fancy, fussy-looking tearoom. From the brief look she got of the inside as they drove by, it appeared as if someone had vomited doilies over every surface. Birdie would love it.

Next, they dropped off Ace and Amira, who shared an apartment, to Sophie's utter shock.

"You guys are roommates? But you two can hardly go a minute without arguing," Sophie sputtered.

"Rent is too damn expensive in this city. I can't afford a decent place without getting a roommate. At least I already know Amira," Ace said. "Plus, she's hardly home. She spends most of her time as the neighbor's pet cat."

"Don't look at me like that," Amira said after Sophie's incredulous stare. "Bob is really nice. He's not too needy like some humans. It's a pain in the ass to get a human properly trained, and I don't want to start fresh with a new one. Plus, I get free food. It's a sweet deal."

"Oh my god! You're the 'queen of that castle'. Holy shit. I just got that!" Sophie exclaimed.

Amira and Ace got out of the car with a wave and headed into their building.

Fitz lived only a few blocks away in a converted brick warehouse. Once Fitz exited the van, the quiet inside the vehicle started to get on Sophie's nerves. Looking around, trying to find something to discuss, Sophie noticed the dirt smeared all over the upholstery.

"We got dirt all over your sister's car," Sophie said, grimacing at the evidence of their nighttime activities smudged all over the inside of the vehicle.

"I plan to get the car detailed for my sister as a thank you. She'll never see what we did to it. I'm not working today, so it should be easy," Mac said with a negligent shrug.

"Can I ask you something?" Sophie requested.

"Sure," Mac responded, after giving Sophie a quick assessing glance.

"I have no idea if it's rude to ask, but... are you really a fox shifter? I didn't see you last night," Sophie asked quickly.

"Some shifters can get a bit offended when someone asks, but it's easy for them because they can tell what kind of shifter someone is by scent. However, I don't mind. To answer your question: yes, I'm a fox."

"Reggie mentioned fox, but I was so overwhelmed by all the new information at the time, I wanted to make sure. Are foxes from the apex or lesser kingdom?" Sophie asked.

Mac grumbled under his breath.

"I don't like the term lesser kingdom, but I don't know what else the non-apex shifters are supposed to be called," Sophie rushed to explain.

"Sorry, I hate that term. The non-predator shifters aren't 'lesser'. It's just some bullshit prejudice practiced by a few apex shifters and the Fae," Mac growled. "To answer your question, most Mythicals consider fox shifters a part of the apex kingdom, but we mostly straddle the line. It depends on who you're talking to, really."

"Huh," Sophie replied. "It's so weird that even magical beings have to deal with racism."

Turning her thoughts over in her mind, Sophie looked outside, admiring the early morning bustle already starting in the city. One of the dozens of taquerias dotting every corner of the Mission District caught her eye. A Mission-style burrito sounded so divine Sophie almost groaned out loud at the thought. But even the low growling of her stomach couldn't distract Sophie from feeling that she had forgotten something.

"Is something wrong?" Mac asked.

"I feel like I'm missing something. It's there on the tip of my brain." Sophie sighed.

"Do you mean the tip of your tongue?" Mac snorted.

"No, my brain. It's just out of reach. I can't seem to get my synapses firing. What am I forgetting? I know it has something to do with Zhang, but I can't figure it out." Frustration laced her voice.

"Do you want to go drive past the murder scene? It might help jog your memory. We can even go drive around Forest Knolls and look at Sutro Tower. I don't have anything else to do today besides clean up Miranda's van," Mac offered.

"Forest Knolls! Holy shit, that's it!" Sophie exclaimed. "A few days ago, I was in The Little Thumb when I overheard these guys talking about getting pushed out of the Forest Knolls territory. Er, let me think... what did they say?"

Sophie rubbed her forehead, trying to remember the incident.

"There were four men. They looked like maybe they worked in construction or something, you know, paint-splattered clothes and work boots and such. One had shaggy brown hair; another was blonde with hair buzzed close to his scalp. I didn't see much of the other two, they were facing away from me, but they both had darker hair. They were saying they would have to start running in Golden Gate Park and the Presidio because they were getting pushed out of Forest Knolls. They said something about taking it to a conclave," Sophie said. "Oh shit! The blonde warned them that they didn't want to end up like Zee! Do you think that they were talking about Zhang?"

"I don't know, but it's worth checking out," Mac responded, his eyes gleaming with the excitement of the chase. "Would you be willing to come with me to talk to Burg? I think he will be less hostile with you there. The last time we met, I was asking questions about you. I think I pissed him off, so if you're there, he'll realize we're on the same team. I also need you to give descriptions of the shifters to him and help refresh his memory. I want to see if he knows those guys or overheard anything. Could we go now?"

"Sure. I think he lives above the bar, so he should be around.

He usually opens by eleven, but he's often prepping for the day earlier than that," Sophie said, checking the time on the dashboard. It was still early in the morning, but Burg would probably be up. The sun had risen while they dropped off their friends, but most of the city was still just beginning to start its day.

On the opposite side of Brown Betty from the bar was a narrow area reserved for the residents' cars. Pulling into the only open space, Mac turned to face Sophie.

"Thank you, Sophie," Mac said. "Your help has been amazing. I couldn't have done this without you. I know I gave you shit about being a human and saying you would cause problems for shifters. I was wrong, and I'm sorry I was an asshole."

"Don't worry about it. I didn't understand your attitude at the time, but now I get why you were worried. But thank you for the apology," Sophie said. "Plus, I don't think you can help being an asshole. It's just who you are."

Mac chuckled at Sophie's assessment. "I need to head home and get cleaned up. When I get back, we can both talk to Burg. I live in the Outer Richmond, so it'll take me about 45 minutes to return."

"You could get cleaned up at my place, and then we wouldn't have to wait," Sophie offered. "Although I don't know if you can get your clothes clean enough without a washing machine. There is a shared laundry area in the basement, but I don't have anything you could wear while you wait. I mean, you're wearing black – we might be able to get it cleaned up enough with a washcloth?"

"I have a spare set of clothes with me. I've been on the force long enough to always keep a backup. If you don't mind letting me borrow your shower, I'd appreciate a chance to get cleaned up."

CHAPTER 14

◈

*S*ophie and Mac slipped into Brown Betty on silent feet. As Sophie tiptoed down her hallway, Mac followed her with a bemused smile. She turned to Mac, putting her finger in front of her lips to indicate silence. Pointing at the door across from hers, Sophie mouthed the word 'Birdie' to Mac, who nodded his head in sudden understanding.

Sophie ushered Mac into her apartment while looking around the hall to make sure no one noticed their passage. She followed him inside, easing her front door closed as quietly as possible. Once safely ensconced in her apartment, Sophie watched as Mac dropped his backpack on the floor and took in her eclectic space. Most of her furniture was freebies, hand-me-downs, or thrift store finds. Mac walked over to the small table next to her lumpy futon and stared down at her prized lamp. Sophie had found the Victorian Gothic glass lamp at a secondhand store on Haight Street. Vaulted, ornate brasswork worthy of an ancient cathedral framed the jade-green glass shade panels. The lamp's base was a brass skull with a tarnished patina, which gave it an antique mien. The grinning skull always made her smile. Sophie loved the juxtaposition of the fancy lampshade paired with the macabre base. Walking towards the kitchen, Mac stopped in front of two band posters from concerts she'd attended at The Fillmore.

"I've never heard of The Struts or Tune-Yards. Were the concerts good?" Mac asked, looking at the artwork. The Fillmore made beautiful custom concert posters for every band who played at their venue. The few times Sophie had been able to afford a ticket, she enjoyed walking around the building and looking at the concert posters, some dating back to the '60s, plastering almost every square inch of available wall space.

"No, they sucked. I only buy concert posters from bands I hate," Sophie responded with a raised eyebrow.

"Eh, I deserved that."

Looking around her living room in confusion, Mac turned to Sophie with a question in his eyes.

"What?" Sophie asked in irritation.

"Where's your TV?"

"I don't have one," Sophie said with a shrug.

"What? Why not?" Mac asked, looking genuinely confused by the prospect of living without a television.

"Not my thing. Plus, I couldn't afford one until very recently anyway," Sophie responded, feeling a little exposed by the question. No one knew how close she had come to being homeless, and she'd preferred to keep it that way.

"What do you do in your spare time then?" Mac said, not willing to let the subject drop yet.

Sophie picked up a well-worn book from next to her precious lamp and waved it under Mac's nose. Mac looked over at a haphazard stack of books on the floor next to the futon.

"Sometimes I watch reality TV with Birdie. She loves a good bitch-slap fight."

Chuckling, Mac walked into her tiny kitchen and opened a cupboard, peering in at the assortment of mismatched dishes.

"Where's your voodoo shrine to some evil god? The pentagrams for summoning demons? I'm disappointed there isn't a sacrificial altar anywhere," Mac said with a toothy grin, looking around her apartment with mock disappointment.

"Keep annoying me, and you'll get an up-close-and-personal view of my sacrificial altar, asshole," Sophie threatened, making Mac cough out a pleased chuckle. "If you are done being nosy, the bathroom is through there."

Sophie showed Mac through her tiny bedroom into her even tinier bathroom. Pointing out where she kept her spare towels, Sophie quickly headed back to the kitchen to give Mac his privacy.

Scrubbing her arms up to her elbows, she pulled out ingredients to make toast and eggs. She was just finishing buttering the toast when Mac strode out of her bedroom. Silently pointing to the coffee pot, Sophie dished up breakfast onto two plates.

Sitting at the old Formica-topped diner table, Mac plowed through his meal with the single-minded intensity Sophie was beginning to believe inherent to all shifters. Quickly finishing their simple meal, Sophie deposited the dishes in the sink to be cleaned later. With a promise to be quick, she headed to her bedroom to get some clean clothes and a shower.

Stepping into the shower stall, she let out a muffled groan when the hot water hit the sore muscles of her shoulders. She didn't waste any time lingering, well aware of how quickly hot water ran out in Brown Betty. After getting dressed, Sophie stopped in surprise in the doorway of her bedroom, watching as Mac washed the breakfast dishes.

When she cleared her throat, Mac peered over his shoulder at Sophie. "Thanks, Mac. You didn't have to do that," Sophie said, nodding toward the plate in his hand.

"You cooked, so I'm happy to clean. Besides, I'm just trying to avoid being sacrificed on your altar, hellraiser," Mac said.

"Too late. I already put your trip to the altar on my calendar. You don't want to let the cult down, do you?" Sophie tsked.

"No, you're right. Seeing all their disappointed little faces would be heartbreaking." Mac chuckled. "You ready to get out of here and see if we can find Burg?"

Walking side by side down the dingy corridor, Sophie and Mac headed for the stairs at the end of the hall. A strident "ahem" from behind them froze them both in their tracks.

Looking over her shoulder, Sophie saw Birdie standing in her doorway, with her thin arms crossed over her front and her toes tapping in irritation.

"You weren't going to stop by and wish me a good morning?" Birdie asked haughtily.

"Miss Gafferty, normally we would love to visit, but we have somewhere to be," Sophie quickly explained.

"Don't you 'Miss Gafferty' me, young lady. There is always time for a cup of tea with your favorite neighbor. Now, get in here," Birdie demanded imperiously.

"Yes, ma'am. We would love some tea," Mac said, stepping into Birdie's apartment with alacrity.

Birdie pointed to a loveseat for them to both sit in. Sophie knew Birdie purposefully placed them on the small couch so she could take the wingback across from them, allowing her to interrogate them properly. Sophie threw herself into the loveseat with a dramatic sigh of defeat.

"Young man, how does English Breakfast tea sound?" Birdie asked from her kitchen.

"Please call me Mac. Tea sounds lovely, Miss Birdie. Thank you," Mac replied.

Sophie mouthed 'brown noser' at Mac, who nodded his head in happy agreement.

"Oh my. Well, aren't you well-mannered? Whatever are you doing with Sophie?"

"Oh, I don't know, Miss Birdie. Sophie has certain talents I've come to appreciate." Mac gave Sophie an evil grin while Birdie squawked and cackled in delight.

Birdie brought two teacups balanced precariously on saucers

to Mac and Sophie, then retrieved her own from the kitchen counter. Sophie cut her eyes to Birdie and gave her a secret grin when she saw the teacup Mac was holding.

Ginsberg leapt onto the armrest at Sophie's elbow, demanding attention.

"Who's this?" Mac asked, reaching across Sophie to offer his fingers to the cat.

"This is Ginsberg," Sophie said. Ginsberg gave Mac's fingers a very suspicious sniff, but grudgingly allowed Mac to scratch under his chin.

"I noticed you two didn't come home until the wee hours of the morning. Do I need to inquire about your intentions towards our dear, sweet Sophie?" Birdie asked, feigning concern for Sophie's virtue.

"Sweet?" Mac repeated with eyebrows raised comically.

"Too much?" Birdie asked, her eyes sparkling with mirth. "Well, will we be seeing more of you around here? Or was one night enough? I know Sophie is a bit of a prude, so I could show her some moves to help keep you interested."

"Am I going to have to separate you two?" Sophie threatened.

"It couldn't hurt if you could show her some new techniques. I mean, Sophie had the stamina to last all night, but her moves got pretty repetitive," Mac said, pointedly ignoring Sophie while she attempted to murder him with her glare.

"Well, Mac's equipment was adequate enough to get the job done, but it didn't give me much room to get creative. You gotta work with what you have. You know what I mean?" Sophie quipped.

Chuckling, Mac took another sip of his tea. His choking, when he saw the writing on the bottom of the teacup, made Sophie's shoulders shake while she tried to hide her mirth. Birdie and Sophie traded smirks as they watched him reread "Hot Pussy" from the bottom of his cup.

"Oh, did I make the tea too hot?" Birdie asked with sugary-fake innocence.

"No, Miss Birdie. The tea is perfect. So is the company," Mac replied.

"Oh my god! You are such an ass-kisser!" Sophie exclaimed. "Don't fall for this act, Birdie. He's normally a grumpy asshole."

"I can't help that my mother taught me manners. Some people act like they were raised by wolves," Mac said, a mock-serious look on his face.

"Or foxes, perhaps," Sophie whispered back challengingly.

She finished her tea and sat back in the loveseat to watch Birdie shamelessly flirt with Mac, who was eating up all the attention. Sophie shook her head in amused exasperation. Birdie kept calling Mac a "sweet boy", making Sophie want to laugh and throttle Mac's smug face in equal measure.

Mac lounged in his corner of the loveseat like a lion sunning himself on the savanna, relaxed but ready to pounce at a moment's notice. Sophie wondered if Birdie could see the hunter that hid behind Mac's sharp blue eyes. The sensation of a predator's temporarily contained aggression just below his placid exterior made it impossible for Sophie to ever wholly relax in his presence. Mac may have said that he straddled the edge of both kingdoms, but Sophie had a hard time believing Mac was anything but an apex predator.

"Miss Birdie, we really must go. We have an appointment to keep. It has been an absolute pleasure getting to know you. And thank you so much for the tea," Mac said, standing up from the loveseat. He looked over at Sophie, who was busy pretending she was holding in vomit. "Come on, hellraiser. We need to go."

"It was so nice to meet you too, Mac. You can stop by and visit me anytime," Birdie cooed at Mac, walking him to the door, leaving Sophie behind. "Even once Sophie is done with you, you feel free to stop by anytime."

"I will," Mac promised before heading into the hall.

"Thank you for the tea, Birdie," Sophie said, stopping next to her neighbor, who was still making eyes at Mac. "Hey, do you need me to pick up any groceries or anything while I am out today?"

"I'm running a little low on my favorite brandy… Would you be a dear and pick up a small bottle for me?" Birdie asked.

"Of course. I'll drop it by later. Have a nice day, Birdie."

"I really like Birdie. She's fantastic," Mac said after Birdie closed her door.

"Hey! That's my dirty old lady. You can't have her. Go get your own," Sophie squawked indignantly, leading the way down the old stairs. "I have a weird question for you. Birdie's cat, Ginsberg, is he a shifter like Amira?"

"No, sorry, Ginsberg's just a regular cat. He might not be a shifter, but Birdie is definitely a cougar though," Mac teased, making Sophie laugh. "Ginsberg, huh? Was he named after the poet?"

"Yeah. Birdie says she occasionally hung out with Allen Ginsberg and some of the other beatniks back in the '50s and '60s. She says he was very driven and passionate. She named the cat in his honor," Sophie said.

"Did you know Ginsberg coined the phrase 'flower power'?" Mac asked. "He wanted to help inspire the anti-war protests to become peaceful demonstrations and not resort to violence."

"I don't think I've ever heard the term 'flower power' before. It must have been popular before my time." Sophie smirked.

"Hurtful," Mac announced. "Are you trying to imply that I am old? I'm only a few years older than you. Besides, how is it possible you have never heard this term? It's famous. I can't tell if you are fucking with me or not." Mac squinted his eyes at Sophie, who gave an innocent shrug. Then he asked, "Have you ever been to City Lights Booksellers?"

"No, I've never heard of it," Sophie shrugged, while he blinked at Sophie owlishly.

"You've never heard of..." Mac said, shaking his head and looking like he was at a loss for words. "It's a bookstore on Columbus, but it's so much more. Back in the late '50s, they published Allen Ginsberg's Howl. One of the store's founders and Ginsberg both got arrested on obscenity charges. The collection of poems talked about drugs and homosexuality, among other taboo subjects. When the charges got overturned, it helped set a precedent for First Amendment protection of previously banned literature."

"That's cool. And the bookstore is still here?"

"Yes, you should go check it out sometime," Mac suggested.

Striding ahead of Mac, Sophie tried the door to Burg's place, but it was locked. As Mac stepped up next to her, she peered into the gloomy interior of the bar. Spotting Burg rolling up a keg from the back, she knocked on the door and waved to get Burg's attention.

Looking up, Burg's initial smile faded a little when he spotted Mac standing next to Sophie. Setting down the keg, he came over and opened the door.

"Hey Burg, sorry to bother you so early. Do you have a few minutes? We need to talk to you," Sophie asked.

"Sure, come on in," Burg said, holding the door open for them. "Take a seat; I'll join you in a minute. I just need to get this keg in place first."

Sophie led Mac to the table where the possible wolf shifters had been sitting just a few days prior. Sophie took a deep breath, inhaling the yeasty smell of stale spilled beer mixed with lemony hints of wood polish. A moment later, Burg pulled up a seat across from them and sat down.

"What can I do for you both? I've got to say, it is unexpected to see you here together," Burg stated.

"Sophie is assisting me with a case," Mac said. "There were four men, who we believe might have been wolf shifters, having drinks here last Tuesday. I was hoping you could answer some questions about them."

"I can try. I don't remember any specific shifters from Tuesday. Can you describe them for me?" Burg asked.

Mac nodded at Sophie to describe the men to Burg.

"I was the one who saw them. They were here around 7 or 8 that night, maybe? I think they were already here when I came in. One had shaggy brown hair. Another had blonde hair buzzed close to his head. If I had to guess, I'd say they were in their thirties. I think the other two had dark hair, but I didn't get a very good look at them. One might have had the name Marcus, but I'm not positive. They were complaining that some conclave wouldn't help them with their territory. They were sitting at this table, behind me at the bar when you served me a Lullaby Lady. Do you remember?" Sophie asked.

"You drink Lullaby Ladies? That's a kid's drink," Mac scoffed.

"I had to go to work afterward, so no alcohol. And the drink is yummy, so fuck off. The Lullaby Lady is just like me: beautiful but deadly," Sophie retorted, flipping her hair dramatically in a passable facsimile of Amira, making both men shake their heads.

"I think I remember the men you are looking for. They come in occasionally. They visited a couple of times this week. I think they work on a construction site nearby so they stop by after work to share a beer or two. I'm pretty sure they're unaffiliated shifters. I get a lot of pack-less shifters because the bar is considered neutral territory," Burg said.

"I get that. No one's going to fuck with ogre territory," Mac said. "Do you know what construction site they work on?"

After a long thoughtful pause, Burg said, "Hmmm... I feel like they said something about rude, spoiled law students making their job difficult."

"There is the UC Hastings Law school only a few blocks from here. Might be worth checking out," Mac said. "Do you happen to know any of their names?"

"I don't. But let me see if I can pull any receipts from Tuesday. Give me a few minutes."

"What do you think?" Sophie asked Mac when Burg disappeared through a door in the back of the bar.

"I think it's a lead I didn't have yesterday. Perhaps a thread I can follow and hope it helps me unravel this whole thing," Mac responded.

"By the way, what is a conclave? I've heard the term several times now," Sophie asked.

"The Conclave is sort of like the Mythicals' local government. Most big cities, or any area with strong ley lines, have one. Most Conclave members come from founding families, so they're Fae. They're supposed to oversee the Mythicals in the city. If one of us has a problem with another species, we can take it to Conclave. They deal with any problem big enough that might garner attention from the humans. They have people planted in the government, police, hospitals, even the media, to ensure our presence in this realm remains a secret," Mac explained.

"And the morgue! So why did those shifters say that the Conclave wouldn't help them?"

"Conclave doesn't usually bother itself with territory disputes within the same kingdom. Sadly, the shifter you overheard was correct. The Conclave wouldn't trouble itself with a few pack-less shifters getting pushed out of Forest Knolls. That's considered an intra-species issue," Mac said with a grimace which told Sophie that he wasn't a fan of the Conclave.

"What do you do if you have a problem within your kingdom that the Conclave can't help you with?"

"I'm not sure how it works for non-shifter Mythicals. But for my people, most shifters belong to a pack. If a member has a problem, they can take the issue to their alpha. If he or she can't or won't fix it, there's not a lot the individual can do. Usually, they find another pack to join, or they can leave and become unaffiliated. Some shifters do that, but being pack-less is difficult for many people. They won't have the resources and protection that come with being in a pack. But a pack is only as good as its alpha, and that life isn't for everyone. Sometimes, a shifter gets kicked out of their pack by the alpha for causing problems. Those are usually the ones who cause the most trouble for my department. They can be very dangerous. They don't have an alpha to put the brakes on their worst behaviors."

Burg returned clutching a small stack of papers.

"I pulled all the receipts I had starting from 6 until midnight for Tuesday. I'm certain all four shifters were long gone by midnight. I put the three receipts I believe are the most likely ones on top," Burg said, handing Mac the receipts.

"Only three?" Mac asked.

"At least one of them paid in cash, so there wouldn't be a name attached. It might have even been two of them, but I can't say for sure," Burg said. "I do remember that all of them cashed out at the same time and left together. If I had to guess, it was around nine, so those are the most likely culprits," Burg pointed at the topmost receipt in Mac's hands.

"Marcus Lincham," Mac said with a triumphant grin to Sophie, showing her the top receipt. "This lines up with our information."

Mac wrote down the names from each of the receipts before handing Burg back the stack of papers.

"I think you're right, Burg. These two receipts are most likely our guys. Do you think any of your other regulars know these men? Would they be able to tell us more about them?" Mac asked.

"No, these guys mostly keep to themselves. Are they dangerous?" Burg asked, concerned.

"I don't believe so. They may have some information that can help me with a case. If you think of anything else or if they come back, would you give me a call?" Mac asked, opening his wallet and sliding Burg a business card.

"Of course," Burg responded, slipping the card into his back pocket.

"Thank you for your assistance, Burg," Mac said, standing up from the table and shaking Burg's hand. Sophie stood up too, ready to follow Mac out of the bar.

"Hey, Soph. You got a minute?" Burg asked, indicating with a nod of his head for Sophie to sit back down.

"I'll wait outside," Mac said, stepping out with a tinkle of the door's bell. Burg followed Mac with his eyes before turning his attention back to Sophie.

"Everything okay, Sophie? Is that guy causing you problems? He was the one I warned you about. He came here asking a bunch of questions about you," Burg quietly asked.

"Yes, everything is fine. Mac and I have come to an understanding. He even apologized. He was just worried about having a human work in the Mythical division of the ME's office. I was annoyed by him at the time, but now I better understand his concern," Sophie assured Burg. "The reason we're here together is that I overheard something relevant to one of Mac's cases. I'm just helping him track down a lead. You don't need to worry about me. Everything is fine, I promise."

"Alright, if you're sure. I just wanted to check. I already warned him that you're under my protection. If he gives you any problems, you come tell me," Burg growled.

"You got it, Burg. If he gives me any trouble, I will let you kick his ass," Sophie said with a wide grin. "I'm going to head home. I'm wiped out. My sleep schedule is so out of whack; I think I'm going to try to get a nap. See you later, okay?"

With a wave, Sophie headed outside to find Mac leaning against the outside of the bar, attempting to look nonchalant.

"Everything okay in there?" Mac asked with one raised eyebrow. "Is Burg worried that I'm mistreating you?"

"He says if you're mean to me, he will break your kneecaps.

So, you better be nicer to me from now on," Sophie warned, a toothy grin spreading across her face.

"That's not fair. Who's gonna protect me from you? I'm a very sensitive person, and you're mean as hell," Mac complained.

"No one. You're just going to have to toughen up, I guess."

"I was thinking of walking down to the law school to see if I can find any construction happening around the campus. If I'm lucky, they might even be working, though it's doubtful since it's the weekend. Would you like to join me?" Mac offered.

Despite being tempted, she shook her head. "I promised to get a bottle of brandy for Birdie, then I'm heading back to Brown Betty to get some sleep."

"Brown Betty?" Mac asked, confusion coloring his voice.

"You know, like Apple Brown Betty? Old fashioned, classic, boringly uniform brown," Sophie hooked a thumb over her shoulder at the house looming next to her. "The first time I ever had it was at Three Pigs Bakery on Market Street. It may look boring, but it tastes delicious." Mac nodded his head, making a low hum of amused understanding.

"Alright, then. Once I'm done following up on the information you uncovered, I'll message Reggie with updates. Since you, for some fucking reason, don't own a cell phone." Mac shook his head in exasperation when Sophie gave him an unrepentant grin.

"I had a phone, but it broke. I didn't have the money to get it fixed. Now that I'm getting a regular paycheck, I will get a phone soon, so calm down," Sophie said with a shrug.

"Fine. Tell Reggie to expect my call."

CHAPTER 15

*B*y the middle of the week, the high spirits from their weekend caper had started to wear off for Sophie's co-workers. She had heard the retelling of their shared adventure enough times to last the rest of her days, not that she would ruin their fun by saying so. Ace, in particular, seemed to enjoy talking about the close brush he had with a security guard while standing watch. He was in his raccoon form at the time, so Sophie didn't think he had been in danger of getting caught so much as getting chased off with a broom.

During their shared meal break on Thursday night, Amira dramatically announced that she was ready to give up the glitz and glamor of crime and return to the sedate life of a law-abiding citizen.

"It's weird. I don't remember any glitz and glamor when I was kneeling on an open coffin covered in graveyard dirt," Sophie teased.

"Well, maybe not. But I did look fabulous in my black catsuit. Maybe I should start a life of crime just so I can enjoy the fashion," Amira said with a thoughtful expression.

"We should have a gang name. You know, if we're going to

become a crime-solving unit. Something befitting our awesome-ness. Like, The Awesome Ones or The Amazing Ones," Ace suggested.

"If we're going to pick a name which truly represents us, we should be called The Odd Ones," Fitz countered with a smirk, making everyone except Ace crack up.

"You guys aren't taking this seriously!" Ace complained.

After that, the crew turned their attention to the next new thing, which happened to be Fitz's accusation that someone on the day shift had stolen one of his precious sparkling waters. His vow to find the culprit had Sophie and Reggie exchanging amused looks. He even insisted that Sophie touch his cans of water to see if she could get a reading on the thief. Sophie had to give him the bad news that she only got readings off dead bodies.

Picking at her turkey sandwich, Sophie was thinking about the autopsy they had finished before their lunch break. It had been another shifter-on-shifter attack. According to her vision, it was a dominance fight for ranking within a pack. One of the shifters lost control over his animal half and ended up killing the victim. Reggie explained that there was a strict hierarchy based on proven strength and displays of fighting prowess in many packs, especially the more predatory apex shifters. Shifters would often fight to try and improve their place within that hierarchy.

"Do shifters often lose control over their animal halves and kill people? I've already seen several since starting work here," Sophie asked into the sudden quiet of the break room.

"It's something that happens more often with the apex shifters. They're more violent than non-apex shifters. It is especially more prevalent in this realm," Fitz responded.

"Why?" Sophie asked.

"Because the Fae treat this realm like a dumping ground," Ace said, his annoyance wrapped around him like a cloak. Crankiness just seemed to be Ace's baseline state, but Sophie could tell he was working up a head of steam about this discussion.

"I think that's a little harsh." Reggie frowned.

"No, it's not. Most other realms treat Earth the way England used to treat Australia. They send all their undesirables, dissidents, and criminals here. Earth is the 'out of sight, out of mind' solution for those pretentious assholes," Ace responded, running his hands through his variegated hair in agitation.

"Wait... we're a penal colony?" Sophie laughed.

"Plenty of citizens from the Fae realm willingly choose to immigrate to Earth. Lots of Mythicals have gladly chosen to use the ley lines to move here, including my ancestors," Reggie retorted.

"Well yeah, a lot of the 'lesser' kingdom shifters came here because we got sick of all the prejudice against our people. That's why there's such a large population of non-apex shifters in the area. But it doesn't change the fact that the Sídhe court dumps problematic Fae and shifters here. More than half the bodies we see in this facility can probably be laid at the feet of outcasts," Ace growled.

"You've mentioned ley lines a lot. That's how Mythicals get to Earth, right? Does that mean there is a ley line here? Like in the city itself?" Sophie asked.

"Yes, the one here in San Francisco is very strong and one of the closest portals to the Fae realm which is why there is such a high concentration of Mythicals originally from the Fae realm here," Reggie explained.

"So, the Fae realm is close to San Francisco, right? That's why there are so many Fae creatures in the area. Does that mean that the Valhalla realm is somewhere near Scandinavia?" Sophie asked. "And would you find more Valkyries and such there instead of Fae?"

"That's correct. Beings from the other realms have been spilling into Earth using the ley lines, affecting each area's mythology and population for thousands of years."

"If there is a ley line here, would I be able to use it to visit the

Fae realm?" Sophie asked, eyes brightening at the thought of traveling to a place only talked about in fairy tales.

Ace snorted derisively. "No way. Coming to Earth is a one-way trip. There is no way to cross back from Earth to the Fae realm. Even leaving the Fae realm for Earth can be difficult. The Fae court and their sycophants have a stranglehold on the ley line portals. You have to get approval. And no offense, but to them, you're just a measly human."

"When did you guys come here?" Sophie asked.

"We're all several generations out. Back at the turn of the century, a lot of the non-Fae Mythicals, like shifters, trolls, redcaps, and such, immigrated to San Francisco. It was an easy time to arrive and blend in because of the influx of people due to the gold rush," Reggie explained.

"What about you, Sophie? When did you or your ancestors arrive? I wonder if one of your grandparents came around the same time as ours," Amira asked.

"My family is from all over. I wouldn't be able to even guess where I got my ability from. I don't know most of my family since they're scattered all over," Sophie said with a negligent shrug.

"Maybe you aren't Fae then. Maybe you're some other kind of Mythical. The Fae are rather militant about tracking bloodlines," Fitz said with a thoughtful air. "They're all snobs, so they would rarely mix with humans. When a half-Fae baby *is* born, it's usually the byproduct of an illicit dalliance."

"Dalliance, huh? Is this a Regency romance? I suppose that explains why I've never heard about any Fae in my history. Odds are, someone in my family tree was a secret affair baby," Sophie shrugged, not concerned about the origins of her ability.

"Does anyone else in your family get any visions or have any strange powers?" Reggie asked.

"I've never heard or seen anything that would make me think so."

"Well, that kind of thing can stay hidden in the DNA for generations before randomly popping up without warning. It's rare, but I've heard stories about it before."

"Also consider this: I wasn't even aware of my ability until now. I may have family members who have a hidden power they aren't even aware of. If I hadn't been exposed to dead bodies, I might have gone the rest of my life without knowing about my 'gift'. It's the most random, strangest talent ever."

"Maybe you could reach out to members of your family and see if they have any unexplainable gifts or abilities?" Hope and excitement bloomed in Reggie's eyes.

"Not gonna happen. I'm an only child, and my parents are both gone. I'm not close to anyone else in my family, so I'm not going to be calling them to ask them to come touch some dead bodies to see if they get visions. I'm not even sure if I could track them down, even if I cared enough to do so," Sophie stated firmly.

"Okay. It's up to you, of course. You ready to get back to work?"

"Yeah, do you need to grab your phone charger?" Sophie reminded Reggie.

Looking at his phone, Reggie shook his head. "I have enough percentage left to get us through at least one more autopsy."

Each day, Sophie and Reggie still dutifully recorded her stories and forwarded them to Mac. Mac hadn't reached out yet to let them know if he had had any breakthroughs on Zhang Liu's murder case. Sophie tried to ignore the small ball of disappointment growing in her belly at having not heard from Mac yet.

On their way to the autopsy room, movement ahead caught Sophie's attention. Striding purposefully towards them was Mac, making a pleased smile tug at Sophie's lips. Perturbed by her initial gut reaction to Mac's presence, Sophie forced her face into a neutral expression. Glancing over, she smirked, seeing that it didn't even occur to Reggie to cover up his happy expression at Mac's arrival.

"Do you two have a few minutes to talk?" Mac asked quietly with a nod towards Reggie's office.

Reggie eagerly ushered Mac into his office with Sophie trailing behind them both. Reggie sat in his usual spot behind his desk, leaving Sophie to sit next to Mac. She felt awkward and self-conscious perched so close to him. Internally, she lectured herself at the ridiculous reaction to Mac's proximity and forced herself to pay attention. It didn't matter if he was an asshole who made her uncomfortable; for the time being, he needed her to help solve murders.

"Mac, do you need our assistance again? Or do you have news for us?" Reggie asked hopefully. Sophie shook her head at how much Reggie was enjoying their new secret life as crime-solving sleuths.

"I just wanted to stop in and update you on what I've discovered so far. I've been asking too many questions and making suggestions about cases that keep coming true. A few people in my department are starting to look at me strangely. At some point, we may have to discuss making the police chief aware of your gift, Sophie. He's a Mythical, so I believe he would be willing to give you a chance to prove your ability and help solve cases. And I trust him. But for now, I want to continue keeping your gift a secret. Something feels off about all of this."

"What do you mean?" Sophie asked.

"I realized this morning that all three cases your visions say are different from the official police reports are assigned to Lancaster and Hernandez. I'm probably just being paranoid, but we need to be cautious for the time being, just in case they aren't on the up-and-up. I have no proof they are dirty cops, and I'm trying not to let my distaste for them color my perceptions. They're probably just being lazy and not performing their due diligence on their cases, but my gut is telling me we need to proceed carefully. I don't want them to be aware of your involvement with any of this. For the moment, I just need someone to talk to about these cases. I feel like I'm missing something. So, I was hoping we could review them."

"Of course," Reggie responded.

"Alright. Let's go in chronological order. Joseph Henson was killed by his younger brother Floyd. Your vision didn't include a motive behind the murder, so there isn't much to go on. Joseph didn't have a wife or any children. Other than his brother, no other immediate family is alive. There isn't much to discuss." Mac sighed.

"I wish my vision had told me why Floyd killed his brother. I mean, was it over a woman? Greed? Or maybe just plain sibling rivalry?"

"Hmmm. The murder was methodical, well-planned, and precisely executed. That doesn't sound like a murder born from high passions. If I had to speculate, I'd guess greed was the motivation. Without any other immediate family, Floyd will inherit all of Joseph's wealth... And his estate," Mac said with a thoughtful look, tapping his fingers on the desk.

"What are you thinking?" Reggie said in growing excitement, latching onto the air of expectancy hovering over them.

"Sophie has mentioned more than once that these murders had to do with territories and real estate. Could that be the connection?" Mac wondered, looking up at the ceiling as if the answers to his questions were there. "I wish I had a map of the city. If this is about real estate, I'm going to need a map."

"Let me see if Miss Zhao could locate one for us! When the city built this facility a few years ago, there was a lot of debate about where to put the building initially. There might be some maps from that time archived in our records department," Reggie said, hustling out the door before either Mac or Sophie could respond.

After a few minutes of awkward silence, Sophie turned to

Mac. "Am I in danger? If people found out about my visions, would it put me in jeopardy?"

"It's possible, I guess. But I don't think so. However, until we figure out if these three cases are the result of poor police work or something more sinister, I want us to proceed with caution. Just in case," Mac said.

Reggie came bustling back into the room with a stack of maps. He handed the maps to Mac as he started clearing items off his desk. Flipping through the different maps, Mac unfolded the one he thought would work the best and laid it across Reggie's desk.

"Okay. Joseph Henson was murdered in his home here in the Haight-Ashbury neighborhood," Mac said, pointing to an area on the map. "I need some way to put a marker on this map."

"I think I have something," Reggie exclaimed, opening a drawer on his desk and handing Mac a variety of coins.

"Perfect," Mac said, putting a coin down to represent where Joseph Henson died.

"Who's next?" Reggie asked.

"Cynthia Forsythe was a murder-for-hire plot, staged to look like a robbery gone wrong. Her house was in Nob Hill," Mac said, placing another coin on the map.

"Nob Hill, huh? Fancy," Reggie murmured, leaning over to look at the location on the map.

"What was Cynthia? If we were conducting her autopsy, I can assume she wasn't human," Sophie said.

"Fae. A pretty high-ranking one. I can't figure out a motive for her murder. No one benefits from her death. She didn't have any immediate family," Mac said.

"Whom does her estate go to?" Sophie asked.

"I don't know yet. I'm waiting to find out. It will probably go to the next closest relation, a cousin or something. Or it might get turned over to the city, or possibly even the Conclave," Mac replied with a shrug.

"Is there a way you can find out?" Reggie asked.

"I've put in an inquiry, but I did it with someone I trust in the IT department. I didn't want Lancaster or Hernandez to find out that I've been poking around one of their closed cases. They're already aggravated enough with me. I don't want to make it any worse by questioning them directly. Plus, I just don't fucking trust them at this point.

"Okay, the vampire is next. Montgomery was found in Golden Gate Park." Mac placed a coin in the area of the park where the body was discovered. "He was snatched in Twin Peaks on his way to visit his girlfriend." Mac placed another coin on the girlfriend's apartment.

"Sophie said it was because of a real estate deal gone bad. Someone staged the murder to look like a hunter killed him during a dine-n-dash. Did Montgomery own any properties?" Reggie asked Mac.

"I don't think so, but his Domus leader Sebastian does. Their main Domus is in Alamo Square. I'll see if I can find out if Sebastian owns any other real estate, or if the Domus have sold any property recently. I'm going to go back and see if any of our victims or their immediate families have sold or purchased any real estate in the last few months," Mac said.

"Do we want to include Zhang on the map? Did you track down Marcus Lincham?" Sophie asked.

"It took a while, but I finally found him. Marcus believes members of the Sunset District wolf pack killed Zhang Liu over territory and because Zhang was trying to form a pack from shifter outcasts. A lot of the stronger packs don't want the competition from new packs entering the city. Especially a mixed pack like Zhang was trying to create. He wanted a pack that welcomed all species," Mac said, studying the map and placing a coin on West Portal. "Zhang Liu was killed in West Portal by six wolves not far from where he lived. It is possible the murder was over territory in Forest Knolls, though, so I'm going to mark that location as well."

"Huh, besides the coins on West Portal, Golden Gate Park, and Twin Peaks, the rest form an almost perfectly straight line," Sophie said, tracing her finger over the line across the map.

"Sophie's right. Shit!" Mac exclaimed, his face intense with a thunder-cloud expression. "Reggie, are you seeing what I'm seeing?"

"It's impossible to miss. I find it hard to believe, but that has to be the motivation behind all this," Reggie said, running his hand over his face, dazed.

"What's impossible to miss? What does it mean?" Sophie asked in confusion.

"This is the ley line running through San Francisco," Mac said, tapping his finger at a point on the farthest southwest corner of the city, running it diagonally up through the map, ending at the top right corner, where the land met the bay.

"Does this mean someone is trying to take control over the entirety of the ley line?" Reggie whispered.

"Maybe. It could be a single person or even a group. Right now, we have no way of knowing. Why would someone want to own all the property along the ley line?" Mac asked with a thoughtful frown. "As far as I know, the portals from the Fae realm to Earth are controlled on the Fae side. No one even knows how the Fae operate the portals or how they send people through."

"I've heard they have a way to harness the power that emanates from the ley lines. Maybe someone is trying to tap into that?" Reggie suggested.

"So, you think these murders are related?" Sophie asked quietly.

"There is almost no doubt," Mac stated seriously.

Sophie stared at the map for a minute, turning her mind over the possibilities. "How long do you think this has been happening? If this is some kind of conspiracy, then I doubt these four are the only incidents where someone is trying to grab real estate."

"Fuck. You're right. You guys only do autopsies for deaths committed by or against Mythicals. I need to check for all murders committed along the ley line," Mac said.

"You should look into suicides and accidents, too," Sophie suggested. "Joseph Henson's death was set up to look like suicide."

"Is there a way to also check for property recently sold along the ley line?" Reggie asked.

"Shit. This is going to take me forever," Mac sighed.

"Is there any way we can help?" Reggie offered.

"I'm not sure yet. I have to see what information I can uncover first. I need to proceed very carefully. I don't want anyone to realize what I am looking into yet. Not until we know who the key players are. Until I have more facts, let's keep all this between the three of us. Agreed?"

Both Reggie and Sophie nodded their heads in agreement.

"Oh, and I'm picking you up when your shift is over, and we are getting you a cell phone. This is all too important and potentially dangerous for us not to be able to get a hold of you. Don't fucking argue with me!" Mac growled when Sophie opened her mouth to protest.

"He's right, Soph. You truly need a phone," Reggie agreed, making Sophie throw her hands up in annoyed defeat.

~

"GOODBYE, MISS ZHAO," SOPHIE CALLED OUT AS SHE HEADED across the lobby. "Have a nice day."

"Goodbye, Sophie. Have a nice time on your date!" Miss Zhao chirped.

When Sophie looked over at her in confusion, Miss Zhao nodded her head towards the glass entrance doors. Looking out front, Sophie sighed in resignation when she spotted Mac pacing outside, the early morning sunshine reflecting off his dark glasses. Mac came to a standstill when he saw Sophie inside, then pointed at his watch and waved her to join him.

"No, no, no, Miss Zhao. This is *not* a date. He's just helping me get a phone. That's it," Sophie adamantly denied, shaking her head for emphasis.

"Sure. Of course not, dear," Miss Zhao said, disbelief dripping from every word.

"It's not!" Sophie denied.

"Mmhmm," Miss Zhao hummed noncommittally, turning back to her computer.

Looking at Mac, who was tapping his foot in increasing agitation, Sophie was tempted to linger with Miss Zhao for a few minutes more just to annoy him.

"You should go join your man. Before he comes in here to drag you out," Miss Zhao murmured in amusement.

"He's not… Ugh, never mind," Sophie huffed, stomping her way towards Mac.

~

AN HOUR AND A HALF LATER, SOPHIE STORMED OUT OF THE RETAIL store, more pissed off than she'd ever been. Slamming out of the store's entrance with a shiny new phone in her pocket, Sophie whirled on the sidewalk to face Mac as he exited the store after her.

Pointing an accusing finger at him, she bellowed, "Oh my god! You made those people think I'm your 'kept' girl, you prick!"

"What? No. I just told the salesclerk I wanted to get my *best girl* a phone so that whenever I wanted her, she would be able to come take care of my needs immediately," Mac said with an innocent face.

"I'm gonna murder you, and no one will care. I might even get a medal. No one's going to miss you," Sophie stated matter-of-factly, a fire crackling in her eyes.

"Hey, this has been a great day! Do you want to go get some breakfast? My treat, sweetheart," Mac offered with a wicked grin.

"A great day?" Sophie repeated slowly, irritation coating every word.

"Yes! We're getting closer to solving my cases. You got a new phone. I also got to embarrass the shit out of you. And look at this weather," Mac said, indicating the clear sky above them, "just lovely."

Standing in the middle of the sidewalk, blocking the door to the store, Sophie stared at Mac in flabbergasted disbelief. *Who is this cheerful nutjob? Where is the gritty, pissed-off cop who growls at everyone?* Sophie wondered internally, carefully looking around for an escape path, just in case.

"Aww, don't be mad, honey," Mac wheedled playfully.

"Don't 'honey' me. You're a weirdo. Just take me home," Sophie said, shaking her head at the strange turn her life had taken.

"Do you know that when you get angry, you get a tic in your left eyelid?" Mac asked cheerfully before wandering away, leaving Sophie staring after him.

CHAPTER 16

*S*ophie stepped out of her apartment and headed over to Birdie's place. After Mac dropped her off this morning, Sophie had realized that she hadn't visited with Birdie since delivering her brandy a few days ago. As she raised her hand to knock, a masculine voice from inside the apartment had Sophie momentarily freezing in surprise. Once she recovered, she cautiously knocked on Birdie's door.

Sophie relaxed when she heard Birdie's voice call out that she was coming.

When Birdie opened the door, Sophie spotted an older man sitting on the loveseat. The man was wearing pressed tan slacks, a button-up shirt, and a tweed newsboy cap. Thick black-rimmed glasses perched on his long nose. He gave Sophie a sweet crooked grin when he saw her looking at him over Birdie's shoulder. She waved her fingers at him in greeting, also noting that Birdie was wearing a nice floral dress rather than her usual quilted housecoat.

"Who is that?" Sophie asked, trying to see better over Birdie's head into her apartment like the nosy neighbor she was.

"Well... you know how the senior center was hosting those

art museum tours around the city? I signed up to do a group tour at the Legion of Honor." Sophie nodded, remembering Birdie saying something about it earlier in the week. "Well, Milton was in my tour group yesterday morning, and we just hit it off."

"Really? That's awesome," Sophie said quietly. Sophie smiled when she noticed that Milton was balancing Birdie's best teacup on his knee. The Hot Pussy cup didn't look like it'd made an appearance yet. Birdie must have truly liked Milton to be on such good behavior.

"Milton, this is my neighbor Sophie. Sophie, this is my new friend Milton," Birdie said while Milton greeted Sophie with a shy smile.

"I was going to invite you to join me for a drink at the bar, but it looks like you're already busy," Sophie grinned wickedly. "Maybe next time?"

"Not tonight, but maybe we'll both join you on another night," Birdie replied.

"Well, have fun! Don't do anything I wouldn't do," Sophie said in a mock-stern voice.

"Got it. So, everything is still on the table," Birdie sassed back. "Maybe we could have a double date with your Mac sometime soon."

"He's not *my* Mac. He's just a co-worker." Sophie shook her head.

"Don't tell me lies. I could feel the sexual tension between the two of you. You guys nearly set my couch on fire. Besides, if you don't get some action soon, you're going to forget how to use it."

"First of all, there is no sexual tension between Mac and me. There is only good old-fashioned regular tension. I think Mac might have been more enamored with you, anyways. And secondly, I am not going to forget how to 'use it.' That is not how it works, and you know it," Sophie retorted, making Birdie giggle.

"You might be right. He did seem to be very receptive to my flirting. So, forget Mac, but let's find you a man. You need a love life, girl. You are too young to let your assets go to waste. You're young enough that they're still defying gravity, and you'll wish more people got a chance to appreciate them before nature takes its due," Birdie lectured.

"No dating for me right now, thanks. I'd rather live vicariously through you. I'll stop by tomorrow, and you can tell me all about your night with Milton." Sophie winked.

"You really should think about getting laid. Knock the cobwebs out. It might make you less cranky."

"I am *not* cranky, you brat. You need to stop worrying about the state of my pussy and focus on your own. Now, go knock Milton's socks off, you crazy woman," Sophie whispered. Looking over Birdie's shoulder, she waved. "It was nice to meet you, Milton. I hope you both have a nice date."

Birdie stepped back inside, a happy little giggle escaping through the crack as she closed the door.

Smiling in chagrin at the fact that the little old lady across the hall was getting more action than her, Sophie hopped down the stairs and into the cold dusk settling outside. Fog was thick in the air, making the deep breath Sophie took feel damp and heavy in her lungs. The glow of lights emanating from The Little Thumb looked warm and inviting, shooing away the gloom.

"Hey, Sophie! I got a new IPA on draught. You wanna try it?" Burg called out as Sophie entered the bar.

A bunch of the pub regulars – made up mostly of grizzled old men – nodded or raised their hands in greeting as Sophie pulled up a stool at the bar. Hard living had whittled these men down until all that was left was wiry fibrous tissue, leathery weathered skin, and a brusque attitude. When Sophie first moved into Brown Betty and started stopping by the bar, the men looked at her with distrust in their flinty eyes. But over the long months, Sophie's "take no shit" attitude had allowed her to finally slot into a quiet, ignored place in the landscape of their bar. Now she was just another slouched fixture sitting along the bar.

"Sure, Burg. An IPA sounds good," Sophie said, looking around the pub's interior.

When Burg plonked the beer in front of Sophie, she grinned at him in appreciation.

"It's a local brew from Russian River Brewery. I think you're gonna like it."

Sophie took a small sip, then smacked her lips in appreciation.

"Not too bitter, yeah? It's called Pliny the Younger," Burg said.

"Weird name, but I like it. Good crowd tonight," Sophie noted. Most of the stools at the bar were full, and all the tables except for one had patrons seated around them.

"Yeah, The Little Thumb got a write-up on some travel blogger's website. The person wrote how it's one of the oldest continuously operating bars in San Francisco, so we've been getting more traffic lately. Especially on the weekends," Burg blurted in excitement.

"That's awesome. Just make sure you always save a seat for me when you become a hot spot. Has the bar always been called The Little Thumb? I've been meaning to ask. It's kind of a weird name."

"The Little Thumb is an ogre fairy tale," Burg said, leaning on the bar top.

"I've never heard of it."

"You heard many ogre fairy tales, have you?" Burg asked challengingly.

"Um, I think I've heard a few. Gotta be honest, though, none where ogres weren't the bad guys. Like Jack and the Beanstalk and Puss-in-Boots."

"I don't think there are any fairy tales where ogres aren't evil. In most of them, we eat people. I've been advised to say humans taste like chicken," Burg said, giving Sophie an Italian chef's kiss as if humans were just delicious. Laughter caught her so unexpectedly, Sophie almost choked on her beer.

"Alright, tell me the tale of The Little Thumb," Sophie said, once she finished mopping up her face, resting her elbows on the wooden bar top.

"Little Thumb was the youngest of seven brothers in a poor woodcutter's family. He was no bigger than a thumb when he was born. Little Thumb may have been the smallest in the family, but he was also the brightest. Although he hardly spoke, Little Thumb always listened. The family was destitute, and the parents could no longer take care of their children, so they decided to abandon them in the woods," Burg intoned.

"So, the parents hatch a plan to abandon their children. Little Thumb overhears the parents' plot to leave them in the woods, so he gathers a pocketful of little white stones from a nearby river. As his parents lead the children through the forest, Little Thumb uses the pebbles to leave a trail that leads them back home. The boys are able to follow the trail of pebbles to find their way out of the woods. When the children return home, the parents wait a few weeks before once again tricking the boys into the woods."

"Parents of the year," Sophie teased.

"Hey, don't interrupt. You're going to ruin the flow of my storytelling."

"Please forgive me, oh great bard!"

"This time, Little Thumb makes a mistake and uses breadcrumbs as a trail marker instead of pebbles. But birds eat all the breadcrumbs, and the children get lost in the woods trying to return home."

"Like Hansel and Gretel!" Sophie exclaimed. When Burg just stared at her steadily, Sophie mimed zipping her lips.

"Where was I? Oh yes, so Little Thumb climbs a tree to try and find a way through the woods. When he does, he spots a cabin nestled in the forest. The children make their way to the house before realizing it belongs to an ogre. The boys decide that it is safer to stay in an ogre's house than spend the night out in the woods. The forest was teeming with dangerous, man-eating wolves." Burg paused to pour a beer for a customer.

Coming back to Sophie, he continued, "So, they decide to spend the night inside the ogre's house. The ogre lets the children sleep in his daughters' room. The ogre has seven daughters, and each one wears a little golden crown. Little Thumb figures out that the ogre plans to kill him and his brothers in their sleep. So Little Thumb has his siblings switch their nightcaps with the ogre's daughters' crowns. As a result, the ogre, after too much wine, kills his daughters instead. Not realizing his mistake, he goes back to bed. Before he can wake up, the boys sneak out of his house and start to figure out the way back home. When the ogre wakes up and realizes what happened, he puts on his seven-league boots and chases after the children. Little Thumb spots the ogre and has his brothers hide in a nearby cave. The ogre gets tired from running a vast distance in a short amount of time and decides to take a nap not far from the cave. Once he falls asleep, Little Thumb tells his siblings to continue towards home while he steals the ogre's boots. When Little Thumb puts on the boots, they magically resize to fit his feet. They let him travel quickly, and he heads home. Little Thumb uses the magical boots to offer his services as a messenger to the king. Since the seven-league boots allow Little Thumb to travel great distances very swiftly, he becomes a prized messenger throughout the lands. Thanks to the money Little Thumb earns, he and his family are able to live comfortably for the rest of their lives," Burg finished the story with a flourish.

"What. The. Fuck. You – an ogre – named your bar after the kid who got an ogre to murder his own daughters and then steals his magical boots. Did I get that right?" Sophie asked, completely baffled by the pub-naming process.

"I didn't name the bar. My grandfather picked the name. But here's the thing that wasn't in the fairy tale: Little Thumb was an ogre too. He became a pretty famous one in his time," Burg said with a confidential air. "My grandfather swears our family is distantly related to him."

"I feel like you are fucking with me. Is that *really* the fairy tale? Or did you just make up that story to mess with a gullible human?" Sophie asked, eyes narrowed in suspicion.

"That's the real story, I swear. You can look it up," Burg laughed, indicating Sophie's almost empty glass. "Do you want another beer? What did you think of the new IPA?"

"It was good. Not too bitter. I'll take another," Sophie said, finishing off the last dregs of the beer in her glass.

A few minutes later, Burg placed a fresh pint in front of Sophie.

"Why do you have so much crap all over the walls? Don't you get tired of dusting all these ancient knick-knacks?" Sophie waved her hand at the myriad of shelves dotting the walls, heavy with pictures, figurines, statues, and every manner of decoration.

"Those items are not crap!" Burg said indignantly. "Those are treasures my family has collected over the last hundred years. Some of those items are so rare they would blow your mind. Almost every item here is one of a kind."

"Oh yeah? Like what?" Sophie asked, looking around with renewed interest at the bric-a-brac lining the walls.

"See that trophy?" Burg pointed to a golden trophy on the wall opposite of where Sophie was sitting. Squinting, Sophie looked at the "treasure" Burg was indicating. It appeared to be made of gold. On top of a marble pedestal, a figure of a woman held a large cup above her head. Golden wings spread from her back, the plumage arching up behind her to touch the sides of the cup. It looked a little old and somewhat tarnished to Sophie's eyes.

"Yeah, I see it. It just looks like a regular sports trophy to me." Sophie shrugged.

"That is the Jules Rimet World Cup trophy. It depicts Nike, the goddess of victory. They retired the trophy when Brazil won it in 1970. My father stole it in 1984. There isn't another in all the world," Burg said, flipping his bar towel over his shoulder with a dramatic swish.

"Does anyone know you have it?"

"No, it's a secret. Only you and I know now. Well, and my father, but he retired to Florida ten years ago. He's not going to tell anyone."

"Well, it's lovely," Sophie said with what she hoped was the correct amount of awe to satisfy Burg's pride in the trophy. "It still seems like a lot of shit you have to dust. Even priceless items collect dust."

"Mine don't," Burg said with a grin.

"How is that possible?" Sophie squinted at Burg, expecting to be the butt of a joke.

"My grandmother did a brownie a favor a few years after the bar opened. In return, the brownie set a spell here, so we never have to dust," Burg said.

"What? You're so lucky. How do I get a brownie to put a spell on my apartment?" Sophie griped. "Your grandma should have got that brownie to make it so you never have to sweep either."

"Maybe, but how else would I get you to earn your keep around here?" Burg teased. The bar telephone ringing prevented Sophie from giving a snarky reply.

Sophie stood up and wandered over to the pilfered trophy to get a better look at it as Burg went to answer his phone. It was perched on one of the highest shelves on the wall, so Sophie couldn't get as close a look as she'd like. She shrugged in uncertainty as she stared at it. It looked like a plain old trophy to her. Walking around, she tried to look at Burg's cluttered items with new eyes. She walked over and stared at a yellowed circus poster. It showed a man doing a headstand on a tall pole with a strong man looking on. Across the top, it proclaimed "Pablo Fanque's Circus Royal".

Sophie took a sip of her beer, admiring a glossy violin, almost spilling her drink when one of the regulars tapped her shoulder.

The gremlin-looking man told Sophie that Burg was asking for her.

"Everything okay?" Sophie asked, sitting back on her barstool. Burg had a strange look on his face and was pressing a phone to his chest.

"You've got a phone call," Burg said, handing Sophie the cordless receiver.

"Hello?" Sophie said uncertainly into the phone.

"Why aren't you answering your fucking phone?" Mac's voice growled in her ear.

"Oh shit! I forgot it on my dresser," Sophie exclaimed.

"You forgot your phone," Mac repeated incredulously. "The phone I specifically bought you in case of emergencies?"

The calm rasp in Mac's voice made Sophie realize how close he was to actually losing his temper.

"I'm sorry. I'm not used to it yet. I won't forget it again," Sophie said in a rush. "Why are you calling? Is there an emergency?"

"Yes. There was a murder tonight of a Fae who lives along the ley line. I need you to meet me at the morgue. I want to do a reading on the victim asap. I've already talked to Reginald, and he's on his way there now. Can you pull yourself away from the bar long enough to head to the morgue?" Mac said snidely.

"Hey, there's no need to be a dick. I'm allowed to have a fucking night off and enjoy a beer at my local bar. The only thing I did wrong was to forget my phone, and I already apologized for that. So cut that shit out," Sophie whisper-yelled into the phone.

A pause. Then: "You're right. I'm being an ass. I will be nicer from here on out," Mac said, breathing out a long sigh like he was trying to push out stress.

"Don't try to be too nice. You might pull a muscle." Sophie smirked, making Mac chuckle.

"Can you meet us at the morgue tonight? You haven't had too

much to drink, have you?" Mac asked, finally sounding more like himself.

"Only one beer. And yes, I can head out to the ME's office right now. It will take me at least a half-hour to get there."

"That's fine. They're still processing the scene, so you'll probably beat me there."

"I will see you soon, then."

"Thanks, Soph. See you soon," Mac softly responded just before Sophie heard the soft click of him hanging up.

Sophie waved to get Burg's attention. She set the phone and some money down on the bar. She glanced at her full beer longingly for a moment, but got up and headed out the door.

Heading up to her apartment to grab her phone and change her shoes, she smiled as she heard a feminine giggle seep from under Birdie's apartment door.

CHAPTER 17

A little over a half-hour later, Sophie rushed into the Medical Examiner's building.

"Good evening, Miss Zhao," Sophie said, surprised to see the dignified woman behind the counter on a weekend night.

"Good evening, Sophie. Dr Didel is already here and waiting for you," Miss Zhao said as she buzzed Sophie into the back.

Striding up to Reggie's office, Sophie knocked on his door. Reggie jerked it open in breathless excitement.

"Sophie! Is Mac here yet?" Reggie asked, eyes bright and glowing with eagerness.

"I don't think so, but I just got here," Sophie said cautiously.

"I've already explained to the attending ME that we would be conducting this autopsy at Detective Volpes' request. He's a human, so he's used to having some of the autopsies saved for my department because he's under the impression that I am a specialist. He does not know about Mythicals, so we need to be very careful what we say around him, okay? The odds are, you won't even see him. Dr Langston prefers to conduct his work in one of the other autopsy rooms."

"No problem. I won't say a word if I ever see him," Sophie

promised. "Will he think it's weird that we're coming in on our day off?"

"Not really. It's rare, but I have been called in before when an autopsy needs to be conducted immediately. It shouldn't raise any eyebrows," Reggie assured.

"Was Miss Zhao called in too?" Sophie asked suddenly.

"What? No, she was already here."

"She worked this whole week with us. Does she not get the night off?" Sophie asked in concern.

"She doesn't take days off," Reggie explained. "She considers her job and this building her property. Dragons are very territorial creatures. We've found it best to let them have their way once they've claimed something."

"You Mythicals are so weird," Sophie teased, earning a grin from Reggie.

"Like humans are any better," Reggie joked back. Sophie nodded her head in agreement thinking back to the impromptu stoner drum circle that happened on the bus earlier in the week. That was a fragrant bunch – an amalgam of incense, marijuana, and unwashed hair. Sophie was lucky she didn't come into work with a contact high that night.

They both changed into their work scrubs and met back at the main autopsy room to wait for Mac and his incoming Fae victim.

By the time an unfamiliar man rolled a gurney into the room, Sophie was ready to throw something at Reggie to get him to stop his nervous pacing and anxious babbling.

"Good evening, Dr Didel," the man called out. "I have your priority one here." The man rolled the gurney over to the x-ray and weighing station, noticing Sophie standing behind Reggie. "Hey, I'm George. What's your name?" George asked Sophie with what she could only assume he intended to be a charming grin but mostly just came across as a smarmy leer. It perfectly matched the slimy look in his eyes.

"My name's Not Interested," Sophie said dismissively.

"Alright, Not Interested. Be that way," the man turned on his heel and walked out of the room, murmuring "bitch" just loud enough to make sure Sophie heard him.

"I'm going to call Mac and find out how far out he is. I think we should wait for him before we get started," Reggie said, putting his cell phone to his ear.

A moment later, Reggie left a message on Mac's voicemail, letting him know that they would wait for him before they got started. As five minutes became ten and then twenty, Reggie started pacing again, glancing at his phone almost continuously.

"Why don't you call him again?" Sophie suggested, just about fed up with all the night's pacing.

Reggie redialed Mac. A moment later, he looked at Sophie with frustration and worry building in his eyes.

"He's not answering. It went to voicemail again," Reggie said, hanging up the call without leaving a second message.

"That's weird, right?" Sophie asked, Reggie's worry had started to rub off on her.

"Let's just get started. I don't think we should wait any longer. Who knows what's holding Mac up? We will record the session so he can listen to it later."

"I don't mind doing a second reading once he gets here," Sophie suggested.

She unzipped the black body bag and inhaled a sharp breath.

"Oh, jeez," she gasped. "Someone beat the shit out of this guy."

Reggie stepped up next to Sophie to look at the mottled, swollen face of their body. The man had short black hair and a long equine-like nose. It was hard to tell under all the bruising, but Sophie thought he had probably been very distinguished and bold-looking in life. Probably on the far side of his fifties, he had a face that hinted at silver fox status. But whatever happened to him tonight had reduced him to a bruised and broken shell, robbing him of vitality and life.

Getting him weighed and x-rayed quickly, Sophie and Reggie moved the Fae onto the autopsy table.

"Are you ready?" Reggie asked, grabbing his phone and getting it set to record the man's story.

"Yeah, let's get started," Sophie responded, slowly setting her hand on the dead man's arm.

"Mr. Agosti, I'm all finished for today. Unless you need anything else before I head out?" Mary asked.

"Thank you, Mary, but no. I'm all set for the night. I will see you tomorrow. Have a good night," Mr. Agosti responded to his soft-spoken maid. Turning back to the financial report he was reviewing, Atticus absently noted the maid leaving through the front door security camera a few moments later.

Movement on the screen monitoring the front door caught his eyes a few minutes after Mary was gone. Worry settled in his gut when he realized that in order for the men now standing at his front door to arrive so quickly and conveniently after Mary departed, they had to have been outside waiting for her to leave.

Looking closer at the monitor, Atticus grimaced when he realized who was at his door. The Fae standing in the middle of two other men was a recognizable and unwelcome sight. The two men flanking him were unfamiliar. Based on their stances and the way they held themselves – loose and ready to snap into motion in an instant – he would guess they were shifters. That made Atticus raise his eyebrows in surprise. Since when had the Fae aligned themselves with shifters?

He must be genuinely desperate to show up here in person, *Atticus thought to himself. Darting a glance around the room, he stood up and strode over to the safe hidden behind the painting of his late wife. Swinging the frame open on silent hinges, he spun the combination dial. The front doorbell rang as he plucked a gun from the safe. As the doorbell began to ring over and over in growing impatience, he loaded bullets into the chamber, even knowing it would probably not do him any good.*

He stared for a long moment at the intricately carved wooden box sitting in the middle of the safe shelf. Grabbing the box, he opened the top and stared at the large pale green stone sitting on a bed of black velvet, his mind whirling. Pulling out the vermarine jewel by its short brass chain, he grabbed one of his late wife's favorite pendants from its case. The large, honey-colored topaz fit snugly into the box but did not look out of place. Then he closed the wooden case and put it back into the safe, spinning the dial to re-lock it.

He wished, not for the first time, that he had better offensive magic. Being able to heal other people's injuries with just a touch had never served him well in his life. It certainly hadn't helped him save his wife. Without strong offensive magic at his disposal, he had never been allowed to take his rightful place on the Conclave. He'd spent his life attempting to prove his worthiness by serving the Conclave at their convenience. Little good that it did him.

Swinging the painting back against the wall, he stared into his beloved Lizbeth's painted eyes. Gently running a finger across her cheek, he was glad he'd had a life with the one woman who he never had to doubt. It was a life well-lived and well-loved.

With the insistent call of the doorbell beating on his nerves, he glanced around the room. Spotting the floor heating vent next to his bookcase, he remembered that he'd recently kicked the vent and accidentally loosened its mooring from the floor. Prying the vent up, he dropped the stone into the dark depths of the duct system. Putting the heat vent cover carefully back in place, he stuffed the gun into the back of his pants. Then with a deep breath of resolve, Atticus headed to answer the front door.

Peering through the intricate glass of his front door, Atticus composed his face into a careful mask of indifference. Swinging the door open, he greeted the men standing at the threshold.

"Edwyn, it is very late for you to be visiting. I was resting. If you would be so kind, you and your companions can come back tomorrow at a more convenient time," he said.

"Atticus, my friend, so sorry to be a bother, but this really can't wait. May we come in?" Edwyn said with a warm, friendly smile.

"No, I don't think so. I know why you are here, and my answer hasn't changed," Atticus said, pulling the gun on the men. "You need to leave and don't return. Don't make me do something we will both regret. If you bother me again, I will tell the Conclave what you are attempting to do."

Edwyn sighed sadly, "I wish you would reconsider. When history looks back on this time, you will want to be on the side of the victors. On the side of the righteous."

With an imperial flick of Edwyn's hand, a shadow peeled itself from the darkened living room to the left of Atticus and grabbed his arm that was holding the gun. Too late, he realized a fourth person must have snuck into the back of his house while he was distracted by Edwyn at the front door. Atticus desperately tried to bring his arm back down to aim at Edwyn. Struggling to pull away from the assailant, the gun went off, dropping a small amount of plaster and dust from the ceiling onto their heads.

The assailant managed to rip the gun from Atticus's grip, casually tossing the weapon aside. Hauling Atticus up to his toes, the man wrenched his arm up painfully behind his back.

"Make sure we are not disturbed," Edwyn said to one of the men who slipped back out the front entrance, closing the door behind him and sealing Atticus into the trap his home had now become.

"Let's move this discussion to your office," Edwyn said cordially.

The two remaining shifters grabbed Atticus and manhandled him back into his office, tossing him into his plush office chair, which creaked with the force of his rough landing.

"We do not have to make this difficult. Just give us access to this property and give me the clavis," Edwyn said, sitting on the corner of Atticus's desk.

"What you plan is madness. The Fae queen and the Conclave will not allow it. It doesn't matter if you have possession of this building or the clavis or even all of San Francisco. You still have time to step back before it is too late," Atticus pleaded.

"You are wrong. This is... what is it the humans say? Destiny. This is our destiny. My plan is already in motion, and there is no stopping progress. It's a shame you won't be around to see what we create," Edwyn lectured. "Now, tell me where the clavis is."

"It's not here. I put it somewhere safe; someplace where you will never find it. You will never be able to get access to it now," Atticus retorted vehemently, the lie falling easily from his lips.

Edwyn snorted delicately, "Doubtful. I'm sure it's here somewhere. Gentlemen, let's see if we can convince my dear old friend Atticus to tell us what we want to know. Make sure you don't leave any physical evidence behind, please."

The first punch caught Atticus by surprise, the blow knocking his head to the side. After the initial hit, the punches rained down so rapidly that everything just became a blur of pain. Atticus was unable to prepare or recover from the continuous shocks of agony to his body and face. Edwyn's polite, refined veneer never cracked, even when Atticus began to cry out.

Atticus watched Edwyn walk carefully around his office through one swollen eye, as he checked the bookcases and opened various drawers. When he tried to pry his dear Lizbeth's painting from the wall and realized it was on hinges, he gave Atticus a triumphant grin.

Swinging the painting wide, Edwyn turned to Atticus. "What is the combination?"

"I hope you rot," Atticus slurred through swollen lips.

Edwyn tsked with a shake of his head. "Convince him," Edwyn commanded the shifters holding Atticus.

"Tell us the combination," one of the shifters ordered, picking up a letter opener off his desk in a gloved hand. The second shifter grabbed one of Atticus's hands and flattened it onto his desk's glossy wooden surface. He tried to curl his fingers in, but the shifter forced his hand flat.

"Tell us," the shifter demanded again. Atticus shook his head and gritted his teeth. Hovering the sharp end of the opener over his hand, the shifter stared at Atticus expectantly.

Edwyn sighed in mock disappointment from across the room.

When the shifter jammed the letter opener down on Atticus's hand, into the meaty area between his thumb and index finger, for a moment, he felt nothing but disbelief at the action. Before he could even take a breath to recover, sharp burning pain radiated from his hand up the nerves of his body, blinding out his vision. Despite his best attempt to maintain a stoic silence, Atticus screamed out in shocked, choking agony.

"Tell us the combination or your other hand joins the first," the shifter said, his voice dripping with gleeful menace. He picked up a pair of sharp scissors from Atticus's desk, twirling them around one of his fingers as the other shifter forced his other hand next to the first.

"25, 6, 14," Atticus wheezed out.

As Edwyn turned back to the safe, the shifter stabbed the scissors through Atticus's other hand in sadistic glee. His shocked scream rang out through the room. Atticus sagged in his seat, defeat and pain swamping him. Atticus wished, not for the first time, that he could heal himself and not just others.

"Devious," Edwyn said approvingly to the shifter, who chuckled with a sinister air.

"You will accomplish nothing but hasten your inevitable demise," Atticus pushed out through gritted teeth. "You will never get your hands on this home."

"Once you are gone, everything you own will transfer to your cousin. Leandro is a spineless fool. I have little doubt we will have any trouble convincing him to sell us the house. That is a concern for another day, however. The clavis is the only thing I needed to procure this night," Edwyn said as he spun the safe dial. Swinging the door open, he reached in and pulled out the small wooden box with a greedy smile. "And now I have it."

Edwyn opened the top of the box and admired the jewel nestled inside. He stroked one finger over its surface before closing the lid and slipping the box into a pocket inside his jacket.

"Even if you take it to the tower, you do not possess the knowledge to wield the clavis. You are a fool," Atticus warned.

"As usual, you underestimate me, my friend," Edwyn said with a gracious smile, a bright glint of madness shining in his eyes.

The only thing I underestimated was how low you would sink, you halfwit. You don't even know you aren't holding the real clavis, Atticus thought to himself with a small morsel of satisfaction.

"Marcella and the Conclave will stop you. She'll happily pry the clavis from your cold dead hands," Atticus warned.

"That bitch is nothing!" Edwyn screeched, spittle flying from his lips. "Marcella can't even see the rebellion brewing beneath her very feet. The Conclave is ancient, powerless relics from a dying age. They have no vision! Bored and sedate on their fat thrones. They offer no threat against the grand future I plan for our people."

Edwyn turned his back on Atticus, taking a few breaths to calm himself down.

"Gentlemen, you can have anything in the safe and the rest of the house you want. Make it look like a robbery. Just make sure to leave no trace of yourself. I would move quickly before any nosy humans call the police. Also, I want one of you to stay and keep a watch over the property. Call me and let me know who comes and goes," Edwyn said, turning to leave the office.

"Goodbye, Atticus," Edwyn threw over his shoulder as he exited the room with a swish of his long wool coat.

One of the shifters ripped the letter opener out of where it was pinned in Atticus's hand and jabbed it into his throat so quickly he didn't even get a chance to make more than a croak of denial. With one hand still pinned to his desk, Atticus tried to stop the blood flowing from his neck with his free hand. With his hot blood spilling over his fumbling fingers, Atticus quickly felt his strength fading with each beat of his heart.

His last thought was that once Edwyn realized the fake clavis didn't work, he would come back to look for the real one. Atticus hoped Edwyn would be unable to find the hidden clavis and that his death wasn't in vain.

He looked forward to seeing his beautiful Lizbeth once again. Oh, how he had missed her so...

Sophie was shocked to find herself standing in the autopsy room. Tears wet her cheeks as she hugged herself in shock and horror. Never had a vision been so intense, vibrant, and pain-filled. It was as if she had been immersed inside Atticus's mind rather than watching the vision from the sidelines.

"Are you okay?" Reggie asked, grabbing his phone and stopping the recording. Sophie couldn't talk yet, so she just shook her head helplessly. "Come sit down." Reggie gently led Sophie over to a chair across the room like a lost child. "I'm going to call Mac again. He needs to be here."

Sophie's hands wouldn't stop trembling, and she shook them out several times, trying to dispel the phantom pains lingering from the horror of Atticus's death. She pressed her hands against her neck, almost expecting to feel hot, sticky blood spill over her fingers.

Reggie, pressing his phone tightly to his ear, growled, "Where are you? Call us. We have important information you need to hear."

Reggie came back and knelt in front of Sophie, his face filled with concern.

"I'm okay," Sophie tried to reassure him. "Honestly. It was just an intense one."

"How about you sit for a minute and rest while I start the autopsy?" Reggie suggested quietly. "It was strange watching you with this vision. Normally, when you get a vision, you are aware and present the whole time, just recounting a story. This time when you touched the body, you just sort of froze in place like you were in a trance. You also started speaking as if you were talking from Atticus's point of view. Do you know why this vision was different?"

"I have no idea. It was a very bizarre sensation. I felt like I was in his mind. Maybe because his murder happened so recently, it was still fresh. I'm not sure what just happened," Sophie said with a half-shrug.

"Maybe your magic just reacted with his innate Fae magic differently for some reason," Reggie suggested to Sophie, who shrugged in helpless uncertainty.

He told her to stay in her seat and recover while he headed over to Atticus' body to begin the autopsy. The sound of Reggie's phone ringing blasted shrilly through the tiled room, making both Reggie and Sophie jump.

"It's Mac," Reggie said to Sophie, relief evident in his voice as he checked the screen before lifting the phone to his ear. "Where are you?" he demanded into the phone.

Reggie's eyes widened and he stared at Sophie in shock as he listened to what Mac said.

"You got it, Mac. I'll get everyone, and we'll meet you there. After that, Sophie needs to tell you what we learned from the autopsy. You're going to need to hear it," Reggie said. "Yes, okay. We'll get there as soon as we can."

Reggie hung up the phone and turned to Sophie. "Come on, Sophie. We have a situation. We need to go meet up with Mac. I'm glad I brought my car instead of riding BART tonight. I've got to call the crew."

Sophie and Reggie quickly rezipped Atticus' body bag and rolled him into the fridge. She followed Reggie, still feeling numb, as they headed out of the building and towards his car. Getting behind the wheel, Reggie started the car then waited for his phone to connect to the vehicle's wireless system. Choosing Ace's phone number, he pulled out of the ME's office parking lot.

"Hey, Reggie, what's going on?" the rasp of Ace's voice filled the car.

"We have a situation," Reggie said. "Mac called Sophie and me in to do a reading on a murder victim. He was heading to meet us at the office when a shifter started to chase him. They ran into traffic and the other shifter got hit by a car on Geary. The car killed him."

"Shit. Is Mac okay?" Ace exclaimed.

"Yes, Mac is fine. Thankfully, they were both in their animal forms, so the person driving the car thought they hit a large dog. We need you to get Amira and Fitz and meet us behind the Cathedral of Saint Mary of the Assumption on Gough. Can you do that?"

"Okay, you can count on us. Amira's here, and I will call Fitz right now. I'll call you when we get close."

"We will see you soon," Reggie said, letting out a long, relieved breath as he hung up the phone.

CHAPTER 18

By the time they pulled up to the church, both Sophie and Reggie were irritated. Their collective patience had been worn thin from dealing with Saturday night traffic.

"Here we are," Reggie said as they pulled around to the parking lot in the back. "Our Lady of Maytag."

"What?" Sophie choked on a laugh.

"Look at the building," Reggie said, nodding towards the church.

Sophie looked at the modern cathedral with its sleek white façade. The geometric church reached hundreds of feet into the air with graceful curves that met in four flat corners. It looked like the four corners would create the form of a cross if you could see it from above.

"It's very… modern and stark-looking," Sophie responded.

"It also looks exactly like the agitator from a giant washing machine." Reggie chuckled. "So, it has fondly been renamed the Our Lady of Maytag church."

"I'm relatively certain that's blasphemy." Sophie laughed, reflecting that the church truly did resemble the inside of a washing machine. It reminded her of the ancient machine sitting in Brown Betty's tiny laundry room on the first floor.

Parking the car in a spot where the streetlights' fingers didn't reach, Reggie texted Mac to let him know they had arrived. A moment later, Mac emerged from around a corner and waved for them to join him.

Getting out of the car, Sophie shivered, the cold hitting her in the face like a slap. Belatedly, she realized that she had forgotten her coat back at the morgue in her rush to get to Mac. Wrapping her arms tightly around her middle, she followed Reggie around the side of the imposing cathedral.

"I just got a text from Ace, and they should all be here in just a couple of minutes," Reggie informed Sophie and Mac.

"Are you okay?" Sophie asked.

"Yeah, I'm fine. I probably should have called for backup when I realized someone was following me, but I had hoped to catch whoever it was unaware and get some answers out of him," Mac said, frustration coating his words.

"What do you need from us?" Reggie asked.

"Let's wait for the others and then we can figure out how to handle the situation," Mac said.

"Is there a dead body? Do you need me to do a reading?" Sophie asked.

"Yeah, he's dead. Conducting a reading is a good idea. It might give us a few answers. Either way, let's wait for the rest of the crew," Mac suggested.

Sophie tried to keep from shivering and letting her teeth chatter from the cold, but Mac took one look at her and wordlessly dropped his jacket over her shoulders.

"I'm okay. It's not that cold," Sophie tried to protest.

"Shut up, Sophie; just take the damn jacket," Mac growled softly at her. "Shifters run fairly hot, so I'm not uncomfortable. Besides, I don't want to listen to your teeth chattering all night."

"Wow, and here I thought you were being so altruistic," Sophie threw back at him, secretly reveling in the body heat still clinging to the inside of the jacket.

"You should know better than that," Mac said with a challenging tilt of his chin.

"I do, actually. You're no one's white knight," Sophie said, giving Mac a playfully derisive head to toe look.

Reggie's uncomfortable throat-clearing made Sophie and Mac jump back from one another. Sophie hadn't even realized that they had gotten right up in each other's faces. She couldn't let Mac rile her so easily. It was beginning to feel too much like flirting and Sophie wasn't sure she wanted to travel down that path with Mac. So much was happening with her, it felt like a terrible time to contemplate another upheaval in her life. *I'll be cool as a cucumber from now on,* she silently vowed.

"They're here," Reggie announced, unknowingly breaking up the awkward silence that had descended between Mac and Sophie.

They all turned to fetch the rest of their group. Once they located Fitz, Ace, and Amira, Mac led everyone to a dumpster and rolled it away from the wall, revealing a naked man.

"Why is he naked?" Sophie blurted out in surprise.

"When we transform into our animal forms, we can't do it with our clothes on. We'd get tangled up in them," Amira said with a "duh" tone in her voice.

"Oh. Yeah, that makes sense. Sorry, I just wasn't expecting him to be nude," Sophie said with a sheepish shrug. Stepping closer to the body, she leaned over, trying to get a look at the man's face.

"What kind of shifter is he? I'm not familiar with this scent," Fitz asked, taking several deep sniffs, his nose wrinkling so adorably that Sophie had to hide her amusement. Sophie doubted Fitz would appreciate the fact that she found him adorable.

"Jackal," Mac said.

"No shit! They're super rare in this part of the world," Ace exclaimed. "Do you know who he is? Is he familiar?"

"No, I've never seen this guy before. After we figure out what to do with the body, I'm going to see if I can retrace his steps. Hopefully, I can locate his clothes and ID," Mac said. "I can't decide if we should just leave him here or try to dispose of the body. He followed me after I left the crime scene earlier, so it might be better if he just disappears, rather than turn up dead. It might be safer if I'm not linked to this. What do you think, Reggie?"

Sophie's gasp caught everyone's attention before Reggie got a chance to answer. "He was one of the shifters at Atticus' murder. After they killed Atticus, Edwyn told this one to stay and keep a watch on the house," Sophie explained.

She gently placed her hand on the dead shifter's shoulder. The man's final night started to form in Sophie's mind. She forcefully pushed past what he and his companions did to Atticus. She did not need to relive Atticus' final moments again.

"His name was Andrew. After he, and the other shifter Dimitri, killed Atticus, they grabbed some jewels and money from the safe. They made sure to trash the office. They also grabbed some valuables from the master bedroom. After Andrew stashed his portion of the stolen items in his car, he returned to keep an eye on Atticus' place. He waited in the bushes on the side of a house a few buildings down. It was dark where he hid, but it looks like it was a white house with blue trim. Andrew didn't have to wait long for the police to show up. About thirty minutes after the police initially arrived, he saw you pull up, Mac. When Andrew saw you enter the house, he called Edwyn," Sophie told them, trying to focus and absorb as much of the details of the vision as she could. "He described you and your car to Edwyn, and Edwyn thought it was you. He knew your name. He said that you're becoming a problem. You've been asking too many questions and stirring up trouble and drawing attention to their scheme. Edwyn told Andrew: 'Follow him. See if he meets up with anyone or is talking to anyone else. If you get a chance, take him out. Whatever you do, don't let him see you. Call me when you can.' Then Edwyn hung up."

Sophie took a small breath and shook out her hand.

"I think I know what happens next. You don't need to do the rest," Mac offered quietly, his blue eyes dark and serious.

"No, I'm okay," Sophie said, putting her hand back on Andrew's arm. Taking a small breath to center her mind, she continued, "Okay, so when you exited the house again, he watched you make several phone calls. I have to assume that's when you called Reggie and me. Oh man, you looked pissed, Mac. I sure do annoy you, huh?" Sophie chuckled. "Andrew realized that you were about to get in your car and drive away, so he quickly stripped and changed into his jackal form. He growled in his throat, trying to grab your attention and pull you away from your vehicle. He started slinking backward between the houses, making enough noise to lead you away from the area where a few cops were still lingering. You started following him, but he didn't expect you to change into your fox form. He thought that since his jackal is a lot bigger than your fox size, he could probably take you out. Once you started running, Andrew panicked because he realized that he now had to kill you. After all, you're now aware that you're being followed. If you escaped and Edwyn found out that you spotted Andrew, Edwyn would kill him. I think this guy might have been a bit of a dumbass. In his panic, he tried to chase you across Geary Street, but he didn't see the truck until it was too late."

Sophie drew her hand away from Andrew's body and stood up, locking her knees, trying to make sure she looked calm and collected. There was no need for everyone to witness how rattled she was.

"He was in jackal form when he died. But now he is back to human. Reggie told me that's what normally happens when shifters die, is that right?" Sophie asked, grasping for something else to focus on besides her frazzled nerves.

"Yes, we revert to our human form," Mac responded. "Who is Edwyn?"

"He was the man who orchestrated the murder of Atticus tonight. It might be easier if we just listen to the recording of Sophie's vision rather than try to explain it all," Reggie suggested.

Rolling the dumpster back in place to temporarily hide Andrew's body, they all gathered closer as Reggie pulled out his phone and hit play on the recording. Discomfort crawled its way up Sophie's throat as her voice spilled from the phone's speakers, sounding hollow and unfamiliar. The tone of her voice sounded strange and vaguely robotic as if she had been in some kind of trance. When the last of her story drew to a close, everyone flinched a little at the ragged gasps Sophie made as she returned to awareness. Reggie quickly stopped the recording, cutting off the rest of Sophie's choked panting.

"Shit! I need to go back to Atticus' house immediately. I don't know what a clavis is, but we need to get our hands on it before anyone else does. But we need to deal with Andrew's body too," Mac said, looking like he wanted to pull his hair out.

"I can take care of the body." Fitz broke the silence.

"You can? How?" Mac asked.

"My cousin is a mortician in San Mateo. There is a crematorium at his funeral home. He'll let us use it, no questions asked," Fitz said confidently.

"You're sure?" Mac asked.

"Absolutely. My family has had to deal with some 'unsavory' characters in the past, so it won't be the first time my cousin's funeral home has been used to make a body disappear," Fitz replied.

Mac stared at Fitz for a long, pregnant moment before shaking his head in defeat. "Fuck. It's not like I have a choice. I may come back to you with some questions about the funeral home when this is over."

"You know, our department at the morgue has a lot of discretion to deal with the bodies as we see fit. Our main mandate is to safeguard the discovery of Mythicals from humanity," Reggie reminded Mac. "We've had to use his cousin's funeral home on more than one occasion."

"Don't worry, Mac. My family's crematorium has only been used to take care of people who the world was better off without," Fitz reassured him. Unsurprisingly, Mac did not look comforted.

"I guess I'll just have to take your word for it, for now. I trust you. You three," Mac said, pointing at Fitz, Ace, and Amira, "can you guys take care of the body while me, Sophie and Reggie head back to Atticus' house?"

"Sure," Fitz said. "Let's get the body in Ace's trunk."

"Sophie and I will keep watch while you guys pack up the corpse," Amira announced, staring intently at Sophie. "It won't take six of us to get one guy into the trunk of a Saturn."

Amira grabbed Sophie by the shoulder and dragged her over towards the entrance of the church parking lot.

"You okay? You look completely freaked out," Amira asked quietly. "You kind of sounded like you were starting to fall apart at the end of the recording."

"It was awful, Amira," Sophie whispered, her voice shaking. "I felt that man's death. I felt his last moments. I felt his fear and pain. I don't know if I can handle this." Sophie's bones felt like they wanted to vibrate their way out of her skin. She gritted her teeth to keep them from chattering.

"You are allowed to have a freak out about this. You were dealt a shit hand tonight, and frankly, your ability comes with a pretty hefty mental price. It sucks, but right now, you need to put on your big girl panties. If you freak out right now, the guys will coddle you and protect you from all this. But that's not what you need. Something big is happening, and we need you to see it through," Amira said. "After we dispose of the body, I will have the guys drop me off at your place. You and I will drink a bottle of wine – or two – and have a good cry, okay? But until then, you're going to have to hold your shit together. Do you think you can do that?"

Taking a deep breath and staring up at the cold, foggy night above her, Sophie sighed. "Yeah, I can do this. You're right. I can't fall apart right now. I just don't know how to be strong like you."

"Yes, you do. Just channel your inner bitch-goddess," Amira said, startling a shaky giggle out of Sophie.

"My inner bitch-goddess?" Sophie reiterated.

"Yes! Being a bitch is the one true strength of womanhood. The ability to give no fucks about what other people think and forge your own path in the face of doubt. A bitch has to get shit done. So put your bitch face on, and let's go do this," Amira said, bumping Sophie's hip with her own.

"My bitch face?" Sophie said with a grin.

"Yes! Activate that bitch face. We have shit to do," Amira lectured, raising a delicate eyebrow in challenge.

Sophie gave Amira a big grin, feeling relief that Amira was able to help coach her through her mini-meltdown. "Thank you. I needed a pep talk. You're right. I can freak out later, but right now, we have shit to do."

Sophie noticed that Mac was waving them back, so Sophie and Amira rejoined the guys.

A few minutes later, Sophie, Mac, and Reggie were left behind in the empty church parking lot as they watched the taillights of Ace's car turn the corner and disappear into the night.

"I have a question," Sophie said as they headed toward

Reggie's car, needing to erase the worry clouding Mac's eyes as he looked at her questioningly. "Why aren't you naked, Mac? I saw you transform into your fox form in Andrew's vision, so how are you dressed now?" She wisely refrained from mentioning how adorable she found his fox form.

"Once I dragged Andrew's body behind the dumpster, I transformed back and ran back to my clothes. After I got dressed again, I called Reggie and met you guys here," Mac explained.

"Ah, that's why you weren't answering your phone when Reggie called. You left your clothes and phone behind when you transformed. Wait... Does that mean you were nude when you had to drag Andrew behind the dumpster?" Sophie asked, sniggering behind her hand. When Mac nodded his head, Sophie chortled loudly in amusement.

"It's not funny," Mac grumbled.

"Hmm. It kind of is. What if someone had caught you, the All-American cop, bare-assed while dragging a naked dead man through a church parking lot? You must have been quite a sight to behold," Sophie teased.

"Sorry to disappoint you that you won't ever get a chance to see for yourself. I guess you'll just have to use your imagination. Do you need a few minutes to compose yourself? Reggie and I can wait in the car," Mac retorted.

"You wish," Sophie scoffed. "You are such a dickhead."

"That's Detective Dickhead, remember? You keep forgetting," Mac reminded Sophie.

Getting into the front passenger seat, Sophie glanced back and spotted Reggie looking like he'd rather be anywhere else in the world than stuck in a car with Mac and Sophie. She mentally reminded herself not to let Mac get her riled up with his remarks. Listening to them bicker had to be uncomfortable for innocent bystanders.

It only took a few minutes to get to Atticus' home. As they drove slowly past the darkened house, Mac announced that it looked like the forensics team was gone. Parking around the corner, he asked Reggie to keep a watch on the street.

As they walked up the sidewalk leading to the house's front door, Mac handed Sophie a pair of latex gloves from his pocket. He pulled out a second pair and donned them.

Approaching the front door on silent feet, Sophie hovered nervously behind him while Mac fiddled with the front door lock. He quietly cursed the door out under his breath, but after a minute, the door swung open on a slow creak. He ducked under the yellow police tape crisscrossing the threshold, disappearing into the black interior of the foyer.

Sophie tiptoed in after him, rushing in to make sure she didn't lose sight of Mac.

"Hey," Sophie whispered. "Did you just pick that lock?"

"Yeah," Mac tossed over his shoulder as he headed toward Atticus' office.

"Can you show me how to pick locks?" Sophie whispered excitedly.

"I don't know if that would be a good idea. You're dangerous enough as it is."

"Please?"

"I don't think so."

"Pretty please?" Sophie begged.

"I already know I'm going to regret this, but you win." Mac sighed in defeat. "I will show you sometime soon. I might as well. I have a feeling you won't stop bugging me until I do anyways."

Sophie wisely refrained from assuring him that she would indeed bug the shit out of him if it would get her what she wanted. Torturing Mac would just be a bonus.

Mac flicked on a small penlight when he got to the office door. He quickly skimmed the light over the interior of the room. Sophie made sure to avert her eyes from the imposing wooden desk facing them, not wanting to revisit what occurred there.

"Where is the heating vent where Atticus hid the clavis?" Mac asked.

Stepping into the room, with Mac warning her to watch her step and not leave behind any evidence, Sophie pointed to the base of a bookcase to her right. While he pointed the beam of light so she could see where she was walking, they headed over to the clavis' hiding spot. Tiptoeing through strewn books, papers, and blood splatter, Sophie led Mac over to the floor vent.

Carefully working her fingers under the metal edge of the vent housing, making sure not to rip her gloves, Sophie slowly pried up the cover. Slipping her hand into the dark hole, she concentrated on feeling around the space and not thinking about monsters waiting in the dark hole to grab her hand. Finally, her finger snagged on a length of chain, and she drew the mystery stone out of the duct system. While Sophie cradled the jewel in her hands, Mac shined his flashlight on the stone. It was oval-shaped and about the same size as a golf ball. The flashlight made the facets of the green gem sparkle, the light refracting in a glittering array.

"Do you know what it is?" Sophie asked Mac. "In the vision, Atticus called it a clavis. He also thought of it as vermarine. I've never heard of clavis or vermarine, have you?"

"No, but we can go online later and see if we can track down any information."

"Do we need to grab anything else?" Sophie asked, giving the clavis one last look before slipping it into her pocket.

"No, let's get the fuck out of here."

They quickly snuck back out of the house and rejoined Reggie on the sidewalk.

"You got it?" Reggie whispered.

"Yeah, Sophie and I need to grab Andrew's clothes. We'll meet you back at the car," Mac said. "Sophie, can you show me where he left his stuff?"

Sophie led him to where Andrew's things were hidden. Mac

parted some bushes at the base of a white and blue Marina-style house. Sweeping the pile of clothes into his arms, he turned and jogged to where Reggie was waiting with the car running. Sophie swallowed her huff of annoyance at having to run after Mac to keep from getting left behind.

"Where should we head?" Reggie asked nervously once Sophie and Mac got into the car.

"I had to leave my car just around the corner when Andrew chased after me. Can you drop me off there?"

"Afterwards, we should all meet at my place," Sophie suggested. "These guys know about Mac, so we need to keep him from being located for the time being. None of these Mythicals seem to pay humans like me any attention, so it might be the best place to go."

Mac didn't answer as he was too busy pawing through Andrew's things.

"Okay," Reggie said after a beat. "Let's do that."

Mac pulled out Andrew's wallet and flipped quickly through it. Next, he held up a cell phone.

"Shit, I need a fingerprint to unlock it," he growled in annoyance. Mac grabbed his phone and quickly dialed a number. "Hey. Have you cremated the body yet?" He paused for a moment, then said, "Good. I need you to save his thumbs first then burn the rest. I need them so I can access his phone. When you finish up there, can you bring them to Sophie's apartment? Good. Text me when you're on your way, and I will send you her address."

Reggie pulled over, and Mac jogged over to his car. "See you at Sophie's!"

It was a silent ride back to the Tenderloin, except for Sophie's occasional instructions on what turn to take. Before long, they were pulling up to an empty spot next to Brown Betty.

Reggie turned off the vehicle. Sitting in the quiet, listening to the soft pings of a cooling engine, both Reggie and Sophie looked up at the placid face of Brown Betty. Sophie noted the window to

Birdie's apartment was dark. She hoped Birdie and Milton had a lovely evening.

"You okay?" Reggie asked softly into the silence, his eyes full of worry.

"I think so. I'm glad you're here with me: you and the rest of our gang. Thank you for being my friend, Reggie," Sophie said, staring intently at her knuckles, vague discomfort at showing Reggie her vulnerable side.

"I'm glad you're my friend too," Reggie responded, placing his hand over hers and giving it a gentle squeeze.

Getting out of the car, they waited for Mac to pull up. Once Mac parked his vehicle, Sophie led them into Brown Betty. They tiptoed their way up the stairs, Sophie pointing to the squeaky step so they could avoid it. She didn't want Birdie to witness her leading two men into her apartment in the middle of the night. She'd never hear the end of it.

Letting Reggie and Mac into her apartment, Sophie flipped the switch to turn on the skull lamp next to her couch, wanting to keep the lighting to a minimum. She immediately headed over to the coffee pot. She was used to the late-night hours now, thanks to the job at the morgue, but fatigue was starting to drag on her shoulders.

"I've just texted Ace. They have started the cremation process. Ace said Fitz's cousin estimates that it will take four hours to finish," Mac announced. Sophie looked over her shoulder, watching as the glow from his cell phone lit up Mac's face garishly in the dark of her apartment. Reggie was sitting on the futon, looking around Sophie's apartment, his face bright with curiosity.

I had no idea a cremation took so long, Sophie thought in surprise.

"You guys want coffee?" Sophie called out. When both Mac and Reggie affirmed that they did, Sophie started prepping the drinks. She already knew how Reggie liked his coffee, but not Mac, so she called out, "Do you want cream or sugar, Mac?"

"Black, please," Mac said, making Sophie shudder in disgust.

She poured the drinks and then brought them over to where the guys were waiting. She handed Reggie his beige-colored coffee with three teaspoons of sugar.

"Black as your soul." Sophie smirked, handing Mac his mug.

Heading to the kitchen, she grabbed her own coffee and returned to the living room to take the only seat left: an ancient rocking chair she had found on the sidewalk a few months ago. She had painted the chair black and replaced the destroyed cushion with a new one in a navy and silver damask fabric.

"Now what?" Sophie asked after taking her first sip.

"We need to come up with a plan," Mac said, leaning forward in his chair.

"Alright, what kind of plan?" Sophie asked.

"Let's review the facts." Mac reached into the inner pocket of his suit jacket and pulled out his ever-ready flipbook. "First, we need to figure out who Edwyn is. Once Ace brings me Andrew's thumbs, I should be able to pull Edwyn's phone number from the call log. I'm hoping I'll be able to do a look-up on the number. Then we need to decide what to do with the clavis."

"Don't forget about Conclave and Marcella," Reggie piped up. "I think I know who that is. Marcella Venturi: she's a very powerful Fae who practically heads the entire Conclave. When we had the grand opening of the new Medical Examiner's office a few years ago, she was there in an official capacity. Our team met her briefly, but I have no idea if she would remember any of us."

"I think you're right. The Marcella that Atticus mentioned in the vision has to be the same woman. I've met her once or twice myself," Mac said.

"Atticus said Marcella and the Conclave would stop Edwyn. Do you think we should try to warn them that Edwyn is up to something?" Sophie asked.

"I wish we knew who Edwyn is. Any ideas, Reggie?" Mac asked. When Reggie shook his head, Mac turned back to Sophie. "Can you describe what he looked like?"

"Uh, he looked like he was maybe in his late forties. He had ash-blonde hair; I think it was thinning a bit on top. He was thin and tall. I'm not sure how tall, but maybe around six feet. He didn't have any moles or tattoos or any distinguishing marks that I can remember. Light blue eyes, wide forehead; when he smiled, he had a dimple in his right cheek. He seemed very proper, almost scholarly," Sophie said slowly, closing her eyes, trying to recall as much of the man as she could. She could hear the scritch of Mac's pencil as he wrote everything down in his notebook.

"Anything else?" Mac asked.

"He had some kind of ring on one of his thumbs. I think it had a red stone in it. It was a big ring, thick and heavy. I don't remember any other jewelry," Sophie sighed. "Damn it. I can't think of anything else."

"That's okay. What you gave me helps," Mac assured her.

"I think we need to take what we have to Marcella," Reggie suggested.

"We don't have much. Certainly no proof," Mac said. "But she would probably know who Edwyn is."

"I don't think we should tell her we have the clavis," Sophie interjected. When both men raised their eyebrows at Sophie, she continued, "Okay. We know all these murders have something to do with the ley lines, right? We also know that Edwyn, who I think is behind it all, murdered Atticus specifically to get his hands on the clavis. Whatever it is, it's important. Edwyn thinks he has the clavis, so I think we should hide the real one until we at least know what it is. It could be something dangerous, and I don't know that we should just hand it over to anyone without an idea of what it can do."

"I concur with Sophie. We should hide it," Reggie agreed.

"These guys know about you, Mac, so I think I should be the

one to hide it. I'm 'just a human', so no one's going to be looking for me. Wait. I know just the place!" Sophie exclaimed, thinking of the stolen soccer trophy high on a shelf in The Little Thumb. To look inside the trophy's golden cup, even a very tall person would need a ladder. No one even gave the tchotchkes in The Little Thumb a second look; plus it never had to be dusted, so it hadn't been disturbed in decades.

"You're sure it'll be safe?" Mac asked skeptically.

"Yes. I've got the perfect spot," Sophie assured him. "Once we know what the clavis is, we can figure out what to do with it."

"Okay, it's agreed. Sophie, you hide the clavis. For now, don't even tell us where it is, just in case. I should be able to connect to the police database and find Marcella's phone number. I will call her and tell her about Atticus' death. I can see if she knows who Edwyn is and if she has any information that can help us figure out a way to thwart his plan. Perhaps with her help, I can get more proof of what is occurring along the ley line. It will take more than just your visions if I want to go through the proper channels to bring Edwyn to justice," Mac said, pulling a laptop out of his messenger bag. "I need proof."

Setting the computer across his lap, Mac grumbled when he realized Sophie didn't have an internet connection or any wifi in her apartment. He fiddled with his cell phone, saying something about a "hotspot". Anything to do with technology generally went over Sophie's head, so she just shrugged in amused acceptance when Mac glared at her because of her lack of technological savvy. With a few clicks on his keyboard and an annoyed murmur about slow connections, Mac announced that he had found Marcella's home number.

"I'm going to call her now. I'm going to put it on speaker so you can hear what she has to say. But I don't want either of you to say anything," Mac said.

"Do you think it's wise to call her this late?" Reggie asked worriedly.

"I don't give a shit. All this feels too serious. I don't want to wait until the morning."

"What are you going to say about my visions?" Sophie asked.

"I'm going to tell her I have a person who has death visions but that the person wants to remain anonymous to protect their identity. I'm not even going to let Marcella know your gender. The less anyone knows about any of us, the better," Mac said.

"Sounds good to me," Sophie said, while Reggie nodded his head in agreement.

"Okay. I'm going to call her now. There is no reason to wait," Mac said, placing his cell phone on the coffee table between them. He quickly dialed the number and hit the speaker button on his phone screen.

The phone rang several times before the click of someone picking up sounded from the phone. "Hello?" a slurred female voice said into the bated silence of Sophie's apartment.

"Hello. This is Detective Malcolm Volpes. Is this Marcella Venturi?" Mac asked in a stern, professional voice.

"Yes, this is Marcella. Is everything okay?" Marcella asked, the sleepiness in her voice evaporating.

"I'm sorry to have to call you so late. However, I needed you to be aware that Atticus Agosti was murdered in his house earlier this evening," Mac said.

A soft gasp broke the quiet hush of the room. "Atticus is dead? What happened?" Marcella said, her voice trembling.

"That is something I do not want to discuss over the phone. I would like to meet with you in person as soon as possible. I have information about his murder that is extremely sensitive in nature. I suspect only you can help me with it," Mac stated.

"You can't tell me anything over the phone?" Marcella asked, suspicion flavoring her voice.

"No, ma'am. The only thing I am willing to divulge over the phone is that I believe the murder had something to do with the ley line," Mac said, biting his lip and looking worriedly at Reggie and Sophie. Sophie understood that Mac needed to take a calculated risk to make sure Marcella would listen to what he had to say.

When the beat of silence stretched for a moment, Sophie began to worry that Marcella was going to hang up the call.

"Atticus was murdered because of the ley line?" Marcella finally asked, her voice full of concern.

"I have reason to believe so," Mac replied.

"That's not good. Can you meet me first thing in the morning?"

"Yes, that would be good. I want to deal with this situation as soon as possible."

"Can you meet me at Buck's in Woodside at 8?"

"Yes. I will see you then. Thank you for agreeing to meet with me." Mac hung up after they both wished each other a good night. Blowing out a breath, he said, "Well, now we will see what happens."

"We should come with you as a safety precaution. We have no reason to trust this woman except that Atticus thought she would be willing to stop Edwyn," Sophie said.

"I don't want her to know of either of your involvement. Especially yours, Sophie," Mac argued.

"She doesn't need to know we're there. Let's go early and stake the place out. I can hang out inside at a different table – just a regular, boring human having breakfast. Easily overlooked and ignored. And Reggie can keep an eye on the street outside the restaurant since she might recognize him. Maybe we can even have the rest of the Odd Ones come too, if they're done with Andrew before 8," Sophie countered.

"Odd Ones?" Mac repeated.

"It's our gang name!" Sophie said, making Mac shake his head in bemused exasperation.

"I agree with Sophie. You shouldn't go in there alone," Reggie said, making Mac huff in resigned vexation. "Although I don't know that we need to include the rest of the crew. They will probably be exhausted by that time."

Mac leaned back on the futon, cradling his cooling cup of coffee. Mac shook his head and snorted in amusement.

"What's so funny?" Reggie asked.

"It just figures that she'd want to meet at Buck's," Mac said.

"What's special about Bucks?" Sophie asked.

"All the rich Silicon Valley VC's and tech entrepreneur billionaires eat there. It's the place deal makers and tycoons eat pancakes," Mac responded. Sophie had never heard of Buck's, but she did know that Woodside was the town where San Francisco's wealthiest citizens erected their back-up mansions.

After debating for several minutes, they finally settled on a plan. Mac would type up and give Marcella a transcript of Sophie's vision, leaving out the part where Atticus switched out the real clavis for a fake. Until they knew who to trust, no one needed to know they had possession of the real thing. Reggie and Sophie would drive up to Buck's early. Sophie would get a table, and Reggie would set up a watch outside.

The big disagreement was that Mac wanted to go home to sleep. Both Sophie and Reggie argued that it might not be safe for him after the thwarted attack earlier in the evening. After Reggie and Sophie threatened to tie him up and throw him into Reggie's spare bedroom, Mac finally relented.

Sophie saw both men out, promising Reggie she would be ready to go and waiting for him outside in the early hours of the upcoming morning. She grabbed her phone to find out when Amira was heading over.

Sophie: *How's it going? Are you going to be heading over soon?*

Amira: *It's taking FOREVER. I had no idea it took so long to burn a body. I don't think I'm going to make it over tonight :(*

Sophie: *Don't worry about it. We can get shitfaced some other time.*

Amira: *I'm holding you to that!*

Once she realized that Amira wasn't coming over, Sophie

headed over to The Little Thumb. With the clavis tucked securely in her pocket, she hung out at the bar, drinking Lullaby Ladies until the final patron, on weaving legs, exited the bar. Sophie offered to sweep the floor "for old time's sake". When Burg headed to the back to finish cashing out his register, she quickly grabbed a barstool and used it to get her high enough to drop the clavis into the waiting arms of the goddess Nike and the Jules Rimet World Cup trophy.

CHAPTER 19

With gritty eyes, Sophie stared unseeingly out the car window at the passing scenery on the drive down to Buck's. She was glad Reggie wasn't feeling very talkative either. After barely three hours of sleep, Sophie didn't know if her brain was up for the task of forming words and putting them into an order that would hopefully resemble a sentence.

Pulling into the restaurant's parking lot, Sophie's eye got caught on a giant, weathered wooden fish laying prone in the dirt by the entrance. The carving was longer than Reggie's car and, based on its gray, scoured surface had been guarding the entrance to Buck's parking lot for decades. The nondescript restaurant was not what Sophie had been expecting. Nestled on a street crowded with tall, twisting oak trees, the low chocolate-colored building was hard to spot at first.

Sophie's initial impression was that the town of Woodside appeared similar to any other sleepy rustic town peppered down California's coast. But then she noticed a Ferrari pulling into the restaurant's parking lot, followed by another sleek, glamorous vehicle that looked like something from the future. It oozed luxury and wealth.

Walking towards the entrance, Sophie gave Reggie a discreet wave. He was staying in the car while Sophie waited inside for Mac and Marcella to arrive. She opened the glass door of Buck's and entered the restaurant, freezing just inside the front door and accidentally blocking the entrance. She had expected a restaurant that catered to the rich and powerful to be sophisticated, refined, and opulent, something with luxurious fabrics, soft lighting, and white tablecloths, maybe even some tapered candles for ambiance. Instead, the inside of Buck's looked like the cluttered lovechild of a toy store and a wild, eccentric museum.

As the hostess led Sophie towards an empty table, she passed by a six-foot replica of the Statue of Liberty holding an ice cream cone instead of a torch and wearing a sombrero. Next, she passed under a silver zeppelin hanging from the ceiling, then a full-sized spacesuit, followed by an orange derby car hovering at a jaunty angle. The hostess led her to a table next to an assortment of ancient-looking swords tacked on the wall. As Sophie took her seat, the woman handed her a menu, leaving her to the perusal of decorations.

Sophie ignored the menu in her hand to look around the décor of the restaurant. She wondered briefly if the owner might have been related to Burg since their design aesthetic ran in a similar vein. "Treasures" were on almost every inch of the walls: toys, black and white photographs, model planes, even a taxidermied alligator riding a surfboard. Sophie laughed when she spotted a tarnished golden trophy almost lost in an assortment of figurines in a glass case. Her eyes widened when she saw the enormous head of a bison mounted to the mirrored wall behind a small bar on the far side of the restaurant.

A few minutes later, the waitress stopped by, and Sophie ordered a cup of coffee.

Sophie was distracted from her perusal of the menu – showcasing a variety of standard American diner-style food – by the ding of her phone. *Damn, sixteen dollars for granola and yogurt? It better be the world's best granola.* Sophie huffed as she looked at her phone. She saw that Mac had sent her and Reggie a message stating that he was in the parking lot and was about to head inside. When the waitress dropped off her coffee, Sophie put in an order for huevos rancheros.

Just as the waitress started to turn and walk away with her order, Sophie spotted Mac entering the restaurant. Out of the corner of her eye, she watched as he pointed to the empty table next to Sophie's. Sophie pretended to studiously examine the menu in front of her as Mac approached. She couldn't help but notice that he looked great in his dark jeans and charcoal Henley shirt while she felt vaguely like sun-warmed roadkill. *It's not fair,* Sophie thought sourly, *he should look like shit, too.*

The waitress approached to refill her empty coffee cup and let her know that her food would be arriving soon. When the waitress left, Sophie put tiny earbuds into her ears. Though there was no sound, Sophie softly bopped her head along to imaginary music.

"She's here," Mac said for Sophie's ears only. The approach of the waitress with a tray holding Sophie's breakfast gave her an excuse to look briefly toward the woman joining Mac at his table. The Fae woman was made entirely of sharp angles, even her straight steel-gray hair. She reminded Sophie of a raptor. She could imagine this sharp-eyed and sharp-clawed woman curled over a nest, ready to grapple with her enemies.

Mac stood up from his seat, ready to greet the approaching woman.

"Magistrate Venturi, thank you for meeting me," Mac said formally, holding out his hand for the woman to shake.

"Please, call me Marcella. Based on what you've told me so far, I think we can settle on a first-name basis," Marcella said, taking the offered chair across from Mac.

After the waitress got their drink orders, Mac said, "Let me cut to the chase, Marcella. I have with me a transcript of Atticus

Agosti's murder last night. Based on what happened, I believe it is of the utmost importance you are aware of what transpired."

Pretending to read the travel article written on the back of the laminated menu, Sophie watched Mac hand Marcella a small sheaf of papers.

"How did you get a transcript of his murder? Was it recorded?" Marcella asked.

"I have been working with a psychic for some time now. This person has visions of deaths and has been helping my department solve murders."

"How have I not heard of this person? I would like to meet them."

"That is not possible at this time. This individual only works with me under the promise of complete anonymity. If anyone was to discover the psychic's identity, it could possibly put them in danger from the criminal elements within the city," Mac said, shaking his head. "My contact's cooperation is predicated solely on staying anonymous."

"Hmmm. How can you trust this person's 'visions' then? How can you guarantee this supposed psychic isn't just a talented scam artist?"

"They have gained no profit from their visions. In over forty cases, their visions have been completely correct. I am hard to fool, as my record with the department will show. There is absolutely no doubt in my mind that this person is trustworthy, and their visions show true. Here, read the transcript. You will see what I mean."

As Marcella read the papers, she occasionally made a quiet noise of distress or anger. The buzz of conversations and laughter from other tables floated over Sophie's head. Regardless of Buck's somewhat garish appearance, the food was excellent. Despite the early hour, the building was already almost filled to capacity, and not just with the area's rich and powerful. Families comprised much of the clientele. Children ran between tables, laughing over the strange and wonderful decorations. Old-timers debated politics over diner fare and steaming mugs of coffee. Still, many booths were filled by serious men in sharply pressed dress shirts, each with an open laptop at their elbows and intense expressions, talking animatedly over their eggs and toast. It was a place for intense conversation where titans of the world made plans for economic domination.

"Edwyn," Marcella suddenly growled. "That bastard."

"Do you know who Edwyn is?" Mac asked with quiet heat in his voice. Sophie could detect his hunting spirit had arrived in full force. She suspected it was his predatory nature that made Mac such a good detective. The scent of prey was in his nose, and his teeth wouldn't let go of Edwyn now that he was in Mac's sights.

"I'm certain this must be Edwyn Nothus. I can't believe it. I knew he had ambitions, but I never thought he would stoop so low. How could he commit such a heinous act?"

"Do you know what the clavis is? He murdered Atticus to get his hands on it. I have also found evidence of at least three deaths committed in the last few weeks in an attempt to gain properties along the ley line across the city. My research isn't complete yet, so it's impossible to determine the total number of properties that have been sold or transferred to new owners. Once I finish my investigation, I suspect that I will find many."

"Edwyn and his followers have been suggesting we should secede from the Fae realm for some time now. He has been advocating secession for the last several years. If he needed the clavis, I have to assume that he is trying to close the portal from the Fae realm permanently. The clavis is the anchor that lets the Fae realm open a portal to Earth. It is not widely known how the portal works. Both sides of it need a clavis to hold the pathway open, even though you can only travel from Fae to here. If he permanently closes the portal, it would be like closing and locking one side of a gate."

"The portal can be closed permanently," Mac repeated, surprise flavoring his voice. "Would it be such a bad thing? The Fae have been dumping their most dangerous and unwanted citizens here for well over a century. I have to deal with those criminal elements almost every day."

"I don't disagree that the Fae pawn their problems off on us, and it is a continual source of trouble for our people. But Edwyn doesn't just want to stop at cutting us off from the Fae realm. He and his followers want to claim the city as their own country, push out all the humans and rule over it. What they propose is suicide for our kind," Marcella explained. "I believe both the Fae realm and humans will rise up to squash all of us should he attempt it."

Mac made a low sound of surprise. "That's insane. He would kill us all. How could Edwyn possibly believe he could push three-quarters of a million humans out of the city? There are barely eighty thousand Mythicals here."

"I can't begin to imagine what is going through Edwyn's head." Marcella sighed.

"How can Edwyn use the clavis to shut the portal permanently?"

"Tomorrow is the vernal equinox. On the vernal and autumnal equinox, the ley line is at its most powerful. He will be able to magnify the power of the clavis to close the portal. Very few people know the process, but I have to assume he has someone who can do it, or has somehow attained the knowledge to complete the ritual himself. The transcript said something about taking it to the tower," Marcella said. Sophie could hear the rustle of papers as Marcella flipped through the transcript to double-check.

"Yes, a tower was mentioned. The only two towers I could think of are Sutro and Coit. Both fall on the ley line, so I assumed it was one of those two," Mac said.

"We can assume it's Coit Tower. A second, weaker ley line

intersects that spot, increasing the lines' power and making it the perfect place to open a portal. Coit Tower is where most of the portal activity from Fae occurs. It's why that location was chosen for the tower in the first place," Marcella said, tapping her nail thoughtfully on the table.

"So, we know when and where. Can the Conclave stop Edwyn?" Mac asked.

Marcella blew out a slow breath. "I don't know if I can trust all the members. Some of them must be aware of Edwyn's machinations, especially if a lot of real estate has been changing hands. I have a few people I know I can trust. If I can thwart Edwyn before he activates the clavis tomorrow, I believe I can carve out the discord from within the Conclave. I wish I knew how many people Edwyn has swayed to his side. If this transcript is right, he has recruited some shifters."

"I have a few people I trust implicitly that I can bring in on this effort. I think the best way to stop Edwyn is to intercept him at Coit Tower. We can stake out the tower and grab him there tomorrow. I do not have proof, but I believe he is possibly working with the Sunset District pack."

"The Sunset pack? I can't decide if I'm surprised or not. The alpha, Alphonse, is a separatist and xenophobe, so I can see him wanting to push out humans. But I have a hard time picturing him working with Edwyn or any other Mythicals that aren't apex shifters."

Marcella and Mac formulated a plan to stop Edwyn while Sophie eavesdropped. Marcella informed Mac that Edwyn would attempt to activate the clavis at the top of the tower. The open air of the observation deck gave the best access to the energy of the ley lines. They both agreed that Edwyn wouldn't risk drawing attention to himself during regular operating hours, so he would sneak into the facility after it had closed for the day. Mac suggested that most of their allies could wait in the alcoves around the observatory, ready to grab Edwyn the moment he emerged from the elevator. Marcella assured Mac that her position on the Conclave would allow them access to the entire building so they could get into place long before Edwyn would arrive.

When the waitress dropped off the check for her meal, Sophie lost the thread of the conversation. Not wanting to draw any attention to herself, Sophie paid her bill. Standing up, she walked around the restaurant lobby, pretending to admire the decorations with a few other tourists. She desperately wanted to know what Mac and Marcella were saying but was worried she'd blow her cover if she wandered back over towards them. After a few minutes, Mac and Marcella shook hands. Slowly, Sophie drifted over to the bar area of the restaurant. In the bar mirror, she watched Marcella head to the exit. Sophie sent Reggie a quick text message letting him know that Marcella was heading out, telling him to keep an eye on her.

Sophie waited a few minutes and exited the restaurant alone. Letting herself into the passenger seat of Reggie's car, Sophie sighed in relief once she closed the door behind her. She was not made for this clandestine, cloak-and-dagger bullshit. She would *much* rather employ the straightforward approach of tracking Edwyn down, punching him in the throat and prying the clavis from his still-twitching fingers.

"How'd it go?" Reggie asked with repressed excitement. Reggie looked like he wanted to wiggle in his seat with enthusiasm. Apparently, he was more a fan of this spy stuff than her.

"I think it went well. Marcella is in," Sophie was about to tell Reggie more when both their phones dinged with an incoming message simultaneously.

"It's from Mac," Reggie announced unnecessarily. "He wants us to meet at his house. He says we need to pick up some items for tomorrow. What's happening tomorrow?"

"I will catch you up," Sophie said. "Let's make sure Mac gets to his car and on the road safely. Then we can head out too."

On the drive to Mac's place, Sophie recapped the meeting between Marcella and Mac.

"If Edwyn only needs to go to Coit Tower to close down the portal, why did he need to grab all those properties along the ley line?" Sophie asked after she finished her recap.

"I'm not sure. It could be for several reasons. Mythicals, especially the Fae, own many properties along the ley line. They siphon power off the ley line for spells and such. He may just be trying to push other Mythicals away from the source of their magic so that he will be the most powerful Fae in the city. But what I really think is happening is that he needs access to the ley line to power up whatever spell he's planning to use to close the portal. But I'm only guessing since I don't know a lot about Fae magic," Reggie explained.

Following the directions of the tinny voice from the map program, Reggie turned one street early. Mac had texted them earlier to let them know that they should be able to sneak through the neighbor's yard behind his house. He was friends with the homeowners, and they had a small gate in the fence between their yards. Mac believed that if anyone was watching his house, they wouldn't expect him or anyone else, to sneak in through the back.

Sophie's curiosity had bubbled over with excitement. She could hardly wait to see what Mac's house looked like. She had pictured a cluttered mess, with walls covered in mug shots of criminals with long red strings connecting them. A conspiracy theorist's design aesthetic mixed with a filing clerk's nightmare.

Reggie parked on a street filled with tightly packed, single-family homes. Getting out of the car, Mac waved them over to a side gate of a two-story house the color of sweet butter.

"George and Anne are probably not home, so we don't need to worry about disturbing them," Mac assured them when they glanced at the house worriedly. Reggie and Sophie followed Mac along a narrow, paved pathway next to the house. The path opened up to a matchbook-sized backyard. They scurried across the yard, and Mac unlatched a tall wooden gate. Pausing at the entrance, Mac turned his nose up to the sky and took long, slow breaths. Out of the corner of her eye, Sophie saw Reggie doing the same thing.

"Nothing. Are you picking up anything, Reg?" Mac asked quietly. Reggie shook his head. Mac opened the gate slightly and peeked through the crack for a moment before slipping through the opening. Reggie and Sophie quickly followed him into another small yard. The backyard was enclosed on all sides by a tall privacy fence. Sophie walked past a circular gravel area with a fire pit, surrounded by Adirondack-style chairs. She glanced at the pit with a bit of envy. It would be the perfect place to enjoy a cold beer and warm her feet on a cold, foggy San Francisco night.

The house was covered in cream stucco and topped with rust-colored Spanish Mission tiles. Reggie and Sophie hurried to catch up to Mac, who was at the house's back door. When he unlocked the door, he held up a hand to indicate that they should stay back. Pressing close to the cracked open door, he once again did his sniff test. Satisfied with whatever his nose detected, he opened the door and they followed him as he slipped silently inside.

The back door led them into a galley-style kitchen. The kitchen was small but neat as a pin. Sophie peeked into the vintage farmhouse sink expecting to see it piled high with dirty dishes, but the well-worn porcelain basin was empty. Other than a toaster, a coffee maker, and a roll of paper towels, the counter-tops were bare of clutter.

The floor was covered in terra cotta squares interspersed with bright hand-painted tiles. Sophie admired the kitchen; it was old and careworn, but also filled with an old-world warmth and charm. She could picture a sweet and plump grandmother spending hours in this room, creating delectable treats for her loved ones. It certainly beat Sophie's chipped Formica counters and cracked linoleum floors.

As Sophie and Reggie followed Mac out of the kitchen, the tile gave way to dark hardwood floors. Mac's living room was neat but spartan, the furniture heavy and functional. Remembering how pristine Mac kept his car, Sophie realized that she should have known his house would be the same.

Teach me to believe in stereotypes. Of course, Mac doesn't live in your typical bachelor pad, Sophie thought.

Several large framed posters – the only real decoration in sight – drew Sophie's feet across the living room. She stopped in front of one of the posters with "Cry of the City" in large yellow letters splashed across the top of a dark waterfront scene. A man's anguished face stared across the film title. The next poster showed a dashing mustached man clutching a blonde woman as a suspicious-looking fellow in a brown trench coat watched from a distance. On a block of red, the movie title read "Touch of Evil". Before Sophie could take a look at the third poster, Mac called her over to him.

"You like old black-and-white crime films?" Sophie asked curiously.

"I love film noir. Hard-boiled detectives falling for duplicitous dames, all wrapped in cigarette smoke and shadows. What's not to like?" Mac smirked.

"I can see why that would appeal... to you," Sophie teased. "Is that what you based your cop persona on? I could get you a trench coat to complete your world-wearied, fatalistic gumshoe image. Maybe I'll buy a zoot suit so I can be your gangster nemesis. I don't think I could pull off femme fatale. We can have clandestine meetings on dark street corners, plan jewelry heists, followed by car chases and shoot outs!"

"Zoot suit? You've never watched any of these films, have you? No, I'll find you something slinky to wear. You'd make an excellent treacherous dame." Mac laughed.

"You caught me. I've seen brief clips of a few of them, I guess, but I've never watched any of those old black-and-white movies," Sophie confessed.

"Well, we'll have to rectify that."

Sophie only got a brief glimpse of some dark wooden furniture and a navy comforter covering Mac's bed as she followed him into the room's walk-in closet. The space smelled faintly of Mac's cologne, some kind of woodsy masculine scent, that made Sophie want to rub her face in his hanging dress shirts.

"Hold this, please," Mac asked. He set an empty duffel bag in Sophie's arms before facing the large safe sitting in the back corner of his closet. With a quick flick of his wrist, Mac spun the dial and swung the large, heavy-looking door open. He waved Sophie closer and started dropping weapons and various electronics into the duffel bag.

"Is this where you store the dead bodies?" Sophie asked, peering theatrically into the safe with its neatly organized shelves and racks.

"Oh no, I use the crawl space for that," Mac said, making Sophie laugh. "I'm not a monster."

She loved how Mac was so quick-witted and never took her shit. It was nice to be able to go toe-to-toe with someone and not have to worry about hurt feelings or jokes being taken too seriously. Plus, Mac could dish it as well as he could take it.

It only took him a few minutes to fill the duffel bag to his satisfaction. Lifting the bag from Sophie's hands, he zipped it up and slung it over his shoulder. He grabbed a second smaller bag and stuffed it with a few changes of clothes. Sophie and Mac headed back out to the living room to catch Reggie appreciating the movie posters.

"I like your house," Sophie told Mac, looking up to admire the dark exposed beams stretching over his living room.

"It belonged to my grandparents. I wouldn't be able to afford a house in the city if I hadn't inherited it," Mac said with a shrug, taking no credit for his part in property ownership.

"I see you have a television," Sophie said with a toothy grin, nodding at the large flat screen, thinking back to Mac's horror that Sophie didn't own one.

"Have you ever seen *The Maltese Falcon?*" Mac asked. When Sophie shook her head, Mac clicked his tongue in disapproval. "Humphrey Bogart as Sam Spade is Bogart at his best. Let's have a movie night soon."

"Sounds like fun, Detective Dickhead," Sophie said with fake confidence, not wanting Mac to notice the small kernel of nervous want blooming inside her when he grinned widely. The feeling as if Mac had tugged on a loose thread inside her rib cage left a strange discomfort beneath her sternum. Sophie swallowed the feeling down, saving it to pull out later and examine when she was alone.

"Do you want to meet at my place or Sophie's?" Reggie asked, not realizing he was interrupting a charged moment. "I think we should go to Sophie's place. No one would think to link you with her."

"I agree. I need to call Ace and have the crew meet us there with Andrew's thumbs," Mac said, looking away from Sophie's dark eyes toward Reggie.

Sophie cracked a smile when she saw Reggie shuddering over the mention of the thumbs. Did he forget what he did for a living?

CHAPTER 20

They decided to leave Mac's sedan behind and take Reggie's car to Brown Betty because Reggie was concerned that someone might be looking for Mac's vehicle. Mac had tried to argue that all this subterfuge was overkill, but Sophie had told him to shut up and deal.

"Imagine how upset Birdie will be if I let something happen to you. I'll never hear the end of it if you get your stupid ass killed. This is what happens when you let people care about you. Just deal with the tiny inconvenience of taking your safety seriously," Sophie lectured a sulking Mac.

"If Edwyn was looking for Sophie, what would you have her do?" Reggie asked, which seemed to settle Mac down better than Sophie's argument.

The rest of the drive to Sophie's place was completed in an atmosphere of good-natured bickering. Both Sophie and Mac tamped down their usual level of snark in deference to Reggie's sweeter nature.

As Sophie unlocked her apartment door, she turned to them and said, "Hey, I want to check in on Birdie. I'll be right back."

"I'd like to say hi myself. You should come to meet Birdie, Reggie. She's something else," Mac said.

With a resigned huff, she led them over to Birdie's door. Birdie practically shoved Sophie aside to pull Mac into a tight hug.

"Mac, my sweet boy, how are you?" Birdie said, pulling back to pat Mac's shoulder.

"I'm good, Miss Birdie. How are you doing?" Mac asked sweetly, making Sophie roll her eyes at Reggie.

"I got some, so I'm doing great." Birdie giggled. Reggie's shocked choking pulled Birdie's attention away from Mac's wide grin.

"Miss Birdie, I'd like for you to meet our friend Dr Reginald Didel," Mac said, stepping aside so Birdie could approach Reggie.

"Birdie, this is my boss, so please don't do anything to get me fired," Sophie warned, only half-joking.

"I would never! Aren't you just adorable? And a doctor to boot, oh my," Birdie said, pinching one of Reggie's round cheeks. "And you have to put up with Sophie every day, you poor dear. You must be a very patient man."

"I'm not going to introduce you to any more of my friends if you keep being mean to me," Sophie warned facetiously.

"Working with Sophie is great. Just her presence at the morgue brightens everyone's day," Reggie said to Birdie earnestly. Birdie cooed over Reggie's sweet statement while Sophie found herself blinking rapidly, trying to contain the sudden burst of emotion bubbling up inside her.

"Speaking of introducing Birdie to more of your friends, Ace, Fitz, and Amira are here. I'll go let them in," Mac announced, looking up from his phone.

Soon everyone was crowded into Birdie's nonexistent foyer, introducing themselves to her. The group appeared to be on their best behavior. Ace was even being charming, something Sophie wasn't aware he was capable of. Fitz was his usual reserved self, but Sophie noted how gently he treated Birdie. And Amira took to Birdie immediately. When those two began whispering and giggling behind their hands to each other, Sophie broke out in a nervous sweat. Nothing good could come from them hitting it off.

"Would you all like some tea?" Birdie offered.

"Can we have a raincheck? We have some work-related things we must finish. You know I would normally love to stay and share a cup of tea with you," Mac said.

"I'm holding you to that," Birdie warned Mac.

"Hey guys, I want to talk to Birdie for a sec, and then I'll meet you at the apartment, okay?" Sophie said.

Everyone carefully shook Birdie's hand while letting her know how much they enjoyed meeting her. When Mac hugged Birdie goodbye, she sassed him for missing his chance at being her "boy toy", now that she had Milton.

"So really, how was your night with Milton?" Sophie asked excitedly once the door to her apartment closed behind the crew.

"A lady never tells," Birdie demurred.

"Perfect, that means you can tell me everything." Sophie smirked.

"Only if you tell me what is going on with you and your sexy detective," Birdie countered.

"Nothing is going on with Mac and me."

"But you want there to be."

"No. I don't know. It's—"

"If you say complicated, I'm going to kick your skinny ass," Birdie warned with a raised finger.

Sophie blew out a softly, frustrated breath. "I don't know if it's a good idea. But... there's something there, you know? He mentioned maybe having a movie night together sometime."

"Girl, I never thought you'd be a chicken shit. You're gonna regret it if you don't at least try to see if there's more between you than just quips."

"You're right. I need to put my bitch face on," Sophie said.

"Your bitch face? What in the world?" Birdie cackled.

"It's something Amira says. It's better than 'man up', don't you think?" Sophie asked, her lips curving up into a mischievous grin.

"Good point," Birdie snorted. "Alright, girlie. Go put on your bitch face."

"I'll try, Birdie."

"By the way, I'm thrilled you're making some new friends. I was starting to worry about you. A young woman shouldn't have an old lady and a surly bartender as her only friends," Birdie lectured softly.

"Hey, don't sell yourself short. Anyone would be lucky to have you as a friend. I'm glad I've made friends with my co-workers, but you're always going to be my bestie."

"Alright, Sophie, you sweet talker. Go hang out with your friends," Birdie said, gently pushing Sophie out the door. "You want to come over later and enjoy some trashy television with me?"

"Of course! The trashier, the better." Sophie grinned, before walking into her apartment to see that everyone had made themselves comfortable. She realized that she needed to get some more furniture if she continued to hang out with her co-workers.

Mac was seated at her kitchen table, fiddling with a phone.

"It worked. I'm in," Mac announced, his words drawing Sophie over to his side.

Sitting down next to him, she complained, "You left a dead man's thumbs on my fucking table. I eat here."

"You cut up dead people five days a week. Stop whining," Mac grumbled, not looking up from the screen in front of him.

"Yes, but I don't do it on the same surface where I eat, you jerk," Sophie protested. Walking into her kitchen, she grabbed a container of bleach wipes and plopped it in front of Mac expectantly.

"Fine," Mac grunted, putting the thumbs into a baggie, now

that he had access to the phone, and gave the table a cursory wipe-down.

"Anything helpful on the phone?" Reggie called from the living room.

"Not really. Nothing we weren't already aware of," Mac said. "It looks like Andrew was just hired muscle. I was hoping we could link him to a specific shifter pack, but no such luck."

While Mac continued to swipe through Andrew's phone, he caught everyone up on the plan for the next day.

"We are there as back-up. Marcella's people will be at the top of the tower waiting for Edwyn to show up. Ace and Amira, I want you positioned near the base, hidden near the entrance to the Filbert Street stairs. Fitz and Reggie, you two will be on the other side of the tower. We will keep in constant contact via our phones," Mac stated.

"Where will I be?" Sophie asked.

"Uh… at home, probably," Mac said slowly, pointedly not looking in Sophie's direction.

"The fuck I will. You are not leaving me behind," Sophie said, leaning over in her chair, forcing Mac to look her in the face.

"These people are dangerous, Sophie," Mac barked.

"I'm aware, dickhead! I've *seen* what they can do. I know better than you just what they are capable of. That's why I'm going. I know what Edwyn looks like. I know what Dimitri looks like. You're not leaving me behind."

"They're not human. You are. They're going to be faster than you, stronger, have magical powers. It doesn't matter how tough of a human you are, you're still just *human*." Mac stood up, leaning over the table, bringing his face closer to Sophie's.

Lean in a little closer so I can punch you in your big dumb face, Sophie thought angrily, hurt and a little betrayed by Mac's lack of faith in her.

"I'm not planning on trying to fight anyone, you dipshit. I can keep watch and stay out of the way just like everyone else. I'm not going to fucking sit at home and just hope you guys are going to be okay. You can just pull that thought right out of your pretty little head. I'm going, and there is nothing you can do to stop me. We are a team, all of us, and we fucking stick together," Sophie growled back, standing up and getting even closer into Mac's face.

Mac threw his hands up in frustration, looking like he wanted to pull out his hair. "Imagine how Birdie will feel if you get hurt. This is what happens when you let people care about you. We give a shit about your safety. So, you just have to deal with the itty-bitty inconvenience of keeping yourself safe. Sound familiar?"

"Maybe we could put her in a vehicle in the parking lot? They'll just think she's a regular human, and if things get hairy, she can escape in the car. They're not going to pay any attention to a single human," Fitz suggested from his perch on Sophie's futon.

Mac rounded on Fitz, looking as if he wanted to tear his head off.

"Good idea, Fitz. That's exactly what we're going to do," Sophie announced, bringing Mac's attention back to her. "I will sit in the parking lot, with a weapon or two from your duffel bag within easy reach. I will stay in the car like a good girl and just keep an eye out for the bad guys."

Mac growled, his blue eyes flashing with ire. Sophie could almost see Mac's animal side peeking through. Staring into his blue-steel eyes felt like staring into a glacier.

"Good girl, my ass," he griped.

"Are you trying to intimidate me?" Sophie snorted, pretending that it wasn't working just a little bit. The predator within Mac looked like it was ready to pounce and rend flesh with its claws and teeth.

"I'm not trying to intimidate you!" Mac exclaimed in irritation. Taking a slow breath, Mac visibly reined in his anger, a calm mask sliding over his face. "Can I speak to you alone for a minute?"

Sophie led Mac to her bedroom in a huff. When she closed the door, Mac leaned back against it, blocking her only means of escape unless Sophie was willing to throw herself out the single bedroom window next to her closet.

"Okay," Sophie said. "What did you need to say to me that you couldn't say in front of the others?"

"Sophie, how can I get you to stay here, away from the danger? I don't want you to put yourself in harm's way."

"I don't want any of you to put yourselves at risk either, but we don't have much choice. Why is it okay for everyone else, but not me? And don't you dare fucking say it's because I'm human."

"Damn it, hellraiser." Mac sighed. "It's because I care about you. I don't want to risk losing you. You are important to me."

"You're important to me too. That's why I have to be there. You can't ask me to stay home," Sophie said, putting her hands on her hips in a defiant stance.

Mac started pacing around her tiny room. There were only a couple of feet of walking room around the perimeter of Sophie's bed, and Mac seemed to fill up all the available space. He strode around the foot of her bed, came to a stop in front of her night-stand, then swiveled on one foot to make his agitated way back to her bedroom door. Sophie climbed onto her bed, out of the way of his path, to let him work through his agitation. She watched as he prowled around her bedroom like a captive lion testing the boundaries of its cage.

"Hey, I got you something," Sophie interrupted.

"You got me something?" Mac repeated in bafflement as Sophie picked up a brown-wrapped package off her nightstand.

"Yeah, I've been waiting for the right time to give it to you. Here, open it," Sophie said, offering up the item. Taking it, Mac sat near her feet on the patchwork quilt, staring sightlessly at the package in his hands for a moment. "Open it," Sophie prompted.

Tearing open the brown paper, Mac stared at the book titled *The Wild and Weird History of the City by the Bay.* He trailed his finger slowly over the title, then flipped the book over to read the back cover.

"I know you like history. So, I took Birdie to that bookstore you told me about, City Lights," Sophie explained.

"Soph... Thank you. This is... this means a lot to me," Mac said softly, looking up from the book to gaze at her.

"You haven't read it before, have you?" Sophie asked, trying to understand the look in his eyes.

"No, I haven't. What did you think of City Lights?"

"I loved it. At first, it seemed like an ordinary bookstore. But as we walked around, this sense of history permeated the entire place, seeping out of every corner. It was how I imagine a coffee shop in Paris during the French Resistance must have felt. I don't know how to explain it, like ideas were primed and ready to take flight, a revolution of thought. Each book there a gateway into change. It was just kind of magical." Sophie stared at the book in Mac's grasp, trying to capture how the bookstore had felt with inadequate words.

Looking up from Mac's hands, Sophie's breath stuttered in her throat to see the heat in his eyes. Her mind was still wandering through a faraway bookstore, and it took a frozen, breathless moment to realize what was happening. The last thing Sophie saw before closing her eyes was Mac's ocean-blue ones crackling with silent electricity. His lips brushed butterfly-soft against hers. Once. Twice. The touch plucked the guitar strings in her heart, pulling a chorus of sound up Sophie's throat, ending in a low groan slipping softly out of her mouth.

When Mac parted her lips with his, desire slipped its leash and came roaring up through her body. Without conscious thought, Sophie's hands found their way to Mac's jaw, fingers gently scruffing through his bristles. The prickly strands of facial hair buzzed sensation into her fingertips. Following the contour of his angled jaw, Sophie tunneled her fingers into Mac's tousled hair.

Mac's mouth pulled slightly back from hers, clinging for a moment while whispering her name. Sophie lured him back with the plush invitation of her lips. Turning on the mattress, she was starting to climb onto his lap when Amira and Ace's raised voices broke into Sophie's awareness.

Pulling back with a gasp, Sophie was momentarily suspended between the conflicting desires of wanting to retreat and needing to grab onto Mac and not let go. She had not realized her skin was so touch-starved until Mac removed his hands from her waist.

"Sophie, I–" Mac started to say, but Ace and Amira's quarreling voices interrupted again, causing him to give the door a dirty look. He leaned his forehead against Sophie's, rolling his head gently against hers, his bright eyes staring into hers.

"Now isn't the time. But... we have things we need to talk about. About us. Once we get through tomorrow, I want some time alone. I like them," Mac said, nodding toward the living room, "but we need some time to figure out what we want to be to each other without an audience."

Overwhelmed with conflicting emotions, Sophie could only nod in agreement. Standing up, Mac turned toward her bedroom window and let out a long breath like he was trying to blow out his thwarted lust and annoyance at the interruption.

Sophie couldn't believe she'd forgotten about her friends, who were only a few steps away. Only a thin particle-board door separated them from discovery. Helping her to her feet, Mac led Sophie across her bedroom. Before opening the door, he leaned in and brushed another butterfly kiss on her lips.

"Soon," he promised, clutching the book to his chest.

Twenty minutes later, Mac was still griping about Sophie's participation in the next day's plan but seemed resigned when he, Reggie, Ace, and Fitz prepared to leave.

"Are you coming?" Reggie asked when he realized that Amira was still lounging on Sophie's futon.

"No, we have some girlfriend time planned," Amira announced, fishing a bottle of wine out of her designer bag and holding it up triumphantly.

Reggie reminded them that they still had to work later that night, so they both promised not to overindulge.

"There's plenty of time to have a little bit of wine and get some sleep before work," Amira assured him.

As Sophie and Amira escorted the boys outside, Moe stuck his head out of his first-floor apartment.

"Who are these people?" Moe sneered.

"Just some friends. Not that it is any of your business, Moe," Sophie replied with a frown.

"You have friends? I don't believe it. What are all these people really doing here?"

"You're right, Moe. We were shooting a porno in my apartment," Sophie taunted with a wide grin.

"Her, I can believe," Moe said pointing a finger at Amira, "but no one wants to see you in action."

"That's not what your dad said last night," Sophie chirped.

She turned her back on a blustering Moe to finish walking her friends to the stoop.

"Who the fuck is that guy?" Mac growled in Sophie's ear, glancing back at Moe's red face. The look on Mac's face said he was imagining Moe's murder.

"My landlord, Moe. He's harmless. Just ignore him," Sophie assured him. "He likes to spar with me verbally. He doesn't seem to realize that I keep handing his ass to him."

"I can't decide if I'm flattered or offended," Amira murmured.

"You can be both," Sophie offered.

After the guys drove away, Sophie suggested they include Birdie in their female bonding time. Heading over to Birdie's door, she was happy to have company. While they watched cheesy television and made laughing commentary, Sophie felt like her soul was floating slightly above her body, tethered by the weakest gossamer thread. So many thoughts were swirling around in her mind; they felt like dust motes caught in a fan, hardly allowing her to concentrate on the catfight on the show. Her thoughts and her spirit kept pushing her to seek out Mac.

Cracks had appeared in the dam Sophie had built around her heart – the mortar created out of pride and self-preservation – ready to burst entirely with the smallest touch from Mac.

CHAPTER 21

"Some superhero gangs get jets, headquarters on spaceships, maybe a yacht, but no... Not us. We get your sister's minivan as our official means of transport." Amira laughed from her seat in the back of the van.

"I thought you were going to clean up the minivan for your sister as a thank you?" Sophie said from her passenger seat.

"I did," Mac said with a grin. "With three kids under the age of eight, I imagine my nieces and nephew erased all my hard work within an hour of returning Miranda's car to her."

Pulling onto the gently curving Telegraph Hill boulevard, Coit Tower appeared high above the surrounding trees' canopy. The slender, fluted tower made of white concrete sat on one of the highest peaks in San Francisco, making it stand out from the surrounding area like a lone sentinel standing guard over the bay.

"Have you ever visited the tower?" Mac asked.

"No, in all the time I have lived here, I've never visited. As often as I've seen the Coit Tower over the cityscape, it never occurred to me to check it out." Sophie shrugged. "I don't know why."

"I visited a really long time ago, in my teens on a school field trip. The murals painted inside are pretty cool. Plus, the top of the tower is an open-air arcade with views of the entire city and bay. See those cut-out arches? You can walk around the top and see the whole city from up there."

Mac pulled the van into a small round parking lot near the base of the tower. Sophie squinted at the statue in the center of the parking lot. It was a lone standing man with a billowing cape clutching a piece of paper, or a rag, in one hand.

"Who's that?" Sophie asked, pointing at the greenish-cast statue towering over the parking lot.

"Christopher Columbus, if I remember correctly," Reggie said.

"What does Christopher Columbus have to do with the Coit Tower?" Sophie asked curiously.

"No idea. Columbus never even set foot on this side of the continent," Mac said, shaking his head.

Steeling her nerves, Sophie turned her attention away from the statue. Mac pulled the minivan into a spot facing away from Columbus. Glancing out the front window, Sophie saw that they were pointed outward toward the vista looking over the bay.

"How long until Marcella and her people get here?" Sophie asked.

Mac glanced at his watch. "About forty-five minutes. Let's familiarize ourselves with the area before the tower closes."

Getting out of the vehicle, Sophie walked over to the fence encircling the round parking lot. The hill they were on was so high above the bay that, on a clear day, Sophie would be able to see Oakland on the far side of the water. If the view was so fantastic from the ground, Sophie couldn't imagine how good the view from the top of the two hundred foot tall tower would be.

Despite the dense fog sitting on the city, Sophie could see Alcatraz Island floating in the bay like a lone lily pad on the indigo water. Mac called Sophie back to the minivan, pulling her from her reverie.

He started handing out equipment and the radios that would

let everyone hear one another. Placing the small earpiece into her ear and the radio in the pocket of her jacket, Sophie listened as everyone did a mic check.

Following Mac, the group strolled around the manicured landscape surrounding the base of Coit Tower, looking like any other group of tourists wandering around. Mac pointed out where he wanted everyone to position themselves once Marcella arrived. Even with the tower closing in less than an hour, the park surrounding the structure teemed with tourists. They crawled all over the area like ants on a carcass. At least the line of people waiting to ride the elevator to the tower's peak had started to dwindle as the closing hour drew near.

Once they finished scoping out the surrounding area, everyone took their assigned positions.

Mac pulled Sophie over next to the minivan. "Be careful, okay? Don't do anything stupid. If you try to act like a hero, you will probably get hurt. These are powerful shifters and Fae. Do you have the taser I gave you?"

Sophie patted her pocket, where the taser was resting. "I will stay safe and out of the way. But you have to promise to try and stay safe too, okay? You better not get hurt."

"I will do my best to be safe, I promise."

"If you get hurt or worse, I'm going to kick your ass so hard," Sophie warned, making Mac chuckle. He leaned in and brushed a soft, fleeting kiss against her lips.

"Okay, then. I have to head over to the entrance to wait for Marcella and her people," Mac said. When Sophie nodded her understanding, he squeezed her hand then turned towards the entrance, murmuring something into the radio channel.

Sophie stood lost for a brief moment, staring after Mac like a lovelorn maiden watching her sailor head off to sea. She shook off her stupor, internally calling herself all manner of names, and took her position by the fence overlooking the bay.

It was easy to blend in with the other tourists admiring the view of the city, despite their thinning numbers. After thirty minutes of pretending to take photos of the area with her phone, Sophie heard Reggie's voice whisper in her ear, "Two cars are pulling into the parking lot. One looks like the same vehicle Marcella drove to Buck's."

Wandering over to stand in front of the statue of Christopher Columbus, Sophie watched as Marcella and seven other people got out of their cars and headed toward the entrance. Sophie was glad that she had thought to wear sunglasses so that she could disguise her intent stare. Pretending to read the plaque on the statue's base, Sophie watched as Mac greeted Marcella. After shaking her hand, he called over Reggie, Fitz, Ace, and Amira to meet everyone.

Concentrating on her earpiece, Sophie listened as Mac introduced her friends. He explained that they were the team that would keep a watch on the surrounding area for potential problems and act as a backup in case things went south.

Sophie headed back to the minivan, pretending that she was getting ready to depart along with the final straggling tourists. She watched as Mac, Marcella, and her crew filed into the building's entrance while the rest of her friends melted into the surrounding foliage.

"Do you have an idea how many people Edwyn will be bringing with him tonight?" Sophie heard Mac ask Marcella through her earpiece.

"We don't believe he will bring many supporters. He should not be expecting us. He is not foolish enough to bring a large group and risk alerting the general public," Marcella responded, confidence ringing in her voice.

Drumming her fingers on the car's steering wheel, Sophie listened as Mac got everyone into position inside the tower. She hated that she had to sit on her ass and stay out of the way.

This sucks. They treat me like I'm made of glass, Sophie thought.

Soon, all the chatter fell silent over the radio channel. As the sky started to darken and the fog began to settle more deeply over the city, Sophie scrunched down in her seat to wait with a defeated sigh.

An interminable amount of time later, spent staring intently at the entrance to the parking lot, Sophie finally spotted a bright beam of approaching headlights.

"I believe a car is pulling into the parking lot," Sophie announced over the open channel.

A chorus of whispered confirmations came from Mac, Reggie, and the rest of the team.

"Wait. It's more than one vehicle," Sophie said urgently. Scooting down further in her chair, Sophie watched as a small caravan of vehicles pulled into the parking lot. "Shit. It's five cars."

"Can you tell how many people Edwyn has with him?" Mac asked urgently.

As each car emptied of its passengers, Sophie did her best to count them.

"It's around fifteen people," Sophie whispered, carefully peeking her eyes above the edge of the car window.

"Shit. Do you see Edwyn?" Mac's urgent voice crackled in Sophie's ear.

Sophie watched as Edwyn started to head towards the tower entrance. There was no mistaking the thin-faced man with his carefully sculpted head of ash-blonde hair. Even from her hiding spot, Sophie could feel the false warmth of his charming façade. She shuddered slightly, remembering what lay beneath his mask.

"Yes, he's here. They're heading towards the tower entrance now," Sophie warned.

"Okay, new plan," Mac announced. "Once Edwyn enters the building, I want Reggie, Fitz, Ace, and Amira to follow him in and sneak up behind him. Make sure you keep the element of surprise. Have your weapons ready, and be prepared to use them. You guys got it?"

Sophie listened while her friends quietly confirmed their orders.

"Is there anything I can do to help?" Sophie pleaded.

"Just keep an eye out for any more trouble. You're our only lookout now," Mac said.

Sophie watched as her friends emerged from their hiding spots to head up the wide cement stairs and into the entrance hidden between two thick columns.

Pulse quickening, Sophie watched the tower and listened to her earpiece. She plugged her left ear with a finger so she could concentrate all her senses on the soft noises coming through her receiver. Mostly the sounds appeared to be softly whispered instructions and the brush of clothing against microphones.

A sudden shout in her earpiece made her jump so high in her seat that Sophie almost hit her head on the rear-view mirror. More yells and grunts began to filter through the mics. There were so many layers of sound coming through the earpiece, Sophie couldn't separate any single person from the cacophony.

The blast of a gunshot made Sophie cry out, then clamp her hand over her mouth to muffle the sound. Opening her door and stepping halfway out of the car, with one foot on the pavement and the other still in the vehicle, Sophie stared toward the top of the fog-covered tower in horror. Fear for her friends held her immobile, filling her with uncertainty on what to do. A shift in the fog revealed the top of the tower for a brief moment. Against the darkened sky, flickering lights, looking vaguely like arcs of electricity, sparked from within the opening of the building. She wanted to call into the open channel and ask if everyone was okay, but was scared that she might distract her friends when they needed all their concentration.

A horrible, gurgling scream filtered into Sophie's ears. It had her moving further out of the car, taking a step closer to the tower. Indecision and terror for her friends dueled in her mind, making her unsure what to do.

"Freeze! Hands in the air! This is the police!" A deep male voice bellowed from her left.

Turning her head, she instantly recognized the detectives from the night she did the autopsy on the vampire Montgomery.

"What are you doing here? This area is closed for the night. You are trespassing!" The Hispanic detective bellowed. As Sophie slowly raised her hands over her head, she racked her brain, trying to remember his name.

Hernandez. And the other one was Lancaster.

"Detective Hernandez, Detective Lancaster. Good evening," Sophie greeted them loudly, hoping her friends could hear her in their earpieces.

"How do you know our names?" Lancaster demanded, pulling his gun out of his holster and pointing it at Sophie's chest.

"Wait... I recognize her. We've seen her before. How do we know you?" Hernandez growled.

"Uh, I work at the morgue. We met once."

"What are you doing here?" Hernandez demanded.

"I was visiting the tower. I was just about to leave when I thought I heard something weird. I'm glad you guys are here; I think some teenagers snuck into the tower to have a party or something. You should go check it out. Make sure they don't vandalize the murals or anything," Sophie said, hoping that they buy her lies.

"Just get rid of her. Edwyn doesn't want anyone interfering with his plans. She's just a human," Lancaster said to Hernandez.

"What? That won't be necessary. I'll just leave," Sophie pleaded.

When Hernandez leveled a gun at Sophie, she suddenly wished she had a bulletproof vest. As he brought the gun up to point at her face, she realized it was too much to hope for a body shot.

A bellowing roar made Sophie drop to her knees and cover her head with her arms. Peeking between her forearms, she saw a blur of motion hit the detectives as they turned in shock towards the noise. The sound of a gunshot made her duck again, but luckily, she remained unscathed.

A creature hit the detectives like a giant bowling ball smashing into pins, tossing them into the air. Sophie started crab-walking backward, attempting to crawl away unnoticed. As she watched, the enormous ghastly creature snatched up a screaming Hernandez off the pavement. With a crunching twist of its hands, Hernandez's screams cut off like a switch. Lancaster was trying to pull himself away from the monster on his forearms, dragging one leg behind himself. The giant, pale-fleshed creature vaulted towards Lancaster, stepping on his back. While Lancaster gurgled pleas for mercy, the beast twisted his neck like a chicken being prepared for the dinner plate.

The monster casually dropped Lancaster's broken corpse and turned toward Sophie. She was frozen in place on her hands and knees in the parking lot.

The giant creature had pale, greenish-tinted skin with whorls of what appeared to be brown war paint decorating its chest and shoulders. Sophie's eyes didn't know where to settle, since there was a lot of skin on display. The monster appeared to be wearing only an elaborate, armored loincloth. Sophie's gaze traveled up past the massive slabs of muscle covering the monster's chest to its hideous face. Small beady eyes stared at Sophie from under a prominent brow, lowered in a permanent scowl. Two large pointy tusks thrust up from his lower jaw.

When the monster took another step towards Sophie, her brain finally engaged, and she started to scramble to her feet in a futile attempt to escape.

"Sophie! Are you okay?" A familiar voice asked.

"What–" Sophie started to say, but her mind got stuck and fluttered around her skull like a moth trapped inside a glass window, rendering her mute.

"Sophie, it's me, Burg. Are you okay?"

"Burg?" Sophie repeated dumbly.

"Yeah, it's Burg. Did those guys hurt you?" the monster asked in Burg's voice.

"Burg?"

"Sophie! Get it together. This is my true ogre form," Burg said.

Sophie stared up at the ten-foot monster in front of her silently, her brain trying valiantly to fight the dissonance of her friend and the monster.

"What are you doing here, Burg?" Sophie finally asked.

"Yesterday, Mac and Reggie stopped by the bar and asked me to keep an eye on you in case things went badly. Looks like they did," Burg said with a shrug.

"Burg! The guys!" Sophie exclaimed, the shock of coming face-to-face with an ogre suddenly replaced by fear for her friends.

Quickly searching the ground, Sophie found the radio where it got knocked out of her hand. Calling into the microphone, she listened intently, but didn't get a response from anybody. Shaking the device, Sophie couldn't tell if it had been broken during the scuffle or if everyone was too busy to answer her call.

"I think they might be in trouble, Burg. We need to go help them," Sophie said.

"I think you're right. The bad guys showed up with a lot more people than Mac thought they would bring. Come on. Let's go take care of this before anyone gets hurt," Burg said, turning towards the tower.

"Should we go up the stairs? I don't want the elevator to announce our presence," Sophie said, eyeing the tower with trepidation, mentally picturing herself passing out from exhaustion on the stairs halfway to the top.

"No, I have a better idea." Sophie scrambled to keep up with his long, lumbering stride as he turned and hurried toward the tower.

"What are we going to do?" she asked breathlessly.

"We're going to climb," Burg said with a confident air.

"Climb? You mean the stairs?"

"No, I mean the tower," Burg said, pointing up the side of the slender, narrow tower rising above them.

"I can't climb that."

"But I can. You just have to hold on to me."

"You're like ten feet tall and probably weigh a ton. How are you going to climb the tower? The whole surface looks smooth. There are no handholds," Sophie argued.

"Ogres are excellent climbers. We're renowned for our climbing ability," Burg assured Sophie.

"Uh, I've never heard any fairy tales that talked about ogres' climbing abilities."

"Bullshit. You've never heard of Jack and the Beanstalk? That whole story is about climbing up a giant plant," Burg pointed out.

"There's no way that fairy tale was a true story. You're just making shit up," Sophie said, stomping her foot in irritation as they stood at the base of the tower, arguing about fairy tales. Looking way, *way* up the flat surface of the tower, she swallowed thickly.

"We don't have time to argue. Do you trust me?"

"Shit! Fuck! Yes, I trust you. Don't make me regret it."

Burg squatted down so Sophie could climb on his back. Filled with trepidation, she stepped up to Burg's broad, shirtless back. Wrapping her arms around what little neck he had, Sophie noted that his enormous trapezoid muscle somehow decided to skip his neck and connect directly to the base of Burg's skull. His skin was thick and felt rubbery under her hands. Sophie decided to take the fact that Burg had bristles like a wild boar to her grave. No need to hurt his feelings.

"Burg, I mean this in the best way, but I want to tell you that you are completely terrifying as an ogre. I almost pissed myself," Sophie said in Burg's ear. "Thank you for being my friend and for saving my life."

"You're welcome. You're my favorite human, so I couldn't let anything happen to you," Burg said with evident warmth in his gravel-rough voice.

As Sophie wrapped her legs around Burg's waist as best she could, Burg stepped up to the base of the white surface of the Coit Tower.

CHAPTER 22

❧

"*W*on't people see us climbing the tower and call the police?" Sophie asked worriedly.

"No, I doubt most people will be able to see us through all this fog and humans are very good at explaining away things they don't understand. Besides, the Conclave has a couple of Fae on staff who can erase and replace memories," Burg said as he placed his hands on the surface of the tower.

With the smallest lurch, Burg started scaling the vertical wall at a steady pace. Sophie focused her gaze on Burg's hands, which were defying all laws of physics and somehow gripping the flat surface of the concrete bricks. Hand over hand, Burg steadily climbed up the face of the tower.

With her stomach left behind somewhere in the bushes below, Sophie clung to Burg's back like a tick to a dog. She was thankful there wasn't much of a breeze to test the strength of her grip. However, it got colder and colder the higher they climbed. Sophie couldn't believe that Burg didn't even sound out of breath.

Like an idiot, Sophie glanced over to the side to see how far they'd come. When she saw how high they were – the minivan looked like a toy in the parking lot – Sophie gasped and squeezed her arms more tightly around Burg's non-existent neck.

"Oh fuck. Oh *fuck*," Sophie chanted quietly, clamping her eyes tightly shut.

"We're almost there, Sophie. Just hang on a little bit longer," Burg assured her.

"I don't like this one little bit. This sucks so bad. Jack and the Beanstalk can bite me," Sophie whispered furiously. "I don't want to die here. Please, please, *please* don't drop me."

A few minutes later, they paused just under one of the cutout arches at the top of the tower. The flickering light was still flashing out above their heads like an electrical storm, and Sophie could hear the faint sounds of battle being swept away on the air currents above them.

"I'm going to peek into the tower to see what is happening. Don't make a sound," Burg warned.

Creeping slowly up the last few inches of the climb, Burg and Sophie raised their heads above the rim of the cement until just their eyes peeked above the ledge.

A flash of reddish-grey fur flew past the window, making Sophie and Burg duck back down briefly. The creature tumbled past them, scrambling to find its footing. When it did, it arched partway up, front paws grazing the floor, a menacing growl rolling out of its muzzle. Sophie made a muffled, gurgling sound against Burg's shoulder when she realized that she was looking at Mac. She'd recognize those ocean-blue eyes anywhere.

"I thought he only turned into a regular fox. When I saw him in Andrew's vision, I swear he looked like a normal-sized fox," Sophie whispered in awe as she stared at the meld of fox and man charging back into the fray. For a moment, just before he tackled a wolfman, Mac stood to his full height, and Sophie could see his face in profile. Pointed black-tipped ears topped Mac's face, which was a blend of fur-covered human features melding into a short muzzle. Mac's blue eyes flashed as he swiped at a larger opponent, a dark-furred wolf shifter, with wicked black claws that looked sharp enough to carve initials into stone.

"Holy shit," Sophie whispered in awe as she watched Mac quickly and efficiently dispatch his adversary. Seeing Mac with his aggression fully unbridled was shocking: a hunter free to unleash his predatory nature against his enemies to ferocious, devastating effect.

Sophie tore her attention away from Mac as he ripped into another wolf shifter with a triumphant roar, taking in the scene before her. Reggie and Fitz were pinned to the side of the staircase railing by several shifters. Reggie appeared to have partially shifted into his opossum form while Fitz was fully human. She couldn't see Amira or Ace in the rapidly swirling movement of battle.

Edwyn and Marcella faced off just in front of the wide opening of a set of curving cement stairs. Cackling like a madman, Edwyn's genial mask had finally cracked. Reaching into his pocket, he held the fake clavis out in front of his chest, showing it off to Marcella.

"You're too late, Marcella. You can't stop me!" Edwyn screeched, cradling the clavis to his chest like a precious child.

He began to chant in some unfamiliar language, each word growing in volume. While two of Edwyn's goons pushed Marcella back with their guns, Edwyn raised the pendant high above his head. Blinding sparks of electricity shot out of Marcella's hands. The bolts streamed from her hands, punching the two henchmen off their feet, tossing them across the tower floor where they landed in a crumpled heap. Edwyn must have had some kind of invisible shield around himself, because when Marcella redirected the lines of her electricity towards him, they stopped a few feet from touching Edwyn, illuminating a bubble of protection surrounding him. The lightning bolts sparked and fizzled along the surface of his shield, lighting up the ecstatic, manic look on Edwyn's face.

"We need to get in there and stop him now," Burg said urgently.

"No, we should wait a moment. When he finishes his incantation, everyone will have a moment of distraction when they think the clavis will close the portal. We can jump in then," Sophie suggested.

"It will be too late to stop him by that point," Burg argued.

"No, it won't, I promise. I can't tell you how, but I know the incantation won't work. Do you trust me?" Sophie asked, turning Burg's earlier question back around on him.

"I do," Burg whispered back. "When we go in, I want you just to try to stay out of the way. I can take care of these assholes. Deal?"

"Deal," Sophie agreed, happy to not have to wade into the fight. It wasn't like she thought she could hold her own against shifters and Mythicals anyways.

They watched as Edwyn continued to chant until he was screaming the words. With a final incomprehensible screech, Edwyn thrust the clavis high into the air above his head, an invisible wind whipping his blonde hair wildly.

"Okay, let's do this in three... two... one," Sophie whisper-yelled. As she said "one", Burg surged up and over the wall of the tower as if a spring launched him. A shockwave of screams fanned out like a rock dropped in a pond, as Burg landed in the middle of the melee.

For a brief moment, Sophie saw the stupefied look on Edwyn's face as he stared at the fake clavis clutched in his hands. He hadn't even noticed the giant ogre landing only a few feet away yet. As someone stepped in front of her view of Edwyn, trying to face off against Burg, Sophie let go of Burg's neck and slid down his back to land on her feet with a jarring thud. Luckily, no one seemed to notice the tiny human scurrying away; everyone's focus was on the roaring, rampaging ogre.

Sophie darted over to a wide column where she could mostly

hide while still keeping an eye on the fight. Burg tore through the crowd, swinging his giant fists like a hammer, leveling foes like a machete through weeds.

Sophie covered her mouth to muffle her gasp as Burg tossed a huge shifter high over his shoulder, right out the top of the tower. Sophie caught a brief flash of horror across the shifter's face before the fog swallowed him, his fading screams the only sign of his fate. Thankful that she couldn't hear his landing two hundred feet below, Sophie turned her attention back to the scene before her.

Now that he had mowed through most of his foes, Burg approached the Edwyn-bubble in the center of the observatory floor, stalking over to it in a lumbering gait. Raising his clasped hands high above his head, Burg brought his fists down on the top of the invisible shield with a resounding boom. The reverberation from the hit made Sophie's teeth vibrate in her skull. Edwyn was kneeling on the ground with raw animal fear plastered across his face. As Burg continued to bash the invisible barrier over and over again, Marcella rushed up next to him and added blasts of electricity to the onslaught between Burg's hits. Cracks in the shield started to become visible as thin fingers of Marcella's electricity snaked their way in through hairline fractures, reaching for a still-kneeling Edwyn.

One of the henchmen Marcella knocked out earlier slowly got to his knees, shaking his head as if he was trying to clear the fog of unconsciousness away. Once awake, he crept his way around the outer rim of the observatory, stealthily making his way around the perimeter until he was at Burg and Marcella's backs. The man hadn't noticed Sophie hiding behind a column a few feet away.

As he began to raise a gun with a still-shaking hand towards Burg and Marcella, Sophie peeked further out from the column, ready to call out a warning. Right as Sophie opened her mouth to alert her friend to the danger, her eyes locked with Mac's in his half-fox face across the open space. With a loud growl, Mac raced toward the henchman in a bounding sprint. Spotting Mac, the man took an unconscious, fear-filled step away from him, bringing him a step closer to Sophie. The goon started to swing the gun towards Mac's approaching form.

Without thought, Sophie leapt out from her hiding spot and threw herself on the man's back, trying to grab the weapon out of his hand. With a startled yelp, he reached his free hand over his shoulder, grabbing a fistful of Sophie's hair. With a ripping yank, he pulled Sophie over his shoulder and tossed her to the ground. As she slid to a tumbling stop, scraping her hands and left side on the cement floor, she scrambled back around to try and locate the gunman. With horror, she watched as Mac took a leaping tackle, driving the man to the floor.

A sharp, cracking noise and a strobe of light flashed between the two men as they grappled over the weapon. Sophie clambered quickly to her feet. Pulling the taser out of her pocket, she circled the two wrestling men. When the henchman's back turned toward Sophie, she rushed forward and pressed the two sharp electrodes of the stun gun to his back, then deployed the voltage.

The man jerked uncontrollably in Mac's tight grip. Thankfully, the voltage didn't seem to be affecting Mac as he put the man in a chokehold. A moment later, Mac dropped the unconscious man unceremoniously to the ground before falling heavily to his knees, one hand clutching his upper chest where blood was quickly spreading across his shirt.

Sophie screamed his name, grabbing for his shoulders as he started to slump over. Splatters of blood covered Mac's face and hands, but the worst area was his chest. With Mac's wheezing assistance, Sophie laid him on the ground.

"Mac! Are you okay?" Sophie cried. She started to pull up his shirt, trying to find the source of all the blood on his furry chest.

"That motherfucker shot me," Mac said in shocked wonder as Sophie located the bullet hole in his left pectoral muscle.

"You're going to be okay," Sophie said, not sure if she was lying or not, while she put pressure on the wound in an attempt to stem the blood flow. Mac groaned in pain. "Sorry, I know it hurts."

Looking around, Sophie tried to locate someone who could help. She quickly realized that all of Edwyn's followers had been subdued. Burg and Marcella looked like they were almost through Edwyn's barricade as Burg continued to beat on Edwyn's shield. Hundreds of hairline fractures covered the surface of the bubble. As Sophie watched, the cracks finally shattered, and Burg snatched up Edwyn, whose high-pitched squeal echoed around the cement tower. The clavis tumbled from Edwyn's lax fingers, rolling to a stop near Marcella's feet.

Turning her attention away from Burg and his shrieking prize, Sophie finally spotted a fully-human Reggie near the staircase. He was checking over Amira, who was bleeding from a gash on her shoulder. Sophie couldn't even take a moment to admire Amira's elegant black fur-covered feline face.

"Reggie!" Sophie screamed. "Mac's been shot!"

Reggie's head snapped up from treating Amira's wounds and swiveled around to locate Sophie. He said something quickly to Amira, who nodded her head. Reggie came galloping over to Sophie and practically slid in on his knees next to Mac's prone form.

"What happened?" Reggie asked urgently.

"That dickhead shot Mac in the chest!" Sophie shouted.

"Hey," Mac wheezed quietly, a small sly grin spreading across his face. "Don't call him that. Dickhead's *my* nickname."

"Mac! Please just be okay," Sophie cried. "I'll call you whatever you want."

Mac grinned up at Sophie, his fox teeth on sharp display. "I'm holding you to that. You're my witness, Reg."

He grunted in pain as Reggie prodded around the wound.

"It looks like it just missed the top of your lung, Mac. You're lucky. It means you're going to be fine. I just need to get the bullet out, and your healing should take care of the rest," Reggie assured Mac with a pat on his other shoulder.

"He's going to be okay?" Sophie asked in surprise, tears rolling unchecked down her cheeks. "But he was shot!"

"Mac's a shifter. He'll be back to normal within a few days," Reggie promised. "I left my medical bag in the van. I'm going to go get it. Can you keep an eye on Mac while I'm gone?"

"Are you sure you should leave me alone with her?" Mac yelled at Reggie's retreating form. "She seems dangerous. She's willing to jump on the back of an armed Fae like a dumbass. Even after promising to stay out of danger."

"Are you fucking kidding me?" Sophie yelped. "I saved your ass. He was about to shoot you."

"I'm not sure you helped like you think you did. You know, since he shot me anyway."

"That's not my fault. You were the one who decided to run face-first into the guy with a weapon."

"I had it handled just fine until you decided to try and climb onto him. Then he tossed you onto the ground like some kind of weak kitten and was going to shoot you. Which meant *I* had to leap into action to save *your* ass."

"Were you blinded by my awesome heroic maneuver? The guy had a gun pointed at you when I jumped on his back. *I* saved *you*," Sophie argued in what she believed was a very reasonable tone of voice. It might've been a little on the screechy side.

"No, I remember it perfectly. I saved you," Mac countered.

Sophie started frantically looking around the floor next to them.

"What are you looking for?" Mac growled.

"I'm trying to see if that guy dropped his gun nearby. I want to finish the job and put you out of *my* misery!"

Scooching and rotating his body slowly across the floor, Mac moved so he could lay his head in Sophie's lap.

"What are you doing?" Sophie asked.

"I was injured saving your life. I need comforting," Mac said. Grabbing Sophie's free hand, Mac placed it on his head and moved her fingers in a massaging motion against his scalp.

"You're an idiot," Sophie said, picking up Mac's demand and running her fingers through the rust-colored fur covering Mac's head.

"No, I'm a dickhead. Your dickhead," Mac said with a predatory grin, practically rumbling a purr when Sophie scratched around his ears.

"Yes, you are. I think I'm going to end up regretting it, though," Sophie said softly, enjoying the silky fur under her fingertips. "Are you sure you're going to be okay?"

Before he could answer, they heard Marcella exclaim loudly. Turning their heads, Mac and Sophie watched as Marcella stomped up to Edwyn, where he was sitting restrained with half a dozen of his surviving co-conspirators. A few of Marcella's people were piling up the bodies that weren't so lucky near the elevator.

Pushing the fake clavis under Edwyn's nose, Marcella yelled, "Where is the real clavis? This is a fake!"

Edwyn looked both defeated and defiant in equal measure, sitting with his restrained hands behind his back propped against the wall. He pressed his lips tightly closed until they looked like a flat line.

"I think we can assume Atticus fooled him and gave him a fake jewel," Mac yelled out to Marcella across the expanse of the tower.

Marcella marched the fifteen feet over to Mac, looking entirely too annoyed, considering her team won the fight.

"Why wasn't that in the vision you gave me?" Marcella demanded.

"It was a death vision. My contact only sees a person's final moments, so if Atticus had previously set up the jewel as a counterfeit, the psychic wouldn't have seen that event. If I remember the vision correctly, Edwyn assumed the pendant from Atticus's safe was the clavis. He was never specifically told that the jewel was the clavis."

"Can your contact try and locate the real clavis?" Marcella asked intently.

"Not unless it makes an appearance in another person's death," Mac stated with a figurative shrug. "They don't have the power to locate missing or lost items. They only have visions. If we learn anything about the clavis, you will be the first to know. Does it look like that brown gem?"

"No, it's a pale green vermarine gemstone, also called green amethyst. Very rare and prized for its ability to hold and channel magic. Dangerous in the wrong hands, as tonight demonstrates. You have my number, so if you find it, call me immediately, no matter the time," Marcella commanded.

"Of course," Mac said, blithely lying through his sharp fox canines.

"Is that a human?" Marcella asked in consternation, indicating Sophie with a nod of her head. "Do you think it wise to include a human in Mythical affairs?"

"She works in the Mythical division of the city morgue, so she already knows about our people. She was only here to keep a watch in the parking lot. When things went sideways with the fight, she valiantly stepped in to help, despite being at a massive disadvantage," Mac stated, a growl hidden within the clipped tones of his voice.

"By the way, it was a good idea bringing the ogre. I'm surprised he came to help. They usually refuse to involve themselves in Mythical politics," Marcella said, already dismissing the presence of a human in their midst. Turning to one of her minions, she called out, "We need to have a team recheck Atticus's house for the clavis. It might still be on the premises somewhere."

Sophie settled her face in a carefully innocent look, making sure not to succumb to the urge to give her friends any furtive glances. Sophie belatedly realized that she hadn't needed to bother looking innocent since none of Marcella's minions even gave her a first glance, much less a second. She was more invisible than Edwyn's shield to them.

The blank face transformed into relief when the elevator door dinged open, and Reggie stepped out, clutching a large black case. Rushing over, Reggie dropped the case next to Mac's side and pawed through the bag's contents.

After a moment, Reggie pulled out a pair of long, curved forceps. As he placed the ends of the tool at Mac's wound, pausing to ask him if he was ready, Sophie had to close her eyes.

Despite her tightly closed eyes, Sophie could tell every time Reggie moved the forceps around within the wound because Mac squeezed Sophie's hand in an ever-tightening hold. The squelching noises made Sophie shudder in horror and disgust. When Reggie announced that he almost had a grip on the bullet, a quiet groan worked its way out of Sophie's throat.

"You do realize that you do this for a living, right? Why are you acting so squeamish?" Mac asked with a strained laugh, trying to hold as still as possible.

"Well, I usually don't have the body we're working on sitting on my lap, wiggling around all warm and gross. It's weird. Reggie, can you knock Mac out so this will feel more natural for me?"

"Got it," Reggie announced triumphantly, ignoring Sophie's request. Sophie opened her eyes to see Reggie holding up a bloody bullet, looking it over in the light. She swallowed thickly, thinking about how that little hunk of metal was just in Mac's chest and could have easily killed him.

Together, Sophie and Reggie bandaged the wound on Mac's shoulder and then helped him to his feet.

"I can't believe you called me 'warm and gross'. My feelings are hurt," Mac complained, making Sophie laugh unrepentantly.

Reggie and Sophie headed over to check on Ace, Fitz, and Amira. Mac and Burg peeled away to talk with Marcella after she waved them over to join her for some kind of important-people meeting.

"Hey, are you guys okay? Did anyone get hurt?" Sophie asked her friends, worriedly looking them over. When Sophie tried to check over Ace, he growled about not needing to be mothered.

"Oh, is your mother here? No? Then tough shit. Suck it up and let me make sure you are okay, you pain in the ass," Sophie snarled at him. One of Ace's lips curled up in disgust, but he shut up and let Sophie complete her inspection. Other than the gash on Amira's upper arm, they all escaped the fray with only a few scrapes and bruises.

"You guys are so lucky you weren't hurt worse. Despite being outnumbered, it looks like only Edwyn's people died," Sophie said.

"We had the upper hand: the element of surprise. Plus, Marcella's Fae had better offensive magic than Edwyn's. They took the brunt of the action and protected us," Reggie explained.

A few minutes later, Marcella shook both Mac's and Burg's hands, then turned her attention to one of her approaching minions. Both Burg and Mac turned away from Marcella, heading towards the group of friends clumped together near the stairs.

"Let's get out of here," Mac stated, leading the way to the elevator.

"Should we stay and help?" Reggie asked fretfully, his round face filled with concern.

"Fuck that. We've earned our merit badges for the night. I'm done. I'm sure as hell not joining the clean-up crew without some fucking overtime pay," Ace griped. "Wait... are we getting paid for this?"

"No, you asshole. Your payment is the good feelings you get from helping save the day," Amira said, pushing Ace's shoulder playfully.

"Does saving the day pay my bills? No, it doesn't," Ace complained loudly, making Sophie and Mac exchange a grin.

"I agree with Ace. We've done more than our fair share. Marcella's people are more than capable of taking care of the clean-up," Mac said.

As they waited for the elevator to arrive, Burg flicked his fingers in a complicated pattern over the sigil tattoo on his forearm and chanted some words under his breath. Sophie's eyes widened in wonder as Burg shrunk. His face melted from the ogre she had quickly gotten comfortable with to the recognizable appearance of her favorite bar owner.

"I wouldn't fit into the elevator otherwise." Burg's familiar face grinned at Sophie.

After everyone stepped into the elevator and they started to descend, Sophie looked around at her bedraggled friends. "What happens now?"

"Well, you guys have to go into the morgue in a few hours. Marcella's team is gathering up the bodies to deliver to the Medical Examiner's office. You have to do the autopsies, fill out your reports, and then the Conclave will begin covering up this event. Any evidence from tonight's activities will be gone before tomorrow morning," Mac stated.

"What about you?" Sophie asked.

"I need tonight to recover from the gunshot wound. Then I have to submit a report to the Conclave and the Chief of Police," Mac said. "Marcella wants the chief brought in to help unearth any other of Edwyn's people and to make sure no one else is planning to attempt to shut down the portal."

"Someone should stay with you while you recover from your

injury tonight. There shouldn't be any complications, but it pays to be careful," Reggie interjected. "Sophie, he could stay at your place, and you can keep an eye on him. I don't think Mac should go home until we're completely sure it's safe. Since these corpses won't smell bad yet, Amira can help me without too much trouble tonight."

"I can't tell if you're just treating me like a delicate, useless human or not, but you know what, I don't care. I'm taking tonight off. It's been a very trying couple of days, and I want a break, even if I have to put up with Mac to get it. You guys should do the same. The bodies can wait, don't you think?"

"We have a few hours before we need to head into work. Why don't we all go to Sophie's place to rest and recover?" Fitz suggested.

Everyone agreed with that plan, and Burg offered to stop by his bar and fetch a celebratory bottle of wine. "I also left my sister in charge of the bar, so I'm going to need to check to make sure it's still standing!" Burg joked.

Sophie spent the rest of the elevator ride chewing her lip, trying to figure out a polite way to ask Burg what a female ogre looked like. By the time the elevator reached the ground floor, she had decided to swallow her curiosity for the time being. There was no right way to phrase that question without sounding like an asshole.

As they exited the elevator and headed out the tower's front doors, everyone in front of Sophie came to an abrupt halt. The collective gasps of shock had her peeking her head over Amira's shoulder to see what had everyone so freaked out: there was a corpse splattered over one side of the entrance stairs.

"When I came down to get my medical bag, I tried to examine the scene but it's too much of a mess. How did this happen? Did he jump from the tower?" Reggie asked in horrified fascination.

"No, Burg tossed him over his shoulder like a used tissue," Sophie announced.

"I did? Huh, I don't remember that," Burg said, tapping his chin in thought.

"You did. I promise."

The group skirted around what was left of the shifter, heading toward the minivan with a sigh of relief. Sophie looked back at the plain white column of the Coit Tower. Looking at the soaring spire, the top of the column vanished into the dark foggy sky above. She shook her head in wonder. To think that the simple fluted tower harbored a secret pathway to another realm. *Life is just fucking weird sometimes.*

"What the hell! Is that Hernandez and Lancaster?" Mac asked incredulously as they rounded the car's bumper and spotted the two bodies crumpled in the parking lot.

"Yes, I will tell you all about it on the drive to my apartment. Who's driving? I don't think it should be Mac, and I don't have a driver's license," Sophie said.

"How can you not have a driver's license?" Mac looked at Sophie in shock. "How have you functioned as an adult for so long? You don't have a driver's license. You don't have a TV, or a phone!"

"I am too complicated for someone like you to understand. I am a mystery. I am glorious and unknowable." Sophie sniffed arrogantly at Mac, channeling her inner Amira.

"Get in the fucking car, your gloriousness," Mac sneered, waving Sophie into the interior with a flourish fit for a queen.

On the drive, Sophie caught everyone up on what happened while they were in the tower.

"Wait, Burg scaled the outside of the tower with you slung on his back?" Amira reiterated.

"Yes, it was fucking terrifying," Sophie responded with a shudder.

"I wish I could have seen that. I bet you looked like Yoda on Luke's back," Amira said thoughtfully.

Everyone booed and hissed at Sophie when she confessed that she hadn't seen any of the Star Wars movies.

"We need to make a list of movies that Sophie needs to see. Then we can kidnap her and force her to watch them all," Fitz suggested from the back seat. Everyone started calling out movie suggestions while Sophie just grinned at her friends.

Looking out over the fog-shrouded bay, a strange bubbling happiness filled Sophie; she felt lucky to be alive and surrounded by friends. Before meeting this group, Sophie hadn't even been aware of what she had been missing. She had refused to acknowledge the vague sense of emptiness and longing that had filled her life before finding true friends at the city morgue. Buoyed by the protective warmth of having people care about her, Sophie realized how bleak and alone she had been.

CHAPTER 23

Two bottles of wine, a massive amount of takeout, and several hours later, everyone except Sophie and Mac was getting ready to head back to their respective places of work. As Sophie had moved around her apartment, fetching silverware and pouring drinks, she found that she couldn't stop touching her friends to reassure herself of their safety.

Sophie hugged each of her friends as they headed out the door. She was not normally a touchy-feely person. Maybe it was the wine or the terror of the night, but it made Sophie forcefully shove aside her usual reservation and cling to them a little.

"You sure you don't need my help at the morgue tonight?" Sophie asked, saving Reggie's hug for last.

"We'll be fine. Get some rest, and I will see you tomorrow night, okay?" Reggie said, giving Sophie's hand a brief squeeze. She stared into Reggie's sweet, round face for a moment, just thankful to have such a good friend in her life.

"Thank you, Reggie. For everything. For getting me a job, for being my friend, for helping me figure out my gift. I don't know what I would have done without you."

Reggie snatched Sophie back into a tight hug. "Soph, I'm so

glad you're my friend too," he said, and if Sophie heard a small sniffle, she wasn't going to tell anyone.

After watching everyone disappear into the creaky stairwell at the end of the hall, Sophie walked into her apartment to find Mac wandering around, once again picking up various items and looking them over. When he meandered his way into the kitchen and started opening drawers, Sophie cleared her throat.

"What are you doing?"

"Searching for the clavis. I want to get another look at it," Mac responded, pawing through her junk drawer.

"And you thought I hid a powerful stolen magical item amongst my ketchup packets and paper clips?"

Mac just raised his eyebrow in affirmation, making Sophie huff in irritation.

"You're not going to find it. I've hidden it too well. Leave my stuff alone. Besides, we both already took a good look at the clavis. It just looked like a big green gemstone to me. I didn't feel any kind of power or magic when I held it, did you?" Sophie asked. When Mac shook his head, Sophie shrugged, "Let's just forget about all that for now. Do you want a shower to get cleaned up? I'll make up the futon so you can take the bed."

"No, I will take the futon, and you sleep in your bed. I'm not kicking you out of your room," Mac argued.

"Yes, you are. You were shot less than three fucking hours ago." Sophie clenched her fists in irritation.

"I was, but I'm a shifter. I will be fine."

"And I will be fine on the futon, too. You're going to take the bed, and that's my final word on it!" Sophie yelled.

"Oh. It's your final word, is it? Well then, I guess that settles it," Mac stated too calmly. Sophie didn't move because she could sense the trap. "How about this instead? If you try to get in that fucking futon, I will physically pick you up and toss you in your bed. That's *my* final word on it."

"I have met bulldozers with more flexibility than you. So, you know what? Fine! You can suffer on the futon for all I care, you stubborn mule. I hope you get a crick in your neck," Sophie said as she stomped to the minuscule hall closet to grab her spare sheets.

As she made up a bed on the futon, her motions jerky from her irritation, she heard the water groan on in the bathroom. After gathering up a few of the empty cups abandoned after the impromptu celebration, Sophie was putting them in the sink to deal with tomorrow, when her apartment entry buzzer called out into the silence.

"Hello?" Sophie said hesitantly into the intercom system.

"Hey, Sophie. It's Burg. I offered to drop off some clothes for Mac since my place is right above the bar. It took me a bit to find some stuff that might fit him," Burg's tinny voice said through her intercom speaker.

"That's so nice of you, Burg. Come on up," Sophie said, pressing the buzzer to unlock Brown Betty's front door. Standing in the open door of her apartment, she waited for Burg to deliver an armload of clothes into her waiting hands. Burg quickly headed back down the hall, calling out a need to get back to the bar.

Carrying the haphazard stack of clothing into her apartment, Sophie headed through her bedroom and knocked on the bathroom door.

"Burg dropped off some clothes for you," Sophie called out.

"Can you put them by the sink?" Mac called out over the sound of the shower.

After only a moment's hesitation, Sophie forced her hand to turn the handle and push the door open. Sophie quickly glanced over toward where Mac was separated from her by only a thin, white shower curtain. She made herself focus on placing the clothes on the counter.

"Do you need any help with a new bandage when you're done in there?" Sophie asked.

The rattle of the shower curtain rings had Sophie jerking her gaze back toward the shower stall.

"I won't need a new bandage. The bullet hole has already sealed itself closed," Mac said, his face and shoulder peeking out from behind the curtain. Sophie forced herself to focus only on Mac's eyes, bright blue under the flop of water-darkened hair plastered across his forehead.

"That's not fair. You get shot, and three hours later, the wound has sealed itself closed. If I barely bump into a table, I get a bruise that lasts two weeks," Sophie complained.

"It's not my fault that you are such a delicate human with tender flesh."

"Eeewww. Tender flesh? Gross. You make me sound like a steak." Sophie shuddered with disgust.

"You don't like the word tender? How about juicy? That better?"

"Ugh. That's actually worse."

Mac gave Sophie a long, thoughtful look while she pretended not to stare at the soap bubbles sliding slowly down his shoulder. Finally, with a small, secretive grin, he said, "Moist," drawing the word out, like he was savoring every extra syllable as it passed his lips.

Mac's loud laugh followed Sophie out of the bathroom as she ran through the door with her hands pressed firmly over her ears, yelling, "Blah blah blah!" to drown out any other awful words Mac might think of.

Sitting on the futon, Sophie curled up to wait for her turn in the shower.

The next thing she knew, Mac was gently shaking her shoulder and whispering her name.

"Wha?" Sophie mumbled in confusion.

"You fell asleep. Come on. Let me help you get to bed," Mac said softly, gently pulling Sophie to her feet.

With one hand on her elbow, Mac guided a half-asleep Sophie

into her room. Standing at Mac's side like a lost child, Sophie watched Mac strip back her blanket through half-closed eyes. He eased Sophie into her bed and pulled the blanket up to her chin, completing the feeling of being a tucked-in kid.

"Good night, Sophie," Mac said softly, kissing her on the forehead.

"Night," Sophie said as her eyes closed.

CHAPTER 24

◈

*A*lthough the wig was itchy against her scalp, she decided it was worth it when she caught his eye. She knew he preferred blondes. Ordering her third tonic water with lime for the night, she spotted a small table finally open up across the bar. With a slightly wavering walk, she managed to snag the table before anyone else could stake a claim on it.

Slowly sipping her drink, she kept one eye on the man she had followed here. She nicknamed him Lumberjack after his large size and his penchant for wearing flannel, no matter the weather. Who wears flannel on a hot day?

She had been following him long enough to have him and his mannerisms cataloged and memorized. He was drinking his usual pint of Guinness. She shuddered in distaste. After she first began tracking him, she decided to try the beer out of curiosity. She suspected that dishwater swirled around an ashtray probably tastes better.

Lumberjack looked slightly unkempt, per usual: his clothes creased, and his bushy hair in need of a trim. He was an awkward man. An underachiever somehow imbued with an excessive amount of unearned self-importance. She once heard someone refer to this type of guy as a neckbeard. It was a somewhat cruel moniker, but she couldn't deny it *was also a little funny. She would never call Lumberjack a neckbeard to his face, but in the recesses of her mind, she thought it with a giggle. He was currently lurking, shoulders hunched like he was trying to make himself invisible, near the arch that led to the restrooms in the back corner of the bar.*

Throughout the evening, she luckily only had to shoo away a few potential suitors who approached her. When each one left without any drama or threats, she breathed a small sigh of relief.

As it got closer to midnight, the itching under the wig seemed to get more pronounced. To keep from shoving her fingers under her wig and scratching her scalp like a woman possessed, she anchored both hands tightly around her tall glass.

Glancing at the delicate watch on her wrist, she decided she had lingered long enough in this bar. Taking a final sip of her tonic water, she pulled on her jacket and hat. Heading out the front door, she bumped into the entrance doorframe as she pulled on her gloves. No one was outside in the darkened gloom of the street. A few cars drove past as the city began to settle down for the night.

She took slow, mincing steps down the sidewalk, pretending a drunkenness she didn't feel. Behind her, she heard the buzz of voices blare from inside the bar as the front door opened and then quickly closed. Watching the reflections in the windows across the street, she spotted the bulky form of Lumberjack as he followed her.

Taking a few quick steps, she zipped around the corner into the alley next to the bar. In the dark, it looked scarier than it had when she had inspected the area earlier in the evening. She wrinkled her nose as the smell of urine and rotting garbage assaulted her senses.

Pretending to lean against the brick wall of the bar as if she was having trouble standing upright, she reached into her pocketbook and pulled out the vial and syringe. Quickly filling the syringe, she dropped the now-empty bottle back in her bag.

Holding her breath and listening intently, she heard the moment Lumberjack entered the alley.

"Are you okay, miss?" Lumberjack asked in his strangely nasal drawl.

She turned slightly, dropping her hand to her side, keeping the syringe hidden from sight. When Lumberjack got close, she quickly rotated her body, raising the needle to plunge into his neck. At the same moment, Lumberjack raised his hand to touch her blonde hair, accidentally knocking the syringe from her hand. Both of them looked at the broken syringe, which was leaking its contents on the pavement, in stupefied shock.

She looked at Lumberjack then back at the broken syringe in appalled hesitation.

"You made me drop my insulin!" she exclaimed dramatically. Bending over, pretending to cry, she slid a long thin spike out of the hidden pouch sewn into an inner pocket of her jacket. The spike was about six inches long and had a small handle across the base, making it look like the letter T. She smiled briefly as it fit perfectly in her palm. She made a fist with the spike poking out between her index and middle fingers.

In the seconds that it took her to palm her weapon, Lumberjack's face had transformed from confusion to growing rage.

"You bitc–"

Before he could finish his curse, Sophie darted one step forward and stomped on Lumberjack's foot, driving the sharp point of her heel into his toes with all her strength. As the man reflexively curled forward, she sunk her spike into his neck in a rapid series of jabs. Lumberjack clutched at his ravaged throat. She knocked him over so that he fell backward against a dumpster. Holding the spike up in readiness, she watched as blood seeped over his gripping fingers, flowing over his neck and soaking into his shirt.

"Not bad improvisation, if I do say so myself. Good thing I wore black," she stated with a cheerful shrug, glancing down at the blood splatters speckled soaking into her clothing.

"Why?" Lumberjack whispered, weakness and blood loss making his voice thin and wavering.

"You know why, Troy," she said with a shake of her head, much like a disappointed parent would after catching a naughty child sneaking a cookie before dinner. After using a mirror to make sure there were no blood droplets on her face or neck, she slipped her spike into her purse. The broken syringe and her gloves quickly joined the spike.

Exiting the alley, with her victim's body cooling behind her, she headed out with a pep in her step and a charming smile on her face.

~

"SOPHIE, WAKE UP. IT'S JUST A DREAM," A VOICE SAID, SHAKING HER shoulder.

Sitting up with a gasp, Sophie looked around wildly for a moment, not seeing her apartment, but a dying man sprawled in a filthy alley instead.

"Sophie, it was just a dream. You're okay," Mac said, placing one of his hands over hers. He slowly unclenched her fist, which was tightly clutching her blanket to her chin like a shield.

"Mac?" Sophie asked in confusion.

Looking fearfully around herself, Sophie realized she was wrapped safely in her comforter with Mac kneeling next to her bed, a concerned look across his face.

"Shit. What an awful fucking dream," Sophie whined, scrubbing a fist over her eyes, trying to erase the vision of Lumberjack's murder from them.

"You want to tell me about it?" Mac quietly offered, carefully wrapping her hands protectively in his.

"Not really. I just dreamed I murdered a guy who looked like a lumberjack by stabbing him in the throat. In the dream, I just happily stabbed him in the throat and left him to die in a dirty alley. My brain fucking sucks. I wish these dreams would stop."

"You get these kinds of dreams often?"

"Not very often, thankfully. I just hate them because in the dreams when I murder someone, my dream-self is always so fucking cheerful and pleased about the whole thing. It's a terrible feeling to wake up with."

"I can see how that would suck. I wonder if seeing all the murder victims at the morgue and having death visions are planting these dreams in your head? I read somewhere once that dreams are how your brain processes information from your day," Mac said, rubbing his thumb over Sophie's knuckles.

"You might be right, but it still sucks," Sophie grumbled.

"I bet. Do you think you're okay to go back to sleep? I'll be right in the living room if you need me. All you need to do is call out," Mac offered.

"Actually, could you stay with me? I'd rather not be alone right now," Sophie asked shyly.

"I could do that." Mac slipped under the covers on the empty side of the bed. "As long as you promise not to molest me in my sleep. I'd like my virtue to remain intact."

"I guess I will have to dig deep and find the fortitude to withstand the temptation you present," Sophie promised dramatically with a scoff.

Rolling over to face Mac, Sophie fluffed up her pillow and looked at him lounging in her bed, looking quite pleased to be there. She was reminded once again of a lion as he surveyed his domain.

"How's your shoulder?" she asked.

"It's good. Almost healed. It will still ache for a few days, but almost as good as new," Mac said around a wide yawn.

"Lucky," Sophie complained around a complementary yawn.

"Good night, Soph," Mac said with a low chuckle.

"Good night, Mac."

~

SUNLIGHT SLOWLY CREPT THROUGH SOPHIE'S EYELIDS, MAKING ITS way into her consciousness. She froze when she realized there was a heavy arm slung over her waist, the heated firmness of a body pressed against her back. When Sophie tried to creep her way out of Mac's hold, he wrapped himself further around her and pulled her deeper into the cradle of his body. She stared at the arm curled over her waist in consternation. Watery morning light limned the smattering of hair on Mac's arm golden and fine. Lightly touching the warm skin over his bicep with a single finger, she admired the lean functional strength displayed in his arm even in a relaxed state. Sophie slowly drew circles and whorls on his arm, feeling the fiber of muscle and tendons beneath his tanned skin. Following the path of a meandering vein, Sophie traced a path along his arm to the back of Mac's hand.

Issuing a low sigh, Mac burrowed his face into the back of Sophie's head while she held still and pretended to be asleep. Mac continued to nuzzle his face into her hair, slowly making his way closer to her exposed ear.

Sophie held her breath, reveling in the palpitating anticipation as she waited for Mac to kiss her ear. The heady feeling of electricity between them built until she was practically glowing with it. Ghosting his mouth across the skin behind her ear, he emitted a low groan. Ripples of sensation lapped along her nerves, making a flush rise from her skin. As a gentle wash of breath wafted over her ear, she began to turn in Mac's arms. Pressing a kiss to the shell of her earlobe, he softly, oh-so-gently whispered "Phlegm" into her ear, then chuckled evilly, clearly pleased with himself.

With a war cry, Sophie rolled over, straddling Mac's thighs. The last thing she saw before stuffing a pillow over his face was glowing blue eyes, filled with anticipation.

"Relax and just head toward the light," Sophie advised as he flailed about, trying to pull the pillow off his face while Sophie cackled like a maniac.

Mac disarmed Sophie of her pillow-weapon with the swiftness of a ninja, flipping her onto her back. Straddling her thighs and pinning her arms above her head, Mac gave Sophie a hot look, grinning at her antics. The laughter died a quick death on Sophie's lips as Mac slowly leaned closer, hovering his lips above hers. He brushed his lips over hers softly, back and forth, like he was testing the texture of her lips. Pushing up against his firm hold, Sophie nipped at his mouth, earning a groan and a grin from Mac. At that moment, Sophie decided that having Mac's smile against her lips was the best feeling in the whole world. Desire raced up the length of Sophie's spine like fire along a fuse.

Right as Sophie parted her mouth against Mac's, ready to devour his lips, a shrill noise from the living room jolted through her apartment, overly loud in the quiet wonder of the morning.

"Shit," Mac groaned sadly, dropping his forehead against Sophie's shoulder in a dejected manner. "I have to answer that."

As Mac got up and headed towards the living room, Sophie admired his muscular form clad only in a pair of boxers. Wetting her lips, she let out a shrill wolf whistle, making Mac look over his shoulder at her with a grin as he turned the corner into her living room.

Stretching luxuriously in her bed, Sophie listened to Mac make a lot of humming agreement noises and several "Yes, sir"s and "Right away, sir"s before hanging up and heading back to Sophie's room, only to find her posing provocatively in her bed.

Mac grinned at her when he walked back into the room. "Do you want me to paint you like one of my French girls?" he asked, waggling his eyebrows.

"Uh… sure?"

"Oh my god! You haven't seen *Titanic*! I think we need to break up. Sorry, Soph. It's you, not me," Mac said, dramatically throwing his hands into the air.

"Well, since we haven't actually been on a first date yet, that won't be possible. You can't technically break up if you've never dated," Sophie archly pointed out.

"You're right. Let's go on a real first date, and then I can break up with you," Mac said, nodding like he was being very logical.

"Good plan. Have you ever been to Alcatraz Island? I heard the night tour is supposed to be extra spooky. I could get us tickets?" Sophie suggested.

"I would love that. First, though, how about I pick you up from work tomorrow morning and take you to breakfast?" Mac said, kneeling on Sophie's bed.

"Deal," Sophie said, sitting up and crawling over to Mac to place a kiss on his lips.

Groaning in disappointment, Mac whined that he had to go into work right away. As Mac pulled away, he brushed his nose against Sophie's, bumping the tips of their noses together, making her giggle.

"Marcella has already called the Chief of Police, and he wants me to come in right away. I barely have time to get home and get changed."

Mac quickly pulled on the sweatpants and t-shirt Burg lent him before Sophie walked him to her front door. They lingered as long as they could over a kiss before Mac finally had to tear himself away.

As Sophie watched Mac walk down the hall, she was filled with the sensation of standing on the edge of something so big it made her chest swell. Anticipation for the future suffused her. She wished she could run out and pull him back into her apartment to explore her feelings for him.

As Mac passed Birdie's apartment, he suddenly stopped in front of her door.

"I hope you're having a nice morning, Miss Birdie," he stated blithely.

"Not as good as yours, I bet," Sophie heard Birdie's gleeful voice call out from the crack of her apartment door.

Shaking her head, Sophie firmly closed her door before she had to hear anything else Birdie might have to say about her morning with Mac.

EPILOGUE

"Good evening, Miss Zhao," Sophie called out with a jaunty salute.

"Good evening, Miss Feegle," Miss Zhao said, buzzing open the morgue doors. Sophie gave Miss Zhao's jade green dress a brief envious glance before heading through the double doors.

Sophie found everyone in Fitz and Ace's office still buzzing from the excitement of the night before.

"How was work last night? Were you guys okay without me?" Sophie asked.

"It was fine. We had to push all the previously scheduled autopsies back so we could process the bodies from the fight, but it shouldn't cause us any problems. We'll just have to play catch up tonight," Reggie responded. "Is Mac okay? Did the bullet wound cause him any problems?"

"Nope. By the time he left this morning, he was fine and seemed completely back to normal," Sophie stated, hoping no one noticed her blush.

"Let's get started then. We received a priority one a few hours ago, and then we need to catch up on our backlog," Reggie stated, already turning and heading towards the main autopsy room. "Oh, also Mac contacted me a couple of hours ago. After meeting with Marcella and Chief of Police Dunham this morning; they both want to start receiving transcripts of your visions. Obviously, we still need to keep your identity a secret, so at the end of each shift, Amira will transcribe the recordings of your visions and then email them to Mac."

"Sounds good to me," Sophie said with a shrug, not caring how Mac got the recordings as long as they could do some good.

Checking the docket for the night, Sophie headed into the fridge and grabbed the priority one. Wheeling him into the autopsy room, Sophie parked the gurney by the weighing station and turned to get cleaned and prepped.

Turning back towards Reggie, Sophie watched as he unzipped the black body bag. The first thing that caught Sophie's eye was a flash of red and black flannel. Sophie's breath froze in her throat as she recognized the man's now blue-tinged features capped by a full head of chestnut-colored bushy hair in desperate need of a trim.

Sophie must have made some kind of noise of distress because the next thing she knew, Reggie was in front of her. She could see his lips moving and a scared look on his face, but she couldn't hear his words over the ringing in her ears.

Finally, she got her frozen lips to move, barely choking out the word, "Lumberjack."

"Lumberjack? What does that mean?" Reggie asked.

"Oh shit, Reggie, we need to call Mac."

AFTERWORD

Dear readers,

Thank you for taking this journey with me. I hope you enjoyed Sophie and The Odd Ones. It was a different kind of story for me to write. And I hope you are as excited for the next in the series as I am.

Although all the characters in the book were made up, almost all of the places were real or based on someplace real. I lived in San Francisco for eight years and fell in love with the city. It is a strange city teeming with strange people. So here goes. The Medical Examiner's office is real; it is based in Bayview, and it does have the fence-looking sculpture out front. The Little Thumb is based on my local pub The Little Shamrock. The Little Shamrock is over 120 years old and kinda looks like it. However, I loved it and I miss getting a cheap PBR there. The poster I mentioned was a nod to the poster that inspired the Beatles to pen For The Benefit of Mister Kite. I just loved the idea of Burg having stolen the original poster.

The second-hand shop was based on the Love Project Curio Shop. If you are ever in SF, stop by and check it out. Plus, proceeds from sales go to a good cause. The Fillmore is my favorite music venue in the city. I have several concert posters from my time spent there. Buck's is a real restaurant and it looks as weird as it sounds. It is also a favorite place for Silicon Valley money makers and entrepreneurs (of which I am neither but my husband was). Boudin is one of my favorite bread shops. And it's a great place to stop by if you're playing tourist at Pier 39. The tearoom I mentioned in Noe Valley is Lovejoy's Tea Room. If you want to feel all fancy-schmancy, that's the joint for you. If you don't talk with a fake British accent while eating cucumber sandwiches, what's the point? City Lights Booksellers is exactly as I described it in the story. Who doesn't love a bookstore, especially one with such a rich history? Alcatraz does do night tours, so if you are ever in the city, you should check it out. The night tour is way better than the regular tour, and there is something lovely about watching the sun set over the city. Very romantic – wink wink nudge nudge.

Woodlawn Memorial Park is a real cemetery in Colma. My favorite person buried there is Emperor Norton. If you ever want a chuckle, look up that man's story. I will give you a hint – he declared himself the Emperor of the United States. And people let him. They even issued currency in his name. Also, Colma is real too. I used to get my car serviced there. So. Many. Graves.

As for the elephant seal that killed the mermaid, there are two good places to see them in the city. One is at Pier 39. The other location is my favorite. You can see the seals at the Fitzgerald Marine Sanctuary which is about 30 minutes south of the city. If you go out during low tide, there are fantastic tide pools filled with all kinds of sea creatures. I used to love taking my kids there when they were little.

Russian River Brewery is a killer brewing company based in Santa Rosa. You can get amazing pizza at their restaurant, but my favorite thing is their beer flights. They have these long paddle boards where you can get eighteen(!) samples to try – try their sour beers, they'll lock your jaw they're so sour and yet so good. I recommend sharing with friends! My husband's favorite beer by them is Pliny the Younger which comes out only once a year. People will wait hours to get their growlers filled on the release day.

Lastly, Coit Tower and the Filbert Steps. The Coit Tower is a lovely place to visit. The views (when it's not foggy) are fabulous. The 25 murals inside are great examples of Depression-era artwork showing how people lived at the time. The tower was paid for when Lillie Hitchcock Coit put in her will that the money be used to add to the beauty of the city. Lillie was an eccentric woman known for smoking cigars and dressing like a man so she could gamble at the males-only gambling houses. She also loved riding the fire engines with the firefighters. She sounded like my kind of lady! The Filbert Street stairs also exist and you can take them to reach Coit Tower. But fair warning, you might regret it. It's A LOT of stairs. However, they are also beautiful and you get to see a lot of the city on the way up – you know, if you don't pass out.

Whew! That was a bunch of information. If you ever want to ask me about the city, feel free to email me at gwen@ gwendemarco.com, and I will endeavor to sell you on San Francisco's merits.

I would like to give a huge thank you to my beta readers Paige R, Pam N, Karen R, Casi R, Jessica and Joanne S. I also need to thank Rebeca Covers for the gorgeous cover artwork and my editor Arundhati Subhedar.

Lastly, I want to say thank you to my husband and kids. I would never have been able to get a single thing published without your unwavering support.

ABOUT THE AUTHOR

Gwen DeMarco is an avid reader, wine & coffee drinker, gardener and a lover of all things nerdy. Gwen loves to write paranormal romance novels with a focus on the weird and wonderful. She loves to write a good snarky heroine and a grumpy male lead. Sophie and the Odd Ones is her first foray into the world of shifters, fae, ogres and vampires.

Gwen is happily married to her high school sweetheart and has two teenage children. She can often be found with her nose in a book and a glass of wine or mug of coffee in her hand.

To learn more, please visit my website and sign up for my mailing list to receive updates at www.GwenDeMarco.com

f **𝕐** **◎**

Printed in Great Britain
by Amazon